T0120981

SOMETHING
ABOUT A
PURPOSE

JODY FLYNN AND MARY K MEINZER

authorHOUSE®

AuthorHouse™
1663 Liberty Drive
Bloomington, IN 47403
www.authorhouse.com
Phone: 1 (800) 839-8640

© *2018 Jody Flynn and Mary K Meinzer. All rights reserved.*

No part of this book may be reproduced, stored in a retrieval system, or transmitted by any means without the written permission of the author.

Published by AuthorHouse 02/24/2018

ISBN: 978-1-5462-2859-2 (sc)
ISBN: 978-1-5462-2858-5 (e)

Library of Congress Control Number: 2018901804

Print information available on the last page.

Any people depicted in stock imagery provided by Getty Images are models, and such images are being used for illustrative purposes only. Certain stock imagery © Getty Images.

This book is printed on acid-free paper.

Because of the dynamic nature of the Internet, any web addresses or links contained in this book may have changed since publication and may no longer be valid. The views expressed in this work are solely those of the author and do not necessarily reflect the views of the publisher, and the publisher hereby disclaims any responsibility for them.

What if you could see your reflection through the eyes of others?

Like all real treasures of the mind, perception can be split into infinitely small fractions without losing its quality. Perception...cannot be purchased with either learned degrees or dollars; it grows at home as well as abroad, and he who has a little may use it to as good advantage as he who has much.

Aldo Leopold

This book is dedicated to my family, my 'Superman' and all of the 'life angels' who have continued to support my ideas and dreams. Thank you so much with all my heart!
Jody

Thanks to all who believed in me and especially to my trusty canine companions who were my little lights in the darkness.
Mary

Contents

Introduction.. xiii

1   Promises, Promises.. 1

2   Dishes and Wishes...15

3   Suites and Treats... 27

4   Secrets.. 46

5   History in the Making..................................... 59

6   Shooting Stars... 77

7   Peace and Grace.. 86

8   Life Angels..112

9   A Leap of Faith.. 125

10   Queen of Hearts 141

11   When One Door Closes..................................161

12   Away, But Never Forgotten 182

Monday, July 4, 2011

*H*e let out a low growl. The small scruff of fur at the back of his neck stood erect. As he stiffened his small frame, I looked in the direction of his intense focus. I could see some movement through the trees and across the small lake. His keen sense of sound alerted him to the fact that we were not alone out there.

I quickly bent down to pick him up so I could distract him by carrying him the rest of the way to the RV, but he wiggled out of his harness and darted forward.

"Felix, STOP! Come back here!" *Oh no, not the lake! Not again!* I began to panic. *The dog can't swim! He'll drown*, I thought anxiously. It was too late. He was hot on the trail of a young doe drinking from the far end of the lake. All I could do was to yell at the top of my lungs, "Henry, help! Felix, stop!"

I took off after him, running as fast as I could. Then, he stopped suddenly and pointed his tiny ears straight ahead. He was as focused as if he was now a lion, strategically pursuing a gazelle. He paid no attention to my approach. When I was in reaching distance of him, I took a leap of faith and made a flying tackle for the little guy. I caught him in my arms.

But something was wrong. I couldn't catch my breath! I rolled over with Felix escaping my grasp. I grabbed my chest but hit my head sharply on the rock trim of the pebbled path. Explosive pain in my head and nausea, like from a blow to my stomach, immobilized me. My vision began to blur. I saw only the tail end of Felix as he ran away. Then, all was darkness.

Feeling as though I was drowning, I fought the imaginary waves, flailing my arms in the air in an effort to keep from going under. I heard garbled voices: "Jess, Jessica!" I heard panic in their voices.

"Put something under her head!"

"No! Don't move her; we need to stop the bleeding!"

The voices were now muted sounds. Then, I felt calm and serene. No more struggling. All was silent. No more voices. No pain. No sound or light. All memory of my physical existence was a dream-like fantasy.

Glowing, iridescent, powder-like dust was shimmering down around me like warm rays of sunlight. As I slowly opened my eyes, *she* was there in front of me, all radiance and splendor. Her garments were an unearthly shade of blue. Her beauty stunned me into staring at her, mesmerized, and not without a feeling of a certain familiarity.

She reached forward and took my hand in reassurance. I suddenly had the sense from her that all of my fears and questions would be understood by me in time.

The woman was smiling at me. Now I knew her. We were part of one another. She was that part of me which I thought was lost forever; the part of my being that sadness and despair had eaten away over the years bit by bit, literally tearing me apart.

As my eyes gazed upon her illuminating smile, I felt something resting in my cupped hands. It was a small, velvet box, the color of a blue robin's egg. I tried to open it carefully, but it would not yield. Puzzled, I looked up at her. She held an ancient skeleton key of brass. As I reached for the key, she held it back. On her face now was a mysterious look of sorrow, mixed with wisdom and love.

I started toward her, compelled to stay in her magnetic presence. She turned and held up a hand cautioning me, and uttering:

"Jessie, you have a choice to make. Choose wisely and remember your purpose."

She said it so softly that I had to bend toward her as she pressed the key into my hands.

"What purpose?" I cried. "Am I dead? Where am I? Are you an angel?" All of these questions I had for her, but she started to vanish! I heard only the echo of, *remember your purpose,* again, as she slowly began to recede into the intense brightness. "Wait!" I cried again. "I want to go with you! My life here is over." I reached out my hand and tried to grasp at her flowing blue garments, but she was gone!

Had I not fulfilled my purpose in this life? I was devastated. I cried out again, "Wait!" Yet I was left alone, with only the blue box and brass key. Upon inserting the key into the box and turning it successfully this time, spectacular colors emanated from the opening, blinding me momentarily. I began to feel disoriented, and suddenly exhausted. While in this suspended state, some memories began to return, slowly transporting me back in time to the previous weekend of my life. The scene was near Boerne, Texas. There was something I needed to be shown, or reminded of…*something about a purpose.*

Promises, Promises

Five days earlier. Independence Day Weekend. Thursday, June 30th, 2011

*I*t's a crisp summer morning and I'm standing amidst the trees at my house near Boerne, Texas. I am looking at the man-made lake and estate with a sense of wonder.

My thoughts meander. Some of these trees are young, and just beginning to dig their roots into the earth. Others are historic, with roots and branches so strong that they can withstand storms, winter ice, and even the burning heat of our South Texas summers. It's breathtaking.

It's the Fourth of July weekend and all five of our guest suites are booked. Besides our quirky staff and myself, eight guests will arrive today. Opening up my home as an inn, lovingly referred to as *Luna's Hope*, has been a major task, although incredibly rewarding.

One couple arriving today has chosen to vacation here because they are in dire need of marital reassurance. Their seven-year marriage is unraveling like a ball of yarn in the paws of a kitten, or, perhaps, a tiger.

Two sisters who have not seen each other in five years will be reuniting here today; both holding life and death secrets from each other.

Also expected is a middle-aged, reclusive, cowboy- biker, who is not only a single father but a millionaire workaholic. He is not happy, feeling tricked into taking this getaway by his adult daughter, Ellie.

Next, the eccentric and flamboyant silent partner in *Luna's Hope* will arrive. Now my good friend, Henry never travels without his little dog and best friend, Felix.

Then arriving will be a rebellious, retired, no-nonsense woman who is in remission from cancer and just wants to be alone, 'a la Greta Garbo,' with her thoughts.

Lastly, my two adult free-spirited sons will be coming in from San Antonio. They hope to share their "peace and love, dudes!" It should be a very intriguing weekend, indeed.

It's been a year since I opened my home to guests on this superb piece of land. The beautiful lake, the exquisite custom-built house, and the whole fifty-eight acres of nature's pure glory, was a dream come true. I can only look back and marvel at what took place. It was, and is, a sight to behold. And thus, the story unfolds.

*I*t is such a beautiful morning; and I love my quiet time. Abruptly, my thoughts had a change of direction, though. They returned to *the summer of 1977.* The recollection of Pensacola, Florida was vivid and clear. It was warm and sunny. We were vacationing at my Aunt Beth's house. Aunt Beth was my dad's sister. She and I had just gone to the movies. It was just us girls. She had three sons, but loved doing 'girly' things with me, whenever we could visit our Floridian relatives. After the movie, she suggested that we take a leisurely walk along the beach. It was that day when she proclaimed: "With your roots grounded deep, deeper than the deepest depths of the entire Gulf of Mexico, all of your dreams will come true, Jessie. I promise."

Those words of wisdom were carefully chosen, and the memory of them comes back to me so clearly that I can almost hear her voice. Of course I had no idea what she meant, then.

Aunt Beth, a kind, but forthright type of person, was always there for her kids and me, unlike my own mother.

The skies were clear that summer day and the water sparkled. I saw my dad a bit further down the beach, walking toward us.

"Hey Allen," Aunt Beth called out. "Come join us." My dad continued heading our way, head down, heavy with apparent sadness. Thirty-four years have passed, and I still haven't been able to erase that vision of my father from my mind.

"Hi Daddy," I called out. I tried to run to him in my sundress and bare feet through the sand, towing my Barbie in hand, but it was more difficult than I expected. I fell a few times. He picked me up and hugged me tightly before setting me back down. He took my hand, and we walked back toward my aunt. He released my hand, and leaned in to whisper something in my aunt's ear.

My mom, Michelle, chose not to come with Dad and me to visit Aunt Beth and my cousins on this trip. This was not unusual for her. My mom spent a lot of time in her bedroom at our home, alone. My father had his own bedroom. Sometimes I'd hear Mom cry; while at other times she would sleep the whole day away.

I always thought that it was my fault that my mother was so unhappy. What could I do, though? I was only a little girl. Maybe if I was better behaved, prettier, or something, she would be happy. In fact, the only time I remember my mom smile was when she read one of my stories about animals and children. She always kept those stories for me, as if she knew I would someday value them as much as she did. But well, here we were, on the beach: Aunt Beth, Dad, and me.

Aunt Beth set out a blanket on the sand that day and motioned for me to sit on it next to Dad. I remember the smell of the Gulf and the taste of salt in the air, intoxicating me and lulling me to a sleepy calmness with every wave. I felt so happy, carefree, and safe.

But, when I looked up at them, they had somber facial expressions. Not mad or upset at me; more like the look that my parents once gave me when they had to tell me that my beloved tadpole, Rex, had died.

Oh no, I remembered thinking to myself; someone died? Worse, one of them was dying; or no, maybe I'm dying?

My imagination began to run wild, and they could clearly see the horror that was creeping through my ten-year old mind. They knew me and my every reaction better than I knew myself, it seemed.

Dad spoke first. "Jessie girl, you know how much I love you." Then he hugged me closely, and looked into my eyes. I could feel his heart beating nearly out of his chest, and I saw something in his eyes that I had never seen before: tears.

"Jess, you know that no matter what, I'll love you forever and ever, and you will always be my angel," he emphasized, with tear-filled eyes.

"Jessie," my aunt was speaking softly now, "we love you more than all of the stars in the sky."

All of this 'loving' was nice, but no one was getting to the point, and I was beginning to feel panic welling up in my throat. And, what was the whispering about, and the way they were looking at each other; so sadly?

"What's wrong?" I finally blurted out. "Did I do something bad?" I asked with fear.

Daddy looked away and coughed, trying to cover up his own grief-stricken look.

Aunt Beth pointed out to me how sick my mom had been lately. "Jessie, you did nothing wrong, honey. You know how your mom sleeps a lot and spends so much time in her room, feeling sick?"

I nodded bravely, not understanding where she was going with this. During my whole life my mom slept most days away. This was normal to me; not sick.

Daddy reached over and placed a finger on the gold heart of my charm bracelet. My mother had given it to me last summer.

Dad simply said, "Mommy loves you very much." Tears began to fall down my face. I felt very sad, but also angry. Suddenly, as if a defensive signal was sent to my brain, I wanted to run…run and hide. I didn't even know why, just an automatic fear that was racing through me.

"I want my Mommy!" I stood up and yelled, instead of running.

My father knew just how I felt. Only he was the adult, and had to keep it all together.

"Daddy, where is Mommy?" I pleaded. "Is she okay?"

That day, I learned that my mother had taken her own life in a moment of despair. Dad could barely understand it all himself, let alone explain it to a ten-year-old. When he finally told me how my mother had taken too much medicine, and that the angels then came down to carry her away, I stared blankly at him.

He continued gently, "Remember, honey, when Rex went away to heaven, and we knew that we would see him again one day?" Daddy held me tightly, as the confusion became all too much for me. He told me that all of the angels in heaven had gotten together and decided that they wanted my Mommy to be one of them. It was a great honor, he went on, and one could not refuse such a request from above. He wasn't making any sense to me. I was always told that there were many, many angels already in heaven, so why would they need my mom, too?

"But Daddy, when will she come back and be Mommy again?" I cried.

My dad wiped a tear from his eye and said, "She wants us to carry on just as if she were here," he said gravely, but I could still see the wetness in his eyes.

Aunt Beth, trying to redirect the enormity of the sadness in the situation, added abruptly: "Well now, let's remember; Mommy is now an angel in heaven and free from all her sadness. Let's all pack up our gear and go back to the house. I'll make us some lemonade and we can talk some more." She hurried us along, though I was still in shock.

I tried to contain my tears, but it was impossible. That night, I went to bed an immensely changed little girl.

I finally decided that I wasn't having any of this. When I was a grownup, I would find out the real truth of what happened to my mom and I would write it all down, perhaps even write a book.

I took off the bracelet my mom had given me, and decided not to wear it again until I understood it all.

In those days, my childish yearning was to be a great female detective who solved all mysteries. Figuring out why my mom left us was one of those mysteries that would have to wait. I lay back in bed, full of resolve, but with tears streaming from my tightly squeezed-shut eyes.

*L*ike an unexpected whirlwind that blows debris in every direction without a warning, a new and different kind of life introduced itself to me in those warm sands off of the Gulf of Mexico, back in *1977*. It was a life in which childhood dreams were to be buried beneath the sand; hidden away for future reference in another world, perhaps. Instead, a dark cloud seemed to loom ahead.

After that day on the beach, I remember traveling from childhood to young adulthood in the blink of an eye, without much to show for it. I was what some would call a loner, or, an outcast. As a young adult, I attempted to work and go to school simultaneously, which turned out to be draining, turning me somewhat bitter. I was losing even more of myself. I became what was known as an *underachiever.*

Insecurity and the beginnings of a clinical depression ultimately became my constant, heavy companions. They were destined to keep me grounded. My dream of becoming a great detective would have to be put on hold. Truthfully, I really wasn't dreaming of doing much at all, anymore.

It was then, as a young adult, when the clinical depression completely settled over me, enveloping me like a cloud of fog droplets. Soon, I was no longer able to see in front of me at all. Visibility was zero.

In my early twenties I ended up at Melbourne Psychiatric Hospital for a stay of six months. The depression was so overwhelming that I had to undergo daily therapy.

Those were dark days. Memories are scattered, and nightmares abound. I watched one girl set fire to her closet, witnessed a patient jump over the half-door of the nurse's station to strangle the attendant, and saw one man throw a huge table at the doctor in a fit of rage.

Even though I had psychotherapy, I did not get all that better. After all, I was going back to the same environment where everyone expected me to be 'cured.' This was not such an easy trick/task. Fortunately, I was able to get more help from antidepressant medication and the occupational therapy during which I wrote out my tangled thoughts in a journal, thus learning new coping skills. But, it always took so many minutes, hours, and years, subtracted from my life!

At one stage, thinking that the answer for my depression might be solved by having a family of my own, I married and became a mother in my mid-twenties. Things moved very quickly for me in that department. I met my husband-to-be at a birthday party of a mutual friend, and within a few months we were expecting a son. We were young, and decided marriage was the right thing to do. I neglected to tell him of my history of depression. Things went so well for the first two years of marriage that we had decided to have a second child.

My two sons gave me the temporary sense of purpose and stability that I had searched for since it had been stolen from me at the age of ten with my mother's suicide. I began to focus more on my growing sons, while letting my marriage take a leisurely back seat. My depression inevitably returned, and I couldn't keep it a secret from my husband any longer. He stuck it out with me for many years, but one day I ended the marriage. No talking, no counseling, just the words: "I want a divorce," and it was over.

In my late thirties, I found out what it was like to become a divorced mother. The reality hit me that I was likely heading down the same road as my mother; that same path of despair. Actually, the reality of it all slammed me in the face.

With the end of a marriage to a man who never truly knew me, and my sons now entering into teenage phases of their lives that didn't include 'mom' so much, I was left feeling alone and adrift. It was a familiar feeling.

I had put my own weak identity on hold for so long that I wasn't sure if I'd ever be able to answer the universal questions of, *Why am I here, and what the hell is my purpose?*

Toward the end of my thirties, burying myself in a demanding career, and against all odds, I met someone. He was a co-worker with whom I had an instant and mutual attraction. Tall, dark, and handsome, Mr. Jay T. Alvarez was completely unaware that he was about to be sucked into the vortex of chaos that was my life.

At forty and in love with Jay, I felt some happiness returning; but I was still not able to shake some of my deep insecurities and fears. I began asking myself seriously, and not without some silent, hidden hysteria, *why can't I just be happy and get on with it!* Part of me cursed my mother for the one 'gift' she left behind...heredity.

*A*fter reminiscing about some of my past frailties, I shook off the old memories and forced myself back to the present.

I admired the lake on my estate, and watched the sun start to make its morning appearance. With the water shining like a sheet of glass, I noticed the occasional ripple from a fish surfacing. It was so peaceful; though I couldn't deny that I felt a tinge of sadness from the old memories.

As I stared at the majestic oak tree standing to my side, I could hear a mourning dove above me, cooing to her youngsters who were awaiting their breakfast. A couple of frogs on the lake's edge splashed over the rocks, and the sound of the soft wind traveled between each leaf of the many trees that surrounded me. I felt the warmth from the sun. As its rays began to dapple the grass between the trees, I realized that it was time I headed back to the house. My first guests would be arriving soon.

I turned back on the paved trail. I walked around the largest of the oak trees, and looked across the field where I could see a partial view of the house. With its old fashioned southern porch, it was built so that each guest had his or her own private patio, or porch, area. The house held five guest rooms with master baths, and a two-bedroom upper loft which was my personal suite and office. A huge, open kitchen, a great room, sitting room/library, and a beautiful dining area completed the picture.

*A*s I took a deep breath, I noticed that I suddenly felt a little shaky. I knew the effects that my low blood pressure could have on me, so I sat on the bench nearby, under one of the trees. I watched a small, fuzzy caterpillar, which inched its way up the trunk of the tree. *That little guy sure has patience and perseverance*, I thought.

I then felt myself being drawn back again, into another segment of my life's events. My mind was a wanderer when it came to trying to figure out my life.

It was *August of 2008*. I had the man of my dreams loving me, my sons by my side, and a career I had somehow managed to achieve. However, the light that I had come into this world with was slowly being extinguished again, flickering out like the last few seconds of a fully burned candle. I was too exhausted to care why. Stealthily, my lifelong feelings of dread turned into another convoluted depression, which ominously festered inside of me, like a silent killer.

All I wanted to do was to stop the relentless anxiety, curl up in my bed, and sleep the day away. I did that exactly, on and off throughout my life. I began to push my loved ones away this time, as I became more and more isolated. Life, on the other hand, never ceased its relentless hold on me. It was coiled around me like a snake; either to trap me or to protect me.

That's the thing about perceptions of fate or reality. You never knew when they were going to collide with life, as you knew it. But when they did, your existence would never be the same, such as in the next major storm that hit me.

I dragged myself to work on that day of reckoning, back in the late summer of *2008*. I was forty-one years old at the time, and a manager for a large sporting goods outlet. I had little to no energy left in me. I had been feeling the effects of insomnia taking over my nights; but I didn't think much of it and pushed on.

Looking back now, I should have taken more notice of my excessive sleepiness, and the new tiny heart palpitations in my chest. Ignoring those little clues that my body was giving me, I kept on going through each day; thinking that the alarms had become mistaken signs of anxiety. I took for granted that our bodies were more than capable of giving us a 'heads up,' when things were going seriously awry within.

It was around ten o'clock in the morning. While climbing a ladder at work, I began to feel dizzy. The room started to spin, and I began to perspire; as if I had just run a race. The heart palpitations that I had ignored for weeks were pounding like mad, and not about to be dismissed any longer.

My eyes lost focus, and seemed to lock into place. It was like looking through a kaleidoscope.

The next thing I remembered about the entire episode was waking up in the hospital. The smell of disinfectant in the air, and the sounds of beeping all around me, were the first clues as to where I was. But why was I there?

I couldn't move my hands. That was distressing, and panic was rapidly consuming me.

I could not see anything, and I quickly became aware that there was something covering my eyes. I heard people talking in the distance and tried to yell out to them. Wishing the words to come out, but unable to speak, I became even more frightened. *Why can't I talk? What's happening to me?* I wondered in horror.

I attempted to move my body to the side, in the hope that someone would see my dilemma; but I was unable to budge.

Finally, a break. I was able to move my fingers, so I began tapping them on the bedrails that my hands were secured to. I wasn't able to produce much sound with the tapping of my fingers, but I hoped that someone would see my fingers moving in a type of frantic code.

A monitor that was connected to me had started making more noise, so my inner panic became apparent. My heart, racing with fear, was beating fast. The sounds of machines beeping and buzzing were getting the much-needed attention of personnel.

It was then that I felt a gentle hand take hold of mine. I heard a woman's calm voice say:

"You're okay, dear. You are in the hospital, and your hands are secured so you don't pull out your breathing tube. You've had heart surgery, Miss Aries, and you are just waking up. We will take your breathing tube out very soon. I can promise that. You'll be able to talk then. Please squeeze my hand if you can understand me."

Her voice comforted the fear that was racing through me, as I wrapped my fingers around her soft, warm hand, and squeezed. I didn't want to let go of this stranger's hand. I didn't need to know anything about this person. It was her soothing voice and her gentle hand which softly cradled mine, that made me feel safe, again.

I began to fade in and out of sleep. I remembered waking up; and this time the covering over my eyes had disappeared. Through fuzzy eyesight, caused by the mixture of anesthesia and pain medication, I began to see everything that was happening around me in the large Intensive Care Unit. I closed my eyes and gave in to the weariness of the nightmare.

What seemed like a three-day sleep was only about thirty minutes. Jay, my love, entered the ICU with my two sons.

They looked at me with sad eyes and nervous smiles. I had suffered congestive heart failure from a defect in my mitral heart valve. I had just undergone a transplant and now would be reminded of my mortality by the constant ticking of my mechanical heart valve and lifelong dependency of blood thinners.

I spent two days in that ICU before I was moved to a private room on the cardiac floor, where my physical and emotional recovery began.

I decided, for many reasons, not to return to retail after my heart surgery. The ten-year-old me was still buried deep in the sand back in Florida, still too frightened to face reality. No amount of time passing, or short-lived diversions, such as a life-sucking career, could seem to dig her out. So why go back to what almost killed me? The months that followed my heart surgery were devastating. But I was not prepared for what was heading my way: another severe clinical depression.

It was not an easy time in my life as I pushed away and lost the man I loved, while going through the worst depression I had known, thus far. Maybe using the word, 'pushed,' is an understatement. I actually shoved my loved ones away. After months of psychiatric care and medication, this time, I totally poured my angst into my writing, and somehow managed to finally get a small manuscript finished. I had started it years earlier. There were parts of the novel I completed that I can't remember writing at all, but I did.

After much sweat and many tears, research, and rewrites, it was published in the late summer of *2009*; one year after my heart surgery. I dared to day-dream about what I would do if my book became a best-seller. I started to develop a vivid idea of investing my money into building and owning an exquisite house. It was to be a sort of bed and breakfast; a spa, and resort, rolled into one. A kind of 'shelter from all storms.'

My novel became a modest hit, and it became profitable enough for me to take a chance and form an official business plan.

I dared to venture out of my shell, and began drawing up an outline. I was also taking baby steps back into my first priority: *living my life.*

I printed out a list of different contractors in and around my area. I mustered up the courage needed, and made necessary phone calls from my little one bedroom apartment.

With every call, I hesitantly explained that I was looking to build a home big enough to use as a type of 'bed and breakfast.' I verbally detailed the kind of real estate I was looking to build on.

One by one, contractors told me politely what I would need before they could even sit down and talk with me...more financing and better credit.

I knew that a request for a seven-bedroom, custom built home on approximately sixty acres was not exactly an everyday request. But, their numerous questions on how I would be financing the project was obviously going to come into the conversation at some point. My novel had recently been published and was doing surprisingly well, but not nearly well enough for me to take on this monetary endeavor all on my own. My modest savings for a down payment was not going to be of much help.

Feeling a bit dejected at first, I might have let my journey end there. I could have tossed my dreams aside. But, after surviving heart failure and severe depression, things began to change deep within me. I was left believing that my future must hold a larger purpose; otherwise, why the hell was I still here? The feeling was so intense that I became impervious to the rejections I received.

With one, then two, baby steps toward inner security, I believed that the right contractor would somehow be more interested in my excitement and the reasons for building my dream, than how I was going to pay for it.

With a call to *David and David Custom Homes* out of Kerrville, Texas, things got moving with a startling change of direction.

It was late one afternoon when I spoke with Mr. Henry David for the first time. Henry David II, that is. He had been in the home building business for an amazing fifty years, starting at nineteen, with his late father, Henry David I. His father was a gruff, but kindly man. He was a no-nonsense business man, without the sense of humor which made Henry Junior so customer friendly. Known for designing custom homes with an old-fashioned love for the trade, the father and son team was also gifted with contemporary knowledge in home building and design.

They were leaders in environmental efficiency as well as beautification of space.

Dialing the number late that afternoon, the phone only rang once; then I heard a soft voice on the other end of the line:

"David & David Custom Homes; this is Henry David. How may I help you today?"

He sounded noncommittal at first. I was surprised that the owner of such a prestigious company would personally answer the phone. I shakily uttered my first words to him.

"Ahh, hello? Hello... Mr. David?"

"Yes, this is he; may I help you with something today?" His kindly, but distracted tone of voice almost made me hesitate in continuing with my inquiries.

"Yes, thank you. My name is Jessica Aries, and I am interested in talking to you about building a custom home." Cautiously, but with mustered boldness, I continued, "Would you have any time to talk, sir?"

As hesitant as his response seemed at first, I was slightly taken aback with his next words:

"As a matter of fact, Miss Aries, I have all the time in the world," said the owner of *David & David Custom Homes*.

"Well, Mr. David..."

"Please, call me Henry," he politely, and somewhat whimsically, interrupted me.

"Henry, I need some assistance in designing a house that I will be using as an Inn. I would like the house to be beautiful, relaxing, and inviting, so that people will look forward to reserving their stays for the purpose of rejuvenating their spirits. I've had some medical issues, so my credit is not great anymore, but…"

There it was; those three simple, but magical words: "rejuvenate their spirits," that had Henry now listening intently. One could almost picture him sitting straight up in his chair. He coughed, slightly.

"Henry, each guest room would be one of a kind, with relaxing and gorgeous views of the property," I continued…

I'm looking to build it on about sixty acres, with a lake and walking trails…"

"Excuse me, Miss Aries, so sorry to interrupt, but…"

A familiar feeling crept up inside of me when I heard him say those words.

I was ready to be asked how I was going to be financing all of this, and of course, the same old question: "what is your credit like?" I simply replied with, "Yes, Henry?"

"Again, so sorry for the interruption, Miss Aries, but I am wondering if you might have time to get together for lunch to discuss this vision, in person. I'm quite interested in this 'rejuvenation' idea of yours," he replied, with a new level of excitement in his voice.

With a spark of hope, I happily answered:

"As a matter of fact Henry, I have all the time in the world, too."

Not a procrastinator, Henry suggested that we get together almost immediately. The day we met for the first time, Henry appeared with a little dog in his arms. "So, this is why you suggested an outdoor café." I smiled at him, and Felix.

Henry was as soft-spoken and kind in person as on the phone. He was a nice looking, older gentleman with short white hair, and a white clipped beard and mustache. Very neat. I especially liked his crinkly-eyed smile. His blue eyes almost twinkled. We ordered a light lunch and coffee.

"Tell me, Jessica Aries, a bit more about your vision."

We spoke of business and aesthetic matters concerning my dream estate. He often commented positively on my ideas. He then spoke of Will, his life partner, and Will's heartbreaking battle with an illness that took

13

his life. He told me that Will made him *promise*, after nursing him was over, to go somewhere 'to rejuvenate his spirits.'

"He used those very words!" Henry reiterated with excitement.

"Get out!" I exclaimed, forgetting my manners.

"But yes, my dear," Henry smiled, and went on, "I felt the same strange, but 'right' feeling talking with you over the phone the other day." I stared at this handsome man, absurdly thinking: *He's a sharp dresser.* I searched his eyes. *Yes, it was there; that goodness and joy inside of him was real. I could feel it.*

It wouldn't be until later, though, that I found out the whole reason as to why Mr. Henry David and I were meant to cross paths. He and I were about to embark on a building venture with a purpose; creating a place that would touch the lives of others, unlike anything we had ever imagined. And, my life was to intersect with his in the strangest of ways!

Dishes and Wishes

Walking towards the front entrance of the house, I passed the large outdoor fountain with a bronze statue of the endangered whooping crane. The walkway to the front door wound over the koi pond and passed native plants and flowers. There were hummingbird feeders and birdhouses of all sorts. Along with a birdbath of marble and tile, this was surely a home for nature lovers.

As I entered through the front door, the first thing I noticed was that Dan, our resident chef and manager of the house, had put an amazing fresh flower arrangement in the foyer: a mixture of red and white carnations, yellow roses, and purple iris. *Beautiful flowers for a beautiful home,* I thought to myself.

After taking a moment to stop, and literally, 'smell the roses' in Dan's floral arrangement, I gazed over at the foyer's fountain for a moment. I took out a penny from my pocket, made the same wish I did every morning, and tossed it into the third basin.

The fountain in the foyer is my favorite part of the house. I got the idea for it when my assistant and friend, Aubrey Saunders, and I were out one night.

Aubrey and I had met on an especially bleak day in my career period as a sporting goods store manager. I was just about to strangle one of the assistant managers, when Aubrey waltzed into the store in an outfit full of bling! Everyone eyed her closely, but covertly. I bravely went up to her to see if she needed any help.

"Well, you see," she said with one hand on her hip and the other waving around a Kate Spade handbag, "I do need a bit of assistance. My ex dared to tell me that I had better tone up before I hit the dating scene again. Can you believe that?" she exclaimed, with an honest to God real pout.

"Well that wasn't very nice of him," I commiserated. And, I suggested she might take it in a wiser way than it was intended.

"How about trying some light resistance bands that do exactly that, without a lot of equipment? That way, you will tone up and feel better, and maybe show him a thing or two, while you're at it. And by the way, the bands also work as a great slingshot if he continues his ridiculous verbal assaults. Personally, I think you look great."

Aubrey nearly clocked me with her bag when she turned to me, and put her hand on my shoulder. "My dear, what an excellent idea, and what a nice thing to say. Please show me these marvelous inventions."

I explained the concept to her, and demonstrated some different brands of exercise bands. Aubrey was sold.

"So my dear; I see its Jessica," she peered at my name badge. "Could you actually get away for a lunch…my treat?"

I was so close to packing it all in that I decided, then and there, to go ahead and take a break. Why not. I called Greg over (the assistant store manager), and explained that something had come up and he would have to take care of things.

Needless to say, the lunch was fabulous and we became fast friends.

As far as the fountain in the foyer, my favorite part of the house goes, I thought of the idea for it when Aubrey and I went out to eat at a quaint little Italian restaurant.

The restaurant had a floor to ceiling water fountain that was extraordinary, and I remember commenting to her on how sophisticated and glamorous I thought it was. Aubrey and I sat next to it while having dinner that night, and couldn't help but feel our earthly stresses being almost mystically released into those flowing waters.

I knew I had to have one. My theory was to have three fountains, built into one wall, representing: mind, body, and spirit. The water looked as if it was magically coming through the wall of glass, and collecting into the three different basins.

The basins, with handcrafted polished brass and etched with interwoven circles of three, are stunning. The three of them were positioned side by side, lying flat against the wall and bowing out into oval shapes.

A company contractor for *Flowing Designs* sat with me for weeks developing the wall fountain. They have a huge picture of my fountain displayed in the lobby of their showroom, and get many requests for similar duplications. I once saw one similar to mine at a spa I passed in the mall not too long ago. It had the logo, *Flowing Designs,* etched in the right corner of the glass. I had to smile and hope that maybe I had been a little piece of inspiration in the intricate design of that one.

The fountain in my foyer gives off the continuous sound of gentle, flowing water, while intriguing the imagination with how it's all possible.

Standing or sitting in front of it, closing your eyes and losing yourself in it as your senses provide you with a virtual massage, can be truly relaxing and peaceful.

It seemed a perfect choice for the Inn, because I've always wanted people to come here for a special purpose: to quiet their minds, relax their bodies, and rejuvenate their spirits; whether they are in turmoil, or in need of rest.

"*G*ood morning, Jessica." Dan smiled at me as I turned the corner and entered the kitchen. Standing at the center island, with a spatula in one hand, and a cake stand in the other, he was happily in his element.

"Your sons called while you were out on your morning walk. They said they would be here around noon, just in time for lunch."

"Thanks Dan, that sounds great," I replied, as I took notice of him frosting the delicious looking cake that had the entire house smelling of fresh lemon.

"How was your morning walk?" Dan asked, hoping to keep the conversation off the cake.

"Dan, it was beautiful. The unexpected rain we had last month is showing through in the wildflowers. The lake is so full, and looks incredible. I wish everyone could spend one day on that lake, taking in its beauty. It reminds me of when Jay and I…" And I stopped in midsentence.

Dan knew me so well by now that he knew what I was about to say and why I had stopped.

"Jessica," Dan hesitated for a moment but then continued, "What if Jay is thinking about you, too. He may only be a couple of keystrokes on the computer away." Dan kept his eyes focused on the finishing touches he was putting on the cake.

"Dan, I don't want to talk about Jay, and I'm sorry, but I shouldn't have said anything." I said this with a tone of finality as I made my way toward the cupboard beside him.

Dan was like Aubrey in many ways, one of which was that he was also a hopeless romantic. He thought that if two people truly loved each other, they could get through anything. However, one of the ways those two differed greatly was that Dan could cook, but Aubrey was a disaster in that category, despite all of her great intentions and efforts. Only Dan and I were privy to this tidbit about our dear Aubrey, so we kept it our little secret.

Both Dan and Aubrey were approximately ten years older than I was, and although each of them had been married before, they still believed in the magic of true love.

I also believed in romance, but when it came to talking about my true love and soulmate, whom I had let slip away, my emotions always seemed to overwhelm me. It was common knowledge that I was adamant about not talking about Jay.

As I reached for a glass, Dan kindly changed the subject saying, "by the way Jessica, I'm planning a grand dinner tonight. There will be a buffet of fruits, fresh veggies, and my famous smoked fish and shrimp kabobs. I'm also whipping up some baked potatoes and grilled zucchini to go with the salad, which features a few of my special homemade dressings."

Visualizing the dinner in my mind, I replied with a smile this time, "Dan, you really do spoil us."

"Oh Jessica, you're just saying that. I'll bet you say that to all the guys," he laughed.

I looked around the room, even turning my head looking behind me, and said, "Looks like you're the only guy here, and even if there were a kitchen full of master chefs, I'd still only say it to you."

When it came to planning meals, Dan already knew what our guests' dining preferences would be, as well as taking into consideration my food allergies. Funny how things happened. I developed a bad reaction to gluten a few years back and was diagnosed with celiac disease. Dan came up with the idea of sending out questionnaires to our guests so that he could properly plan meals around any food preferences or allergies.

Aubrey and I sent out those customized questionnaire forms to all our guests before their visits every month. To our pleasant surprise, every one of them had been answered. It was just one of the things we did to set ourselves apart from other inns and resorts. We didn't know how well Dan's idea would go over at first, but it had become a huge part of our success. The questionnaires were totally optional, but they helped us make every stay a one of a kind experience. One could be as loquacious or as discreet as one preferred.

For instance, two of the guests arriving were Jack and Rosemary Hastings. They were married seven years, and both filled out their questionnaires in beautiful detail.

Rosemary loved white roses and red wine. She had wanted to read the book, *"Collected Stories of William Faulkner,"* for years, but had no time. She enjoyed bubble baths and the scent of lavender. Her favorite way of relaxing was sipping hot tea with ginger and lemon, right before bed. She also missed reading. She used to be an avid photographer and would have loved to have more time to get back into taking photos, too. She preferred not to eat red meat, but would still eat fish and dairy.

Jack loved to fish, and hoped to spend his mornings by the lake. He wrote on his questionnaire that he really wanted to unwind, and maybe even rid himself of a temper tantrum that had been brewing within, that was possibly ready to explode. He planned to have his newspaper and coffee by the lake, while letting his overworked wife sleep in during their stay.

He would have loved to spend more time with his wife, without the constant SOS calls from her work. Needless to say, they had added fuel to his fiery temper lately. He also liked a vodka martini now and then, extra dry, two olives.

When Jack called to make the reservation for his wife and himself, he confided in me that they desperately needed some special time together in order to rekindle the spark that their careers were slowly extinguishing.

He heard what a breathtaking place this was, and wanted to know if we could help him put something special together for Rosemary during their stay. I told Jack that I knew just the person for him to toss some ideas around with. That would have to have been Aubrey of course. She was the one person I knew who lived for surprises and was a hopeless romantic. As long as there was no cooking involved with Aubrey, it would turn out to be a great surprise. Jack and Rosemary did have an interesting private life, past and present.

Thou Rosemary and Jack both had some issues in their marriage, they had high hopes for their future together. Jack grew up in Dallas, Texas, in the shadow of his father, a well-known attorney. That was one reason he set out to work for another law office after he passed his bar exam. He became an equally well-known attorney in San Antonio, Texas. Jack never felt complete until he met Rosemary in San Antonio. He had been searching for a soulmate, and he found it in her.

Back then, Rosemary had worn old-fashioned, little white gloves, and a lacey-collared blouse under her powder-blue business suit. She was such a charmer, he remembered with a smile of bemusement to himself. Rosemary grew up as a pampered young lady in an old wealthy Savannah, Georgia family. But she still felt she needed a career of her own and a life of her own. She had received a job offer as a paralegal in one of the most prestigious law firms in San Antonio. She took the job and loved it. Rosemary was always independent and cultured, and was able to 'neutralize' her once, thick, southern accent. However, it was heartwarming whenever she threw in a well-placed 'Sugar,' now and then.

There was a wild side to Rosemary, too, and she was great fun. She was the outstanding partner of his life.

Some things had popped up that had confused both Rosemary and Jack. Rosemary had become friends with a man who shared her passion for photography. Jack took this as an attack on his manhood.

Rosemary and Jack were passionate people: about their careers, their fun, and their deep love affair of many years. So any little threat to this world of passion was taken as very serious business. Rosemary had dared to step outside their little world with brave, trembling, small steps. Something inside of her felt this need. Jack reacted as if stung by a wasp. That was the state of their marriage upon their arrival at the Inn.

Many of our guests who did not hear about us by word of mouth, like Jack did, found out about us through our website. There, they could see pictures of the property and read reviews. We explained that besides their individual suites, house pool, evening gourmet dinners, and the surroundings of nature, the little town of Boerne was only a small drive from the Inn. It had attractions to visit, as well.

However, it wasn't a rarity for our guests to skip the town attractions all together, and just enjoy a piece of paradise right here. We made each stay that customized and special.

The name of our charming getaway was simply: *Luna's Hope.*

Our mission statement:

No matter how much heaviness is on your mind, no matter how much stress is in your body, and no matter how dark your spirit may feel when you arrive here, our hope is that your mind, body, and spirit will leave feeling as bright as Luna, our beloved moon, who shines on brightly through all darkness.

When I say *our* mission statement, I am referring to my collaboration with my silent business partner, Mr. Henry David.

That would be Henry David II, the home builder, who helped me to fulfill one of my greatest dreams.

The day that I first asked him by phone if he had time to talk with me about a building venture, he replied, "I have all the time in the world." It was the same day that Henry David was preparing for his retirement. Of course, that all led up to our first meeting, in person.

*S*till in the kitchen, watching Dan swipe the last wave of chocolate frosting across the cake, I asked him, "That cake wouldn't be gluten-free by any chance, would it?"

"But of course," he replied, as he stepped back, eyeing the completed masterpiece and smiling with pride. "Jessica, my gluten-free cakes are just as delicious as any *regular* cake out there. People wouldn't be able to tell the difference if I didn't tell them, and so far, I've never heard of anyone who is allergic to *not* eating gluten."

I laughed at his quick humor and had to admit that he was right. The man knew how to cook. Gluten or no gluten.

The cake looked scrumptious and I could smell the fresh lemon. "Mind if I give it a little taste test?" I asked, with a thinly disguised pleading in my voice. The truth was that I simply lusted after that cake!

"Sorry Jessica, my dear; this is part of your surprise at dinner tonight." Dan said this as he deftly moved the cake to the counter behind him, out of my eyesight.

"But it looks and smells so good, Dan. May I ask what my special surprise is for?"

"You can ask all you want, Jessica, but you'll get no reply from me. Did you miss the part about it being a SURPRISE?" Dan repeated, with a frown of frustration starting to show.

"Oh please… just a little hint?" I asked, pathetic and borderline begging. I liked surprises, but I liked finding out about them even more.

"I would, but Aubrey is the boss on this one and she has sworn me to secrecy." He spoke firmly and no longer made eye contact with me, as if I could break him of his silence with the look of desperation in my eyes.

"Okay Dan, but if you leave that cake unattended, I can't be responsible for my own actions," I said half-jokingly.

"That sweet tooth of yours is going to get the best of you one of these days. I swear Jessica, if you so much as pick one tiny piece off that cake, I'll let Aubrey make your next cake, by herself!"

Dan laughed heartily as he shook his head. He reminded me of his first experience in the kitchen with Aubrey.

"Madre de Dios," that girl could *cook;* just not in the kitchen," he laughed again.

He told me how he had asked her to cut up half an onion and toss it in the stew. He was called to the phone, and afterwards returned to the kitchen.

"*What*?!" There was a brave attempt at cutting up half of an onion which was left on the cutting board. In the stew was the uncut other half.

"Madre de Dios," he recalled saying, "I never saw anything like that. Where I come from, even young girls know about these simple things."

I laughed too and said, "Well Dan, it's just that Aubrey comes from a part of the south where little girls from well-to-do families learn certain things first. Like exquisite manners, beautiful home décor, flower arranging, and skills such as those."

Dan sighed and agreed, "You know Jess, I've always had sort of a crush on Aubrey, and it came as a shock. But I can take it. I'm a strong man and a good teacher," he joked, pounding his chest.

"Well, let's just try to keep this our little secret okay, TarzDan," I joked back.

Dan nodded in compliance, thinking, *I guess I'm getting pretty good at keeping secrets.*

Several guests asked how Aubrey and I met Dan.

She and I went out to eat a few years ago to celebrate the completion of my novel. We tried out a cozy little restaurant in downtown San Antonio, on the Riverwalk. We first made the acquaintance of Mr. D'angelo Romano (Dan for short), disguising himself as our server. Unbeknownst to us, he was really the executive chef of that fine establishment. He also took a special liking to Aubrey at first sight.

As our 'server,' he came to our table and offered us something to drink, along with explaining the chef specials in mouthwatering detail.

I guess it should have been more obvious to Aubrey and myself that our "server" had only served our table, and no others that night, but we were too awestruck by the food to notice.

At the time, Dan was fifty-two years of age, with shiny dark black hair cornered around his ears. He had expressive, almond-shaped eyes the color of honey. His voice was soothing, and came across as gentle and sincere. Dan was about 5'10 in height, with a medium strong build, and a smile that could light up an entire room. He had been working with innovative cuisine for over fifteen years. But he had been dabbling in the art of cooking since he was a boy.

That night, when he first approached our table, he dazzled us with his knowledge of the menu items and recommendations with his beautiful Mediterranean accent, and then took our orders.

When he disappeared back into the kitchen, Aubrey commented on how handsome he was. Listening to soft music playing in the background, she and I began to talk about our day, as a different server brought out the bottle of red wine that we had ordered. She poured each of us a glass while lighting the candle on our table.

Aubrey and I felt like we had left this world behind and arrived in an alternate reality, wherein she and I were the only people in the restaurant.

A short time later, lost in our conversation, Aubrey and I took notice that Dan had returned to the dining area and was approaching our table. This time he had his creations in hand for us to behold.

"Ladies, your dinner is served," Dan said with a flourish, as he set the tray of food down. He proceeded to place Aubrey's platter in front of her. He then gracefully lifted the shining silver lid off the platter.

If it's one thing that Aubrey could appreciate, it was beautiful food.

Aubrey had grown up in a very well-to-do environment, so eating out at fancy restaurants was the norm for her. I would even go as far as to guess that the mansion's kitchen in the Saunders Estate was seldom, if ever used, except by the staff, when Aubrey was growing up.

Her eyes glazed over and she stopped talking about her day, and simply stared at her plate. Her senses looked to be going into overdrive.

D'angelo then paid me the same courtesies, and my breath was taken away as well.

Aubrey's plate consisted of Duck with a Raspberry-Pecan Sauce. The plate was filled with vibrant color, brought out by fresh raspberries and a sprig of green mint. The duck meat was displayed with crisscross patterns from the grill, and drizzled with a red wine and raspberry sauce. My plate consisted of Tenderloin of Beef with Mushroom Sauce. Buttered Shallots, cooked in red wine and seasoned with black peppercorns, added color. It was like magic. We were speechless!

"Go ahead ladies, please, taste…," he invited us in a voice filled with pride.

After each of us took a bite, and felt our taste buds come alive, we knew that somehow, someway, Mr. D'angelo was going to become our very good friend.

It wouldn't be until after dessert when another server approached our table and informed us that the executive chef had not only created our meals and served us personally, but that Dan had also taken care of our bill, along with formally inviting us back again.

*A*ubrey walked into the kitchen of the Inn where Dan and I had been talking. I was still mesmerized by the cake on the counter, but I didn't say another word about it.

She walked around me and opened the refrigerator, took out a bottle of water, and, with a big smile, she greeted Dan first.

"Hi Dan, I see you are desperately trying to keep Jessica from that dessert you've been working on," she stated with subtle humor. She then took a drink from her bottle, while giving me a whimsical wink on the side.

"Jess, you know he is not going to let you eat any of that cake until after dinner. Besides, I have an idea. How's about you and I go and see how I set up the guest room for Jack and Rosemary?"

With that, Aubrey locked arms with me, as girls in the South still sometimes do. Aubrey led me away from my cake and out of the kitchen. Not without a backwards glance from me, though.

We entered the guest room that was now ready for Mr. and Mrs. Hastings. As only Aubrey had the talent to create the level of comfort the room held for those two people, it just warmed my heart.

She had the king bed made up with Egyptian cotton sheets, and a lovely lace-covered comforter that I had picked up at an antique shop that I frequented in Boerne. It was called, *History in the Making*.

The curtains, a perfect vanilla lace accent to the bedding, let in just the right amount of daylight. During the cooler months, if fresh air was what our guests wanted, the curtains were light enough to sway in the wind from an open window. The only night lights outside during the evenings at the house were the moon, the abundant stars in the sky, the glowing lights from the swimming pool, pond lights, and patio candles.

The Hastings' suite had a table for two in the corner of the room that was made from vintage cherry wood. Aubrey had placed one of Dan's Lenox vases filled with blooming white roses on the little table. At the opposite side of the room was the master bath, with a two-person whirlpool tub encircled with lavender candles. A new bottle of lavender bubble bath sat on a shelf. The two-person vanity, with an entire wall mirror, was connected to the marble walk-in shower. All amenities were included, and were set up luxuriously, along with the fluffy white bath towels.

The attached patio was theirs alone, offering their own view of the property during the day, and a quiet ambiance in the evenings. Their patio had two lounge chairs with a low drink table in between. In front of the loungers were three candle stands ranging from three to six feet, encased with glass hurricane shades. The pillar candles under the glass were vanilla scented.

Each guest room was designed to give an exclusive and brilliant view of the nature surrounding the house. A portable stereo system on the nightstand of each room had headsets, meditation music, and CDs available to use. Unlike most suites in the commercial-type hotels, there were no televisions in any of our guest rooms.

On the nightstand of the Hastings' suite, next to the stained glass lamp, sat a book covered with a pretty purple bow. Waiting for Rosemary, it had been especially picked for her: *Collected Stories of William Faulkner.*

Aubrey took out her camera and walked around the room, looking for the perfect shot. She loved taking photos of the guestrooms right before the guests would see them. She would ultimately frame the picture of their suite and mail it to them as a courtesy gift. It's those thoughtful added touches that made a stay with us so memorable. I was especially happy with the atmosphere of the Hastings' suite, because I knew this weekend was very important to both of them, and to their marriage.

Suites and Treats

*T*he call came in that our first guests were entering through the front gates, so Aubrey and I headed to the front of the house, near the Koi pond, where Dan was already waiting.

The pond was a beautiful touch to the house. With its cascading waterfall, tri-level rock formations, and floating waterlilies, it stretched from one side of the front entrance to the other. The fish would swim in groups under the bridge to the front entrance. The entire pond, surrounded with colorful plant life, was a vision of serenity.

Rosemary (Jack and a few close friends were the only ones who called her Rose) and Jack had had a little tiff on the way to the Inn about Jack's driving. This was a common theme and cause for stress. Rosemary had asked Jack to slow down earlier, and Jack had done a mental slow burn, until he finally pounded the steering wheel. He nearly shouted, loudly and sarcastically, "Rosemary Hastings, are you driving, or is it me at the wheel, hmm?" He did this often, sounding like a petulant child sometimes. Rosemary sat back and sighed.

If only Jack could relax and calm down. Or was this trip all a bad idea? She did not care to even guess. However, Jack's little temper tantrum blew over quickly, as the surrounding scenery began to enchant both of them. Driving in from San Antonio, the changing landscape really was lovely. The Texas Hill Country, with its rolling green hills, began near Boerne. Jack had cooled off by then, and he had recalled some private memories that always made him smile to himself. He and Rosemary again looked like your typical, happily married couple, on the road to a getaway weekend. In fact though, a keen observer might be able to take in the nervous look in Rosemary's eyes, and perhaps a bit of the 'sergeant' in Jack's demeanor.

Jack Hastings stepped out of the driver's side of their new model, jet black, four-door Toyota Avalon, and came around to open the passenger's side door for his wife. Jack was dressed in a pair of golf shorts, a light blue polo shirt, and casual walking shoes. In his questionnaire, he said that he had a passion for his career in law because he enjoyed fighting for patients' rights.

Jack was built as if he had seen a gym or two in his day, and stood about six feet tall. The look on his face, as he took his first gaze of the property, was priceless. Within his smile, it was obvious that his first impression was just what he (and we) had hoped it would be.

Rosemary, on the other hand, slid her legs to the door while adjusting a high-heeled shoe with one hand, and holding her cell phone to her ear with the other.

"I'll call you on Monday, so just focus on the reports for the company president. I left you a list of details to go over at Friday's meeting. The meeting with Mr. Stuart is very important, and I know you will do great. I'll talk with you on Monday…yes, yes, I will try to relax…you have a good weekend, too."

With that, she pushed herself to a standing position, straightened her checkered, knee-length skirt, gave up her cell phone to her husband, as promised, and headed to the trunk of the car for her luggage. She, unlike her husband, had yet to stop and take a look at where they would be staying. Rosemary Hastings took her job very seriously. When asked on her questionnaire about a passion within her career choice, she wrote, "Vacation time is always a plus."

With luggage in hand, Jack and Rosemary walked up to the front door, where the three of us were waiting.

"Welcome to *Luna's Hope*," Aubrey greeted our two guests, and then proceeded to introduce Dan and myself.

"Hello, it's nice to meet you both. I hope you found us with no problems?" I asked, as I shook both of their hands. I was curious to see if my suspicion was right about their relationship being in more trouble than Jack lead on over the phone. I was coy about it, but I did take notice that the two of them didn't seem to look at each other much.

"Yes, your directions were perfect," replied Mr. Hastings.

"And, may I take your luggage to your room for you while the ladies show you around?" Dan asked.

"Yes, thank you, that would be lovely," Mrs. Hastings said, finally beginning to let obvious thoughts of work take a backseat to the beauty all around her, which she was just starting to notice. And did she take notice of the nature! Suddenly, a yellow and black swallowtail butterfly flitted around her like a sign to wake up. Her immediate thought was about where her camera was.

With that, Dan was on his way to deliver their luggage, while the four of us walked into the house. Stepping into the foyer, Jack stopped and looked intensely at the fountain.

"This is amazing. I've never seen anything like it before," he said.

"Thank you, it's my favorite part of the house." I smiled proudly.

"Shall we go to the kitchen so we can get you both something to drink before we give you the grand tour?" Aubrey asked.

"That sounds nice, thank you," replied Rosemary, as she looked closely at the details of the foyer fountain; her mind spinning with ideas again of how she would love to photograph it from different angles.

"Miss Aries…" said Jack as we headed down the hall towards the kitchen.

"Please, call me Jessica, and may we call you Jack and Rosemary?"

"Absolutely, Jessica. I just wanted you to know I have read your book, *"Finding Grace in Pennies,"* and I'm honored to meet you in person."

Rosemary nudged Jack quickly on the arm and gave him a *look*. He cleared his throat and apologized, saying, "I'm sorry; I meant *we* have read your book, and are *both* honored to meet you." Jack's face turned a little red with embarrassment, for he had accidently forgotten to include Rosemary in his compliments about the novel.

"Thank you very much; and it is nice to meet both of you as well," I replied, with a smile, but thought, *"yes, these two are far apart, but I've seen miraculous things happen to people when they came for a visit, so this should be interesting.* I had a pretty good feeling about them, immediately.

We entered the kitchen, *Dan's Place;* as stated by a handmade brass, embossed sign hanging decoratively over the sink. Made by one of our previous guests in appreciation of the care Dan put into every meal, he was really proud of it.

The center kitchen island was four feet wide by six feet long, with a speckled-cream and russet-colored granite top. Above it was a shining steel chandelier of pots and pans, ranging from stainless and brass, to wrought iron.

Next to the refrigerator sat a chilled wine cooler with beveled glass doors. Attached to the wine cooler was an antique stained glass fixture that held an assortment of wine glasses.

"I love this rack," Rosemary stated as she took a closer look at it.

"Thank you, it came from an antique shop in town. Do you like antiques, Rosemary?"

"Oh, please, call me Rose, and antique shops…yes, very much indeed," she said, as she looked around with delight. She removed her jacket and looked more comfortable in her sleeveless silk blouse.

As the couple was avoiding eye contact with one another, I purposely asked them both a question. I also reached for her jacket, since she had a large bag over her shoulder, and a small purse, too.

"Well then, would you two like to check out that little shop while you are here? The shop owner is now a friend of mine, and I think you will be very impressed." Then, we returned to the kitchen tour.

Rosemary just smiled at Jack, but said nothing, as she knew getting her husband into an antique shop would be about as easy as dragging him to get his back waxed.

Oh well, they did make eye contact at least, I thought. Dan kept a spotless, organized kitchen. The appliances were all stainless, including the range hood that looked more like a fireplace chimney. Surrounding the center island were granite counters galore, enough space for a culinary artist to create a masterpiece. There were enough cupboards built floor to ceiling, storing what looked like every plate and glass known to man. This room was Dan and Aubrey's favorite part of the house.

Everyone had iced tea. We went on to the dining room.

This impressive room held a dinner table made of oak that sat up to ten people. A crystal chandelier dangled above the vintage table surrounded with plush, auburn captains' chairs. Each of the three rose-painted walls showcased paintings. They were all originals by Michael Morgan.

Two paintings were of vases filled with fresh flowers so colorful that guests often wanted to smell them. The third work of art undeniably drew the most attention. It was of a woman standing on an upper balcony, overlooking the ocean, holding a glass of red wine in her right hand. Her long, dark, auburn hair flowed in the wind as the sun was starting to set.

She was wearing what looked like a white gown of cotton and lace. Next to her bare feet lay a small dog, curled up and sleeping soundly. The name of the painting was, *A Gentle Breeze.*

Under the dining room table was an Oriental carpet that Aubrey and I purchased from an estate auction.

The owner of the auction house said the carpet came from a famous teahouse in Japan. It was dark maroon, with white lotus blossoms throughout. Aubrey *had* to have it for the dining room, and she is quite the bidding artist at an auction house.

"This is the dining room, where Dan will be tantalizing our taste buds every evening around 6 pm," Aubrey announced proudly.

"Yes, and we are expecting six more guests to arrive this afternoon, two of which are my adult sons. All are invited to dine together," I smiled.

"Dan already has meals planned per your food request, and, as you know, the kitchen is open for self-serve from 7am until 2pm, so you can create a breakfast or lunch as you choose," Aubrey added.

"That sounds delightful," said Rosemary, loving the eye for detail in the rooms.

"There are many options in the pantry and refrigerator, so please make yourselves at home," I repeated as we left the dining room.

Passing through an arched hallway with built-in book shelves filled with volumes of books, we arrived in the sitting room.

The sitting room, with its cathedral ceiling, was as comfortable as it was vast.

Four cozy, Victorian-style chairs and a comfy couch that would seat six, were placed in a 'U' shape in front of the rock fireplace that encased the entire wall. Pillows, hand quilted in earth tones, were tossed in random fashion on the large, rustic, brown leather couch.

On one wall, a two hundred gallon aquarium, filled with colorful fish swimming contentedly in their own underwater world, graced the area.

The windows of the room were ceiling high, letting the outdoors in, and outlined with crown molding. Looking out any of the six windows, you could glimpse the manmade lake, some of the walking trails, and the massive array of beautiful old trees. No trees were cut to build the Inn; rather they were accommodated.

The room had cedar beams and hardwood floors. It was furnished with linen fabric in neutral colors, and casual window treatments. They added some natural elements and directed attention to the views.

Above the rock fireplace hung another original painting by Michael Morgan. This painting, over four feet in height, was entitled *Branches of Time*.

Done in acrylic paints, a senior magnolia tree stood alone under a clear blue sky. Its painted branches, full of lush green foliage and blossoming, peach-colored magnolias streaming out in all different directions, were a symbol of change and growth. Sitting under the remarkable tree on the plush grass, holding a notepad of paper and busy writing, was a woman lost in thought. That woman was me.

My passion for these paintings by Michael Morgan was obvious, and they were commonly a topic of conversation initiated by some of the guests. It wasn't an oddity for a guest to contact Michael to purchase one of his prints for their own home.

He was not only one of the most talented artists of his time, he was also a very close, personal friend of mine.

There were three guest rooms that could be entered through three separate halls from this sitting room. The Hastings' room would be on the other side of the house, so we continued on the tour back through the central hall, and came upon the great room.

The great room, a large open room with a beverage bar that could seat eight, also sports a pool table, a white Steinway baby grand piano, and window views overlooking the swimming pool and verandas.

"Please check out your room; it's the one down the hall after you enter the door on the left. We have a swimming pool, walking trails, and a sweet little lake you may want to explore," Aubrey said, with excitement and pride.

"Thank you so much, we are so excited to see our room," Rosemary exclaimed, very enthusiastically now.

Passing through the door on the left, and down a short hall, they came upon their suite. As they entered the room, Jack was beaming as he looked lovingly at his wife and said, "Rose, look—white roses."

"This is so nice, Jack. How did you find this place?" She asked this as she leaned over, gently grasped a rose in her hand, and took a deep breath in. The soft scent of the rose awakened her senses. It saddened her slightly that Aubrey and I knew her favorite color and type of rose, but Jack didn't, until now. Then, her thoughts briefly strayed to a certain friend of hers, Mitch McCoy, who also happened to be aware of her favorite rose.

"A man at my office brought his wife here last year when they first opened. I'm so glad you like it, Rose," Jack said, as he sat on the end of the bed watching his wife explore the room. He never tired of watching her. He just needed to tell *her* that.

A four-poster bed, with a silk canopy and coverlet strewn with embroidered white roses, matched the other furniture of walnut wood. Lots of comfy, white pillows were casually placed atop the bed. An antique vanity table held a silver mirror and a white, porcelain jewelry tray. An old fashioned, stained glass lamp was another interesting object with an art deco look to it.

Jack hadn't seen his wife's smile in some time, and he couldn't help but feel as if it was going to be a very special weekend for them.

As Rosemary admired their suite and smiled happily, Jack was incredibly relieved. He had hoped for months that Rosemary's internet *friend* that he had accidently discovered, was nothing more. The couple badly needed some time together to talk and relive their best times. Jack needed reassurance.

Rosemary, meanwhile, as she was inspecting the lovely room, smiled and remembered some those special times, at the same moment. However, her thoughts again strayed. She, too, was looking for a certain reassurance.

"I do like it," replied Rosemary, as she made her way into the master bath for a look-see.

Taking notice of the lavender candles that outlined the circular whirlpool tub, Rosemary was almost ready to stop right there, start filling the tub, and step in for a much needed relaxing soak.

"Rose, honey," Jack called out…"you may want to see what has been left for you on the nightstand. I think you are going to be surprised."

With one last, lingering look around the master bath, she smiled. She looked forward to spending lots of peaceful time indulging in the amenities of that room, and sorting through her ambivalent thoughts.

As she walked back into the bedroom where Jack was sitting, Jack motioned over towards the night table and her eyes followed, spotting a book on the stand. She picked it up, untied the lace bow, looked into her husband's eyes, and said, "Thank you Jack; this place is incredible."

Walking past the hall near the kitchen, I spotted Dan out on one of the verandas watering some calla lilies, so I walked out the French doors to meet him. He looked over my way and smiled, as I thanked him for taking the luggage to the Hastings' suite.

"Sure, Jess. They seem like a nice couple."

"Yes, they do. Oh, and by the way, I just got a call that the Embers sisters will be here in about two hours. Would you mind very much telling Aubrey for me, please? I'd like to step away for a little while."

Now watering the purple irises that were emerging from a large planter on the veranda, Dan smiled and said tactfully, "It's good to get Aubrey away from the kitchen to where her real talents can be appreciated, no?"

"Yes Dan, as a matter a fact, I understand completely. Last night I saw one poor excuse for a potato trying to be baked in a small George Foreman Grill. You wouldn't happen to know anything about that, would you?"

I grinned and shook my head in fake 'dismay,' as I turned around and headed into the house. I shook my head again, this time for real. I was thinking how funny it was that Dan actually thought that I didn't know his crush on Aubrey was much more. In fact, I had to bite my tongue and smother a huge laugh.

Heading up the stairs to my office, a two bedroom suite above the kitchen, with my mind full of ideas for my next chapter, I was determined to put my thoughts down in print before they escaped my memory.

That's the unpredictable way my stories tended to unfold. One minute I was thinking about sneaking a piece of cake, while Dan is out of eyesight watering his plants, and the next, I was heading to my computer with new plots and characters filling my head.

My little desk, a vintage maple piece of history that was a gift from my friend Martha, in town, sat directly in front of a huge picture window. I could gaze out and see the lake from it. It held my laptop computer, a small lamp, some notebook paper, and a candle. I often pulled out the bottom drawer on the left side of the desk, (which I found by accident), and propped my feet up on it as I typed.

You couldn't tell that the drawer was even there. It blended into the wood. I moved the desk into my office one day when I saw that the desk had a slight scratch. I thought maybe I had scratched the vintage piece of wood moving it, so I inspected it closer. It wasn't a scratch at all, but a built-in secret drawer. It was stuck at first, but with a little elbow grease, I was able to pry it open. But there was nothing secretive inside, except the carved initials, EB.

I called Martha at the antique shop, and she said that it was vintage from the 1800's, and that the monetary value of the wood was not high, but it was the person who was said to have owned the desk previously that made her choose it for me as a gift. It was rumored to have belonged to an author by the name of *Emily Bronte,* who was a poet and novelist, until she died at the age of twenty-nine in 1849.

Martha had picked the desk up at an auction in New York. She had more knowledge on the pieces in her shop than any other antique owner I had ever known. Going to her place of business, ironically called *History in the Making*, was like stepping into a time capsule and taking a journey to the past. Pieces that were once a part of our history were passed on, becoming a part of our future.

Martha asked me once when it was that I first knew I wanted to become a writer. Reading poetry was one of her favorite pastimes.

I told her that I had always planned on becoming a writer. I had always been a good storyteller, and as a child, I wrote little stories about animals, birds, you name it. One day in 2003, after my divorce, I just started writing out a story that had entered my thoughts. I thought it would be a good outlet when I was feeling sad or anxious. I became addicted to it quickly, and thought about my characters often throughout my day.

I looked forward to escaping my real life when it became stressful. Writing took me to a place where I could create and fantasize.

I finished the first rough draft of my now published novel in 2007. Yes, it took me years of writing, here and there, and making about a million changes along the way, before I finished the story.

Strangely, just as suddenly as I started writing *Finding Grace in Pennies*, I just as spontaneously closed my computer one day, put it away, and left it alone for more than a year.

A few months after my heart surgery in 2008, I decided not to continue with my career in retail, because I felt the stress was going to be too much to deal with, again.

As it was, I was experiencing some post-op depression. One day, I opened my computer to the novel I had finished writing about a year previously, and I read it from beginning to end.

As the story began to unfold once again on my computer screen, the characters started to come back to life in my mind, and I was reading a story that moved me.

As I read, I changed some things, added some things, and without realizing it…I was editing my own story.

It was an amazing feeling that I could take what was in my own thoughts and imagination and put it into words.

I didn't know at the time what was going to happen with the novel that I had written, or the incredible journey it was going to lead me on, but I knew it was something that I had started, and I was determined to see it through. At the very least, I knew my family would buy a copy from me!

Finding Grace in Pennies turned out to be a life changing story.

*P*ulling out my black swivel chair and making myself comfortable at my desk, I put on my headset and began singing to a tune on the radio, as I often did when writing. Little did I know that my singing ability was one huge, ongoing joke between Dan and Aubrey. They would stick their fingers in their ears when I was not paying attention.

I glanced out at the lake as I was about to start typing, and I found myself suddenly distracted, thinking about Jay again. Jay Alvarez, the man of my dreams, who was so close, yet so far away.

He was the one who told me that the world needed to hear Grace's story in my novel. He was always supportive of me, with his optimism and flair for life. I missed that.

Now living across the country, in San Francisco, fulfilling his dream of becoming a successful computer programmer, our relationship had turned bittersweet.

Jay and I had met at work in late 2006. Both in the same type of business, our paths crossed on a daily basis.

Spending everyday working together with someone in a stressful environment can bring people together, or split them apart, quickly. In our case, it brought us together. At work, he was such a strong manager. He was able to leap merchandise hurdles in a single bound, faster than a speeding bullet when he was needed to soothe an irate customer or associate. Jay could also make me, and so many others, laugh harder than anyone I had ever known. His ability to impersonate people, and create lyrics out of the blue, had people in stitches on a regular basis. He was also able to lift my spirits with gentle words of encouragement, and remind me of my inner strengths when I doubted myself. Even though he managed to succeed in retail effortlessly; it was not his dream career, and we both knew it.

After my heart surgery, an opportunity came about for Jay to train in California for a computer programming company. He had turned the offer down at first, thinking that there was no way he was going to leave me behind after all I had been through. I convinced him that he should go, and that I'd be fine while he completed his training. People have long distance relationships all of the time, and our love would get us through anything.

It was painful for me to push so hard for him to go, but I couldn't live with myself knowing that I would be the reason that he passed on a chance to fulfill his dreams. I hid my emotions well, and kept reassuring him that we could get through this, and that I was going to be fine.

Jay reluctantly took the job offer and went to San Francisco. We continued to communicate everyday by phone, talking about our future plans together, and making the best of being apart. I tried to fill my time away from him by writing and editing my novel, but it wasn't working out as well as I had hoped. I began to lose focus, getting frustrated with myself. Then, I regressed back to a state of depression that turned both our worlds around.

My depression had gotten more intense each day, and I finally told Jay that it was nothing he did or didn't do. It was me. How cliché; but so true. I wasn't sure I could be happy anymore, no matter what the situation. I wanted to hide from everyone and everything, especially the dark thoughts that were filling my mind. Whatever it was that was happening to me, I felt little to no control over it.

Jay felt helpless, too, even suggesting he give up his training and come back to be with me. I couldn't let that happen.

Why should he do that? I had nothing to offer him anymore. Depression was talking for me.

I was depressed and damaged, and he had his whole life ahead of him. He could give up everything for me, and I could turn around and have another heart failure and die. He deserved a better life than worrying about me. Those were just some of the dark thoughts that consumed me.

So I told him, "No! Don't come back, please; because if you do, I'll only feel worse. And, I really want and need to be alone right now."

That really confused and upset him. He had never heard me say anything like that before. He asked me if I still loved him, and I answered, "I'm not sure I can love anyone or anything right now; I'm so sorry." And those were the painful words I left him with. I deleted my email account and social media page on the internet, and I let my voicemail take all my calls. Depression and my genetic propensity toward it left me very isolated.

One day, about a month after not returning any of his calls, he left me a particular phone message that repeats over in my mind to this day:

"Jessica, I'll always love you, and I'm sorry I don't know how to make your sadness go away. Tell me what I can do. You mean so much to me, Jess, and I'll be there for you, always. Please call me back. Don't keep pushing me away, Jessica."

I wanted to call him every day to let him know that I loved him, too, but I was still feeling emotionally unstable and unsure of myself. I decided to stay reclusive and hide from that world.

Jay continued to leave me voicemails to let me know how he was doing, and that he missed me and loved me. I heard them all, but did not reply once. I'd pick up the phone and start to push the numbers to call him back, but then I'd start crying and just hit 'end.' I wanted him to be happy, but I just had no happiness to offer him. I was miserable. I can't say that I ever actually attempted suicide, but I will admit that even though I wanted to live, at the same time, if my heart did give out again and I was to die, that would be okay, too. That was my depression talking, again.

Months went by like this, until I finally sought the help of a doctor who was able to guide me through the fog. Slowly, I was able to write again, and I sent out query letters every day for months. I'm not quite sure how, but my query letters got better with each one, and I caught the eye of a literary agent. My energy was surging at the time.

Jay had never left my mind or my heart, and I knew that someday I would find the courage to reply to his calls and tell him why I became so distant. I was so wrong for pushing him away, yet I could not explain to him what made me do it. The only thing that kept me from contacting him was that, and my fear that I might have pushed him too far away.

Jay had kept me informed of his training and his life out in San Francisco for almost three months. Then the calls stopped. By then, I wanted more than anything to share the good news about my book with him. I wanted to tell him that he was a huge part of my believing in my novel and my having the courage to seek out a literary agent.

I wanted to explain the sadness that I finally knew was normal after open heart surgery, and I prayed he would understand and forgive my actions. There were so many things I wanted to tell him!

I finally gained enough courage to attempt to contact him, about eight months later. I sat down and wrote him a long hand-written letter. I had his phone number, but a phone call was not going to be personal enough for what I wanted to tell him. I still had his address in San Francisco, so I sealed the letter and mailed it out before I lost my nerve.

I waited restlessly for weeks for an email reply or a phone call, and I checked my mailbox every day. One morning, about three weeks after I had sent the letter to Jay, it was returned to me, unopened, with a stamp that said, 'return to sender.' That day, I took it as a sign, and realized that I had waited too long. Jay must have moved on, and I had lost the one man that truly ever made me happy.

I decided at that moment that there had to be a way to help others who were experiencing depression, and the emotional ups and downs of the roller coaster ride of post-heart surgery and clinical depression.

I needed to bring awareness to others, so that maybe they would stand a chance against this surgical side effect. I talked to several hospitals to find out what support groups existed, if any, in my area, and after finding out that there were very few, I started one.

Sitting at my desk, thinking about Jay, I could feel a lump creeping into my throat as I remembered the very words spoken to me not so long ago on the cardiac floor by an elderly man named Kenneth.

"Some say everything happens for a reason, little lady. So keep your eyes open, and you will be shown the way."

Those words had seen me through many difficult times since my heart surgery. I thought about my experience at that hospital often, and I thanked God every day for the miracles I had been shown.

I then lit the candle on my desk, took a deep refreshing breath, and began pouring my thoughts onto the keys of my computer.

Typing for about an hour, I heard a knock behind me at my office door. "Come on in," I called.

"Hi Mom, how's the new novel going?" Chase asked, as he walked over to kiss me on the cheek.

"It's going great. How was your speaking engagement in Houston?"

"It was amazing, Mom. We spoke to the largest crowd yet," Trey replied, with his big blue eyes glowing.

My oldest son, Chase, was twenty-three, and my youngest son, Trey, was twenty years of age. Besides their day jobs, they were both inspirational speakers with a local youth group. They started speaking to small groups a few years ago, and that day they spoke in front of a thousand people at Houston's Civic Center.

Trey had reached his full height of 6'5 by the time he was fifteen. With long brown hair and natural waves, and highlights that made many of us women envious, he had a slender build and the most gorgeous deep blue eyes I've ever seen on a human being. It made him hard to miss in a crowd.

Chase stood about 6'1, same slender build, with silky, medium length blonde hair and a contagious smile. Chase could connect with people naturally and effortlessly. Both guys were so sweet and handsome that it made me break into a smile thinking: *these are MY boys!*

Each of them have had their own share of bouts with depression and dismay, but their use of philosophy and insight was undeniably beyond their years.

It was not always easy for us. We grew and changed many times, apart and together, through the good and the bad.

I remembered the first time they signed up to speak with a small local youth group about depression in teens. I didn't know what to expect when I went to watch them. There I was, listening to my young adult sons along with ten others, taking turns talking about life in a way that I wouldn't have believed, if I hadn't heard it for myself. Teenagers and parents were listening intensely, and asking questions and sharing stories. The night ended with many tears and hugs throughout the room.

There happened to be a gentleman attending that night with his teenage son. His son had been suffering with depression for about a year, actually attempting suicide once. At age fifteen, the boy had been fighting a battle within that just seemed too overwhelming to win by himself. He struggled for weeks with depression, followed by weeks of sleepless nights, and thoughts racing through his mind faster than he could process. It wasn't until he swallowed a bottle of sleeping pills, and had an extensive hospital stay, that he finally got answers.

He was diagnosed with bipolar disorder. The night of the youth group's first speaking engagement, that boy opened up for the first time about his inner pain, connecting with my sons and the other teens.

He reached out for guidance and embraced their advice about how to rise above the label that he had felt he had been given. That night had changed the boy's life in a way that was described by his father as, "nothing short of miraculous." His father happened to be on the board of directors for a local hospital, and he began to spread the word about the youth group's inspirational meetings. I'm proud to say my sons have been holding these meetings at schools, hospitals, and auditoriums throughout the state ever since.

Chase and Trey Aires had arrived here at *Luna's Hope* for a relaxing weekend before heading back to work. They had their own apartment back in town, near their jobs, but this weekend, they would be relaxing here with me, and staying in one of the suites for the four-day weekend. They had plans to meet their boss here on Sunday afternoon. That was my good friend, Henry David II. Henry had met my sons when we first started building *Luna's Hope* together. That was when Henry took notice of Trey's talent for detail and passion for design. Henry offered Trey an apprentice position in the design department of his company. He had been a mentor to him ever since then.

Henry may have technically been retired, but he still found a way to keep one hand in the company. At seventeen years of age, then, Trey was the youngest apprentice ever brought into the company. Chase, with his gift to connect with people, joined the sales team and was very successful.

Henry was extremely supportive of their passion for speaking, so he worked around their meeting schedules, even attending them at times.

I had not seen my good friend Henry in about two months, and I was really looking forward to his visit. Henry usually visited for a few days at a time when he came, driving up in his beautiful RV with his little dog, a Yorkshire terrier named "Felix."

Henry and Felix traveled everywhere in their home on wheels those days. That weekend, they were arriving back from a trip to the Grand Canyon, and I was sure he would have some fun stories and pictures to share.

The morning was about to become afternoon. After my sons arrived, I put away my computer and spent some time listening to their wonderful stories from the speaking engagement and meeting in Houston. They were real stories that tugged at my heart strings. Especially upsetting was the story about the young girl who had been suffering with anorexia for three years. It was too close for comfort for me, as I suffered with that illness myself for a short time, as a young girl.

When the call came in that the Embers sisters, Melinda and Kelly, would be arriving shortly, my two sons went to their room to unpack and I located Aubrey. She was trying to make herself a baked potato in a George Foreman grill, again. I could see Dan's predicament. He truly cared for her, but this was unreal. I asked Aubrey to help me with greeting the Embers sisters, and told her that I'd help her with cooking the potato afterwards.

The sisters, who had not seen each other in over five years, were coming to reunite here. From their questionnaires, Aubrey and I knew that Melinda and Kelly had a lot to share over the next four days. Melinda was a twenty-five year old single woman who owned her own floral business in California.

Kelly, thirty-two years old, was a hard-working, stay-at-home mother of two young daughters, ages ten and eight, living here in Texas. It was Kelly's husband, Ben, who orchestrated the getaway vacation for the sisters. Both women enjoyed reading, walking, swimming, and relaxing, so he felt this would be the perfect spot for them to reunite and catch up on their lives.

Melinda's taxi arrived first, at around noon. Aubrey and I were waiting next to the pond at the front door of the house.

The driver graciously opened the passenger door, and out stepped Melinda. She was a beautiful woman of about 5'7" with long, flowing blonde hair, dazzling, hazel eyes, and a shy smile. She was dressed in a loosely fitted, cream-colored, sleeveless dress and sandals. She came directly from the taxi to shake our hands and introduce herself.

"Hello, I'm Jessica, and this is Aubrey, we will be your hosts for the weekend." I gave her a big, welcoming smile.

Reaching out to shake our hands, Melinda replied, "Hello, I'm Melinda Embers."

"Your sister will be arriving soon, so would you like a nice cool drink while we wait for her?"

"That would be great," she said. She seemed a bit distracted, though she certainly looked very together.

Approximately five years earlier, Melinda had moved from her home state of Texas to California, at only twenty years old. Transferring colleges, she finished her last two years of school in California with a business degree, and at the age of twenty-two she was engaged to be married. Her entire life was before her. She had met her Prince Charming while living in her small college apartment. He was delivering flowers to her roommate one day when Melinda smiled at him and said, "Maybe mine will come tomorrow."

To her surprise, her flowers did arrive the next day. A beautiful bouquet of daisies arrived with a card that said: *To more tomorrows…*

Keith Shoji, owner of, and sometimes even delivery man for "Hearts and Blossoms" flower shop, had brought the bouquet of flowers to the beautiful woman he had briefly met only one day prior. When Melinda went to thank the man behind the flowers, they talked for over an hour. From strangers to friends, a spark had flickered. Keith had sent Melinda daisies every week for two months, always with a card saying: *To more tomorrows…*

One week, his card said: *Would you give me the pleasure of taking you to dinner?*

To Keith's surprise, he received a bouquet of flowers himself. The card said: *I would love to have dinner with you.*

The two became closer as the weeks turned into months. Keith asked Melinda to marry him on their one year anniversary from the day they first saw each other. They were inseparable, engaged, and soon running his floral business together.

It had been two months to the day before the wedding, when Melinda, busy preparing dinner, was awaiting Keith's return home after he made one last minute floral delivery. She received a call that there had been a terrible automobile accident.

Melinda lost more than her fiancé that day. She had lost her best friend, her faith in God, and her passion for living. She covered her pain with long work days and a stoic demeanor. She was determined to carry on for Keith.

Surrounded by beautiful flowers in the shop her fiancé had willed to her, she was unable to notice any of their splendors anymore. Melinda had not spoken to anyone about her sadness since his death. Her family tried to get her to talk, but she always told them, over the phone, that everything was going to be okay, and she was just trying to move on. They couldn't see the tears of pain she held in. Melinda made hiding her pain a profession, so she thought.

Kelly, however, knew her sister all too well. The tone in her voice said that she had taken on too much sadness to handle by herself.

After talking over her concerns with her husband Ben, he made the trip possible for the sisters. Kelly's hunch was correct, and Melinda had taken a turn for the worse. She had been falling deeper into the abyss of depression, and began having nightmares and more ominous thoughts of dread. Melinda had been closing the shop more than it was open, and when she wasn't working, she would sleep long hours. She had been so sad, at times, that she even began contemplating suicide.

Melinda told herself that this weekend trip with her sister would be good because she could have some kind of closure with her. All she needed to do was keep herself together for four days, let Kelly know that she loved her, and then go back to California and say goodbye to this cruel world. It somehow made perfect sense to her.

She saw the taxi pulling up the driveway and put on her professional, fixed and phony smile.

The three of us girls waited anxiously beside the pond for the grand reuniting of sisters.

Melinda stepped away from Aubrey and myself, and was walking towards the taxi before it could even come to a complete stop. Melinda opened the door for her sister, and Kelly stepped out. The two sisters embraced in a hug filled with tears of nervous excitement. Aubrey and I could not contain ourselves, and the waterworks began to fill our eyes as well.

As the sisters dislodged from their embrace, Kelly stood in full view of us, and we noticed that there was a bit of a surprise that she had brought along to show her little sister. Kelly was a good five months along in her pregnancy. She looked precious, with her rosy cheeks, and hair up in a ponytail. She was wearing a pair of black maternity shorts, white tennis shoes, and a white flowing top. She, too, looked like a model, even pregnant.

"Oh Kelly, you are simply glowing—I had no idea. Congratulations! When are you due?" exclaimed Melinda. For a brief moment, Melinda felt a spark of happiness.

"I'm due around Halloween. There is so much to talk about, little Sis. But first I really need to use the restroom, please," Kelly said as she hugged Melinda.

"Absolutely ladies," Aubrey hurried us toward the closest bathroom. She then said, "let us show you to your room. You may want to freshen up. The grand tour will wait for whenever you are ready."

Walking with the sisters down the hall toward their suite, I watched as Kelly took Melinda's hand. It made me feel oddly wistful.

"Thank you, we will," said the two, as they spoke in unison.

"The suite down on the right will be yours. Please let us know when you're ready for the full tour," I smiled.

Now it was time to hold up my end of the bargain, and I was off to the kitchen with Aubrey, to show her a better way (the microwave oven) to bake a potato.

4

Secrets

*J*ack and Rosemary were already out by the pool. They had their swimsuits on and a couple of tropical drinks in hand. Rosemary had her new book with her for some reading pleasure.

One of the nice things here was that once our guests were greeted and shown around, they were free to make themselves at home.

Dan was in the kitchen pouring an ice cold glass of sweet tea. Aubrey and I were enjoying hot baked potatoes, loaded with butter and cheese.

"Dan, did you hear from Kathryn DuBois as to her estimated time of arrival today?"

"Yes ma'am, she will be arriving at approximately one thirty this afternoon."

"Sounds perfect. We have some time to relax," I said as I finished the last bite of my potato.

"Jessica," Aubrey asked, "do you by any chance know what the tastes of Kelly and Melinda are, as far as flowers?

"I don't think they specified on their questionnaires, but my guess is that they would be daisy or lily of the valley girls. Gosh, you do think of everything. What about Mr. Tom Hanley's room?" I joked.

Dan was quick to reply sarcastically, with: "I put thistles in all the single men's rooms!"

"You would," Aubrey punched him lightly on the arm.

We were all laughing when the Embers sisters walked into the kitchen.

"Perfect timing, the kitchen is all yours. Maybe when you are finished with your lunch, we can take you on that grand tour. Everything you need to cook or prepare something is either in the refrigerator or the pantry. The dishes, flatware, napkins, and glasses are all in the cabinets. Feel free to use whatever you like," Aubrey offered, as if she was the master of the kitchen. I had to contain my laughter at her magnanimous tone.

I faintly heard the engines of the ATV's starting up in the garage, so I went to see where my sons might be heading. Stepping out into the driveway, I waved towards my sons and asked, "Hey guys, where are you going?"

"We were going to visit *Peace*," replied Chase over the sound of the engines.

Lovingly named *Peace*, the two year old magnolia tree was their gift to me for my 42nd birthday. We planted the magnolia near water and some shade. They are not meant for hot Texas summers, but it has thrived. My sons knew that this species was my favorite type of tree. They explained to me that I was branching out in new directions of my life. By completing my novel, building this Inn, and surviving heart failure, I was starting a new chapter in my own life's story.

The boys also included a hand-written card with words that deeply touched my heart.

The card that came with the little tree read:

> *Dear Mom, it's time for you to grow with*
> *'Peace' in your life.*
> *Thank you for always*
> *loving us unconditionally.*
> *Love always,*
> *Chase and Trey*

My sons and I were not always this close. For a time, after my divorce from their father, Chase took it very hard. He had bouts of depression, anger, and confusion for a few years, and would not talk to anyone, especially me, about his feelings. I remember him telling me after the divorce that he would never get married. He was fifteen at the time.

It took him a few years before he began to talk about the divorce with me. One day, he simply came to me and said, "Mom, I am really angry!"

His younger brother, Trey, was always the quieter of the two brothers. Twelve years old at the time of the divorce, he never showed his anger. Chase held the spotlight with his outward emotions, so Trey just focused on being there for his big brother. That was a very difficult time for them, and for me.

Waving to my sons as they headed down the path, I turned and went back into the house. I felt lucky to have them so close to me, now.

Aubrey was working on the finishing touches in Kathryn DuBois' suite, so I joined the Embers sisters in the kitchen as they were devouring their peanut butter and banana sandwiches. I smiled as they explained that they had many fond memories of eating the odd combination together as kids.

Kelly did not have a lot of time to herself the over past few years. Married to a busy, dedicated police officer of eleven years, with two young daughters and domestic duties galore, she was in comfortable cleaning clothes most of her days. She had talked to her husband many times over the past years about missing her sister. Kelly knew that her sister was hurting, and she was suffering her own type of sadness because of it.

Kelly's husband knew the only way to help his wife and sister-in-law was to bring them together, and that is exactly what he was able to do. The sisters, seven years apart in age, were always close, but Kelly saw herself as more of a mother figure to Melinda. Melinda was fifteen years old when Kelly got married at the age of twenty-one. Having her first child at age twenty-two, and second at age twenty-four, Kelly loved having her younger sister so closely involved with the kids. It wasn't until Melinda was twenty years old that she decided to take a grant at UCLA to complete her bachelor's degree in business administration. It had been the first time the sisters had ever been apart, and they missed each other more than they knew.

"Well, ladies…how do you like your room?" I asked them both.

Melinda smiled and said, "It's beautiful, and thank you for the chocolates, too!"

Melinda's favorite food was chocolate, so we had set a box of gourmet chocolates on her pillow. Also, Aubrey found some tulips in the garden and brought them in. The girls loved this final touch.

"The view on the patio is incredible, and my bed looks so comfortable. I can't wait to get a kid-free night's sleep," Kelly laughed.

"You are very welcome. How about that tour now, shall we?"

"Let's," said Kelly and we were off towards the sitting room.

After the tour Kelly decided to take a nap, and Melinda took a walk to check out the lake.

At the lake, there were two row boats, two kayaks, and a pier. The lake was filled with fish and had poles and bait for fishing. Of course we had one fishing rule. All fish had to be released, and in the event that any fish were caught and couldn't be released, they would be given to Dan to be made into a meal.

Melinda took one of the rowboats out and noticed some wild daisies growing near where the rowboats were docked. She remembered the daisies that Keith had sent her the day after they first met. Quickly wiping away a stray tear, she maintained her plan to keep her pain hidden. However, sometimes things don't always go as planned.

"**J**essica, Kathryn is arriving soon," Aubrey said as we met up in the main hall. "Come see her room quick. It's missing something, and I don't know what."

Aubrey always said things like that when she wanted to involve me in getting the rooms ready. She knew I did not have a big talent for decorating, but she wanted me to feel involved, as if I did.

"It looks perfect, Aubrey," I said after entering the room and glancing around.

The rooms are set up similarly, except some had either a king or two full size beds, but each room had added touches to customize the area for each guest.

Kathryn loved plants and flowers, so we bought her a pink bougainvillea plant. It was a nice, local gift that she could take home with her. Aubrey had it hanging by Kathryn's patio door for her.

Kathryn's suite was elegant like her, yet soft and romantic, too. Pale yellow walls, snow white lacey curtains, a matching coverlet, and a vintage cut-glass vase on the maple vanity table; all served to invite the guest to relax and get comfortable. Fluffy white towels and candles were in the bath, and Aubrey had even remembered to put a soft, white, leather journal and pen on the maple nightstand, since Kathryn had mentioned her intention of starting one.

I asked Aubrey if we should get the fresh flowers that Dan had in the kitchen and set them in the vase on her vanity, since she mentioned that she loved flowers so much.

Aubrey replied with excitement, "That's it! That's what's missing! The yellow roses. Perfect." Aubrey always flitted about like a butterfly. I smiled to myself in amusement. I assumed it was what kept her so slim.

With that, Aubrey ran to the kitchen, before meeting me back at the pond for Kathryn's arrival.

Kathryn pulled up in her little sports car. It was a fire-red convertible Corvette, with music blasting, and personalized plates.

Kathryn DuBois had just turned sixty. She was a newly retired clothing buyer for a high-end chain of department stores.

She had been widowed five years earlier, and had spent the last few years of her career hiding her loneliness in long work hours.

At the age of fifty-five, after a routine pelvic exam and sonogram, Kathryn was shocked with her diagnosis of ovarian cancer. She worked two more years, spending her days at her job, even though she was in and out of the oncology department at the local hospital.

Kathryn, currently in remission, and now living the retired life, had come here with a purpose. She was looking to get closer to nature, and have some time away from hospitals, doctors, and the curious, who kept asking her, "how are you feeling, my dear?"

She confided in us about her diagnosis and remission, but asked us to keep it confidential, so that she could enjoy her vacation without health questions or looks of pity from the other guests.

To see her step out of that little car with her big smile and the pep in her walk, you would never guess what inner and outer turmoil this woman had gone through over the past years.

Kathryn had had an interesting life as a clothing buyer and occasional fashion columnist for the style section of the local newspaper. Though she kept mostly to herself socially, much of it was because of her late husband Blake's anti-social behavior when he drank, which was often. They could never go out without Kathryn feeling on guard for Blake's next blowup.

Kathryn lived a lonely life back in those days, and now that Blake had passed away, she felt confused. Still lonely, but in some ways she felt a relief of a sort. That in turn brought a bit of guilt with it.

She had grown up a smart, precocious little girl who loved playing with her Barbie dolls and dressing them all up. Sometimes she designed her own little outfits for them, not knowing it would lead to a future career in fashion. Many lonely school days were spent at home, for Kathryn had a form of scoliosis and needed to be in a body cast from the age of ten to about twelve. She was homeschooled for two adolescent years. Those two years were difficult to make up socially, so Kathryn was always behind a little in that department. Growing up, she had always felt a bit like a bystander, watching everyone else at the prom dancing the night away.

Kathryn had looked forward to this getaway, and meant to make the most out of her visit to the Inn.

"*H*ello Kathryn, it's so nice to meet you. I'm Jessica, and this is Aubrey. We'll be your hosts for the weekend."

"Girls, you have no idea how happy I am to be here. I have friends who've spent time here, and they can't say enough about how great they feel after staying with you. And they always look fabulous, too. What's your secret," she joked, good-naturedly.

"Thank you Kathryn, we hope you will feel the same. As for the last part, we can't take all the credit, but the air here is wonderful."

Dan walked up and introduced himself, asking if he could take her luggage to her room. Dan had a talent for showing up just at the right moment. Without him, Aubrey and I would be lost. And he was good at keeping Aubrey's cooking challenges a secret, too!

"Yes, and thank you," Kathryn replied. "Nice to meet you, Dan."

"Are you thirsty, Kathryn? We'll be touring the kitchen first, and we have plenty of cool drinks to choose from."

"Why yes, I am a bit parched...do you have Diet Cola? And thank you, for the thought," Kathryn replied.

Passing the foyer fountain, Kathryn paused and commented:

"What a gorgeous wall. I think I'll make a wish."

There were pennies in the basins from past wishes, including my own. Kathryn had read online about our guests making wishes in the fountain when they arrived. She took out her penny, closed her eyes, and tossed it into the second basin that represented the body. Then, on a whim, she tossed in a quarter. *"You never know!"* She thought automatically, not without surprise and amusement at herself.

After touring the house with Aubrey and myself, Kathryn happily went off to check out her suite.

We had one more guest arriving today, but his flight was not due in until three o'clock. Mr. Tom Hanley was a fifty-six year old owner of a famous motorcycle shop, *Hanley's Hogs,* in North Central Texas. He had won a four-day stay with us at a silent auction.

Tom Hanley didn't know what a day off was anymore. He was a workaholic in denial. He secretly thought of himself as the nicest guy you'll probably never get to meet, but others might beg to differ.

He was not an open book, to say the least. His seemingly nonexistent humor, and his sometimes outright sarcastic comments, had people a bit stand-offish when it came to befriending Mr. Hanley.

When it came to relationships, he liked to use the excuse that he had no time to meet anyone because his job was so demanding, but it was just a façade to keep others at a distance.

When Tom Hanley let himself have a few hours off from work, on rare occasions, he sat at home planning the itinerary for his next work day. However, it had not always been all work and no play for Tom. This was only after his bitter divorce. His Ex had left him for her hairdresser. He had only married once, for fear of his heart breaking into even more pieces. He also rarely dated. Yet, he was really a very sophisticated man, underneath. He had quite an education to brag about, if he wished.

Tom had a daughter Ellie, age twenty-three. He had been training her to take over the business for the past three years. For some reason, Tom was not ready to let go of the business yet, and didn't know why, exactly. He suspected it might be due to the fact that he had always been a bit overprotective of his little girl, who had now blossomed into a bright young business woman. After all, he did raise her as a single father, something he was extremely proud of.

Ellie was very capable of taking her updated knowledge of the business world and expanding the company, but Tom just couldn't seem to let go of the reigns yet.

Tom tried to get out of his four-day stay here by offering it to people at work, but oddly enough, no one else could stay this particular weekend.

Unbeknownst to Tom, Ellie had made it very clear to everyone at the office that she wanted her Dad to go on this vacation. So, Tom Hanley was flying in from Dallas, probably worrying about work the entire flight.

"Well Jessica, Mr. Hanley's suite is ready, so how about I school you in a quick game of pool while we wait?" Aubrey smirked.

I looked at Aubrey as she stood in front of the pool table, chalking up her personal pool stick, and replied:

"Sounds like a challenge to me, Miss Saunders, one condition though… the loser does dishes tonight!"

"If you insist, Miss Aries. I'm willing to go easy on you, Aubrey replied, as she positioned the cue ball at just the right spot before breaking.

Don't break a precious nail, is what I jokingly mumbled, under my breath.

I was soon reminded why Dan had warned me so many times never to accept her challenge to the game. I never stood a chance, and it still perplexes me as to how she was so good at pool. She was the last woman I'd ever imagine at a pool hall!

Maybe she was a rebellious teen and just never mentioned it. I can see it now, Aubrey sneaking out of her Fourth floor bedroom window at the Saunders' Estate, and bribing 'Albert' the butler not to tell her parents as he caught her climbing down the rose trellis. Probably to meet up with a dude named Bubba at a small 'hole in the wall' tavern for pool lessons, drinks and a couple rounds of darts! I laughed to myself.

*C*hase and Trey were heading back to the house when Chase pulled his ATV next to Trey's.

"Trey, you can go on back to the house if you want. I think I'll go chill at the lake for a bit. I need to clear my mind."

Flashing the peace sign to his brother, Trey continued on, yelling out above the sound of his engine…"sounds good, see you later, bro."

Chase parked his ATV near the pier and took out the remaining row boat. He began paddling around the big bush near the pier and saw that another guest was already out on the lake. It was Melinda Embers.

Chase pulled his boat next to hers, as he politely introduced himself.

"Hello, I'm Chase. It's a beautiful day to be on a lake, isn't it?"

Melinda had been lost in her own thoughts when Chase paddled near her boat with his introduction.

"Yes, it is a nice day—are you here for the weekend, too?" Melinda inquired.

"Yes, my brother Trey and I are here to visit our Mom for the holiday weekend."

Melinda thought about it for a second and then asked, "Oh, your mom must be Jessica?" Melinda then saw the resemblance.

"Yes, my brother and I have the weekend off from work, so coming here is one of the best ways to enjoy the time. You'll like it here. Will you be staying for the Sunday night barbeque and fireworks display?"

"I have made special arrangements to stay until Monday morning," Melinda answered, looking shy.

"It was a really good time last year. You can see the neighboring town's fireworks perfectly from this lake, and we are supposed to get some much needed rain before Sunday night, so that will be good," Chase enthusiastically added.

"I look forward to it, then. So Chase, I take it since you said you are here visiting your mom, that you and your brother don't live here with her on this rambling estate?"

"No, we keep an apartment in the city, too, near our work and by the skate parks," Chase answered proudly.

"Sounds like you two brothers stay pretty busy. You are lucky to have a place like this to come to and relax, Mr. Aries. It's very nice," Melinda commented, as she attempted to remain polite, even though she really wanted to be alone.

"Yes, this place defines beauty and comfort," Chase said as he took a look across the lake at the property. "Do you live here in Texas, Miss…?"

"Embers, but please, call me Melinda. I grew up here in Texas, but now I own a floral business in Southern California."

"Now that sounds like a cool business; and as for Cali…very cool place to live," Chase smiled. "I'm into nature myself, and I've been to Cali twice with my Mom for some writers' conventions. So, Melinda, when you are not working, do you get to enjoy the beaches there, surfing some rad waves?"

"I have gone to the beaches, but not in a while. How about you…what do you do for fun, Chase?" Melinda inquired, as her gaze slowly lowered to the water again.

She had been an avid surfer with Keith, but didn't let herself revisit those memories, if at all possible. She felt a moment of raw pain. She attempted to hide it from Chase, but her eyes remained a sure giveaway. But, Chase picked it up.

"Actually, my brother and I like to chill and enjoy each day. We also do some volunteer work in our spare time."

"Really? Tell me about it? What kind of volunteer work? Melinda asked, as she lifted her gaze to Chase's eyes.

Chase couldn't remember ever seeing a woman so beautiful, yet with such sad eyes. As they both began to relax in their own boats next to one another, they continued talking. Chase thought Melinda was one young lady with 'flow.'

Melinda was still in her own world, but did notice that Chase talked and dressed differently than anyone she had ever associated with before.

As Chase sat there in his boat, she took notice of his nice posture, and was surprisingly impressed. She looked at his attire; a green t-shirt with a picture of Bob Marley on the front, cut off knee length khaki shorts, white tube socks, and some very colorful skateboarding shoes. His hair was long, wavy, and blonde. He had on black-rimmed prescription glasses, but she could still see the ocean blue of his eyes. Melinda had seen skateboarders on the beach in Venice, so this look was not new to her. She always assumed they were typical beach bums, oddballs, just smoking and 'chillin,' and wasting their precious days and hours.

Chase surely looked that part, too, but something about his gentle voice and respectful mannerisms kept her there, giving him the time of day, so to speak. Besides, he was very sweet looking, she had to admit.

"Well…last night for example, my bro…I mean my brother, Trey, and I spoke with our youth group at the Houston Civic Center. Our topic was called: Jumping Hurdles."

Chase felt comfortable on the lake and around this woman, but he thought he might tone down his slang just a bit. Melinda looked like a classy lady; sad but elegant, and he didn't want to scare her away.

"What did you speak about?" Melinda asked curiously, hoping to keep the questions and focus off of her, although she was somewhat intrigued by him.

"Well, it was about the vast number of hurdles we all face in life, and how jumping them builds our strength. But trying to avoid them just tires us out. You would be amazed, Melinda, at some of the different hurdles people have in their lives. Some are pretty major."

"Sounds like an interesting way to put it. 'Hurdles,' I mean. What about hurdles in life that are too tall to jump; did you address those?"

Melinda spoke the words before she could even realize what she had said. Was she opening up to a total stranger on this lake…and if so, why? She was doing just fine keeping all her feelings inside and hidden, *so why open up now*, she silently asked herself.

Normally, if Melinda's question had come during a speaking engagement, Chase would have answered her question by asking her if she wanted to share a particular hurdle she was facing or had faced. But here on this lake, with just the two of them, and Melinda with her sad eyes, Chase just responded with: "I know there are very tall hurdles out there and sometimes it seems impossible to jump them. But like I said, I've heard some gnarly stories, and people can and do get through some amazing things."

In the back of his mind, Chase had a flashback of a young teenage girl, who shared her story yesterday in Houston. She was overcoming a two-year struggle with leukemia, now in remission. All the while, she was living in foster care, after being dumped like garbage by her drug-addicted, single mother.

Chase looked back at Melinda, and wondered what tall hurdle she was living with that caused such sadness in her eyes. He wanted so badly to ask, but knew that it was not the right time nor place. She didn't even know him, much less want to tell him anything that personal. He felt those vibes very strongly.

But Melinda did like the way it felt to let some of her feelings slip out, so she continued to tell Chase what came to her mind next. "Yes, the tall hurdles…I believe that some hurdles are, well honestly, just not jumpable," Melinda snapped back; this time looking back down at the water next to his boat.

"Yeah, I felt that way, too, at one time. I thought this life was just a bad dream I couldn't wake up from, but anyway, I think differently now. I really believe that the only limits we have in life are the ones we set for ourselves."

Chase challenged Melinda, as he waited silently for her to respond to his comment.

Melinda felt a flicker of anger building inside of her like someone had just put another log on her inner furnace. But, the years of holding emotions in were to her advantage, as she firmly replied: "Mr. Aires, that is a nice optimistic thought, but I'm going to have to disagree. I know people, too, Chase, that have had some things happen in their lives that are so random and debilitating, that they don't have time to jump; and they just crash right into those hurdles, getting very hurt during the process." Melinda was secretly referring to herself. Chase already knew that somehow, but he said nothing.

This time her eyes went cold when she met Chase's eyes straight on. She had made her point clearly, and also showed strength behind it.

She picked up her oars and positioned them as if she was going to relocate her boat, and said, "Well, Chase Aires, you are probably one of the most positive people I have met in a long time, and it's been nice talking with you." She hoped he would take the hint and leave.

"Very cool. And, I have enjoyed your company as well. It's probably time I get back to the house to see what Trey is up to," Chase said, as he took Melinda's cue that their conversation had ended.

"Enjoy your day, Mr. Chase Aries," Melinda said, as she looked behind her and began to row backwards.

"You do the same, and Melinda…"

"Yes," she replied as she kept rowing, still facing away from him.

"Maybe you could let those people you know, the ones with really tall hurdles, not to give up. If they live to love, they will love to live!" Chase quoted his own favorite saying, as he flashed his two fingers up as a sign of peace to Melinda, and paddled back towards the dock. He wasn't sure if she was paying very much attention to him at that point, but he was cool with that, too. He knew that he had all weekend for a chance to talk with her again, hopefully.

Melinda soon heard the sound of the ATV as Chase went heading back toward the house.

*Live to love, love to live…*what the heck does that even mean, she thought with more frustration, as Chase's words repeated over in her mind.

Melinda was now pondering on the fact that she had just barked at a perfectly nice person, and decided on a walk around the lake before returning to the house in order to cool off. Docking her boat and tying it to the pole, she picked a yellow daisy and started walking up the trail as she plucked the flower petals off, one by one.

"To more tomorrows…" the words Keith had written on every card and *"live to love, love to live,"* the words that Chase had just spoken to her, weighed heavily on her mind. She thought again: *And what does that even mean?* She was really pissed off now. *How easy it was to spout phrases that sound 'new age' and catchy. Chase Aries probably never saw, much less jumped, a hurdle in his whole perfect life!* She suddenly became consumed by, and lost in thought, about Keith.

Was losing Keith really a life hurdle that would make me stronger? Really, get real! She thought. Then she saw a yellow and black butterfly land on what was left of the daisy she was holding, and she broke down in pure utter sadness.

"Oh Keith, why can't I talk to you one more time, to tell you how much I enjoyed being with you and how much I miss you?" Then she cried out in pure pain, as if she had been stabbed in her heart.

A single tear escaped her eye, then slowly became a river of tears. Melinda Embers found herself crouching down next to a large oak tree, hands covering her face, and crying silently, but hard enough for it to cause a physical pain in her chest. She had cried like this all too often when she was alone in her apartment in California.

Melinda looked upwards towards the cloudless sky and whispered through her tears: *"Keith, how can losing you possibly make me stronger when all I feel is empty, alone, and weak when I think of life without you?*

History in the Making

"*I*t's four o'clock, Jessica. Mr. Hanley's limo will be arriving soon."

"Thanks Dan. Aubrey's getting dressed for dinner now, so she can assist you in the kitchen later. Could you do the greeting with me, pretty please?"

"Of course Jessica, I would love to," said Dan proudly.

"By the way Jessica, I heard you'll be doing dishes tonight," Dan laughed.

"Yes, word travels fast. I think Miss Aubrey has been practicing her game of pool again. But Dan, don't be so quick to laugh at me. Aubrey is getting ready early so she can 'assist' you with dinner, remember?" I replied humorously, since both Dan and I were well aware of Aubrey's, let's say, *good intentions* in the kitchen.

"No worries Jess, Aubrey can cook with me anytime. I'm a professional, remember," Dan said as he held his head up high.

Thank goodness for that or we might all starve! I thought and smiled.

A stretch black limousine was driving up the long paved driveway towards us, and stopped at the front entrance where Dan and I were now standing. The driver, a young woman in a black suit and leather driving hat, got out of the driver's side and walked around to open the back door for Mr. Tom Hanley.

As Tom stepped out of the car, he said somewhat curtly, "Thanks Suzan, I appreciate the drive in."

With that, Mr. Hanley discreetly handed the limo driver a monetary tip, and wheeled his luggage in our direction.

"Hello Mr. Hanley. My name is Dan, and this lovely woman is Miss Jessica Aires, proprietor of the Inn."

"Nice to meet you both," Tom replied politely.

"Hello Tom, I'm so glad you could make it this weekend. Your daughter Ellie called earlier. She left you a message that she has everything under control; and also left strict orders for you not to worry about work this weekend. She said for you to turn off your cell phone because no one at work is going to be able to take your calls until Monday." Jessica took a deep breath.

Tom half-smiled and said:

"That's my daughter, alright." He expressed himself with a somewhat self-deprecating manner, though he was obviously proud of his daughter.

"May I take your luggage to your suite while Jessica shows you around?" Dan offered.

"That would be nice, thanks," replied Tom, somewhat absently.

"Miss Aries, do I need to give my phone to you, or how does this all work?" he asked.

Tom was not used to being out of his comfort zone of the office, and did not know how to relax in the very least. Even his walk had an uptight way about it. His shoulders were held stiff and high, and he had a very fast walking pace.

"No Tom, this is not that kind of retreat," I said with a smile, trying to keep up with his speed-walking.

"We do have an unwritten house rule about not disturbing other guests with cell phone use, but you can keep it and use it if you really need to. You won't set off any secret alarms," I said jokingly.

"Well, Miss Aries…"

"Please, call me Jessica."

"Well Jessica, since apparently my daughter Ellie has seen to it that no one at work can take my calls until Monday, I won't need this little device on, at least."

With that said, Tom made the first step in releasing some tension. He turned off his phone, placed it in his pocket, and almost immediately, his shoulders lowered a bit.

Tom had an intermittent southern accent, and for some reason, I pictured him out on a ranch with a herd of horses, and not in a stuffy suit.

I could see that he was wearing a pair of snakeskin cowboy boots, and I wondered if maybe he had just been out of his element for far too long. I hoped that maybe a little fresh air would bring back some southern charm to this uptight businessman. I thought about Dan joking about thistles in the single men's rooms, with a silent laugh.

"Well Mr. Hanley, here is your suite. Feel free to settle in, and please, won't you join us for dinner in the dining room at six?"

Tom nodded and said "okay," since he already had other things on his mind. He decided to give his daughter Ellie a ring. He managed to reach her on his first try.

"What kind of damn prison did you put me in?" he asked, in an annoyed tone of voice.

"Dad, it's not a prison, for Pete's sake," Ellie laughed at this gruff side of her father. She knew she could always get her way with her dad, just as she had ever since she was a little girl.

"Just give it a try, and maybe you will get to like it, Dad." She used her most persuasive voice. "Maybe you will meet someone interesting."

Tom grumbled a little more, but gave in to his beloved daughter. He was so happy to have a daughter like Ellie that he would do anything for her.

"Okay babe, but this better be good," he grumbled some more.

"Okay Dad," she giggled, "you've now used your one phone call, so I won't be expecting anymore."

"Very funny, sweetie," Tom replied as he hit 'end' on his phone.

"*R*ose, would you like anything to drink, honey?" Jack asked his wife, as he climbed the stairs out of the pool.

Rosemary was lying on a lounge chair next to the pool, reading her new book and looking even more beautiful than the first time he saw her. The sun shining down on her made her look like an angel, Jack noticed. He made a mental note to complement her more. He didn't know why it came so hard to him. He particularly noticed her lovely hair looking so silky. *And what a body,* he thought with pride. *I must be crazy not to tell her what I see!*

"Thank you, yes, I'd love a cold soda. I'm just finishing this page, and then I thought we could take a swim together." Rosemary flashed a loving smile at her husband. This came so easily to her, she barely noticed it.

"Okay, one cold soda coming up, Mrs. Hastings," Jack said happily, snapping back to reality.

As Jack dried off and entered the house, Rosemary closed the book on her chest and looked up at the azure blue sky with some ambivalent thoughts. Something about the story she was reading, and the beautiful surroundings, made Rosemary start to reminisce about her and Jack's first dates together. She began to do something she hadn't done in a long time. She wasn't thinking about work, or her new friend Mitch. Instead, she remembered how she had met Jack so many years ago. Jack and Rosemary had met at the downtown courthouse in San Antonio.

Jack, already an established and well-known attorney, saw Rosemary's cell phone and various other personal items come flying out of her handbag when some rude and clumsy clown jostled her shoulder roughly. The loser didn't even stop to help her, or ask if she was okay. Jack gallantly helped her get her things back together. As their eyes met while picking up these items, there was a little spark in Jack's gorgeous blue eyes. Rosemary's green eyes met his, and the attraction was mutual and instantaneous.

Jack was thirty-eight, single, and his work was his life. Known to be brilliant in the legal world, he used his talents mostly to help out others less fortunate. Rosemary, tall and slim with super-model legs, was a paralegal working for a large law firm. Her real love was photography, which she longed to make her 'real' job. Extremely talented, she had won some awards for her photos.

"Well, little lady, this here is one enormous handbag for such a dainty woman."

Jack actually struggled a little for words, while looking into Rosemary's eyes. And his old Texas accent could be heard again.

Flustered a little by his verbal clumsiness, he just looked at Rosemary and smiled then, taking in her loveliness as much as possible.

Rosemary was aware that she was pretty, and also knew when a man liked her. She was not above using her charms when she was also attracted. She was from Savannah, Georgia, where she was a much sought after beauty in her day. Now she was thirty-one, and not so naïve anymore about the whole world of love.

She smiled back and put a delicate hand out: "Rosemary Ann Evans, so nice to meet you, Mr.?"

Jack quickly said, "Hastings, and the pleasure is all mine."

Rosemary blushed a little saying, "That was so nice of you, Mr. Hastings. People can be a little bit rude at times, I must say. Where I grew up, men would never be that crude to a woman in public.

"Miss Evans, may I buy you a cup of coffee or a sweet tea? You must let me erase that awful image of Texas men," Jack insisted. He added, "Let me show you how gracious Southern men can be."

Rosemary glanced at her watch, and saw that it was only eleven-thirty. She decided, on a whim, to say "Why yes, Mr. Hastings. I will take you up on that kind offer."

Jack and Rosemary sat in the coffee shop getting to know each other, until soon it got to be two o'clock. Rosemary said "Oh, Jack, I really did stay too long. I'm sorry, but I have to get back to work. The firm will miss me. They are somewhat short today, too."

Jack said, "Don't worry Rosemary. I'll give Matt a call. I'm due to play golf with him soon."

"Why, don't you dare, Jack!" She blushed again and said, "I'm a big girl now, and I can just march right back in there."

That was almost eight years ago; and Jack and Rosemary Hastings had been inseparable since.

*M*elinda, returning from her visit down by the lake, entered her suite quietly, as to not awaken her sister. She wanted to keep her sad face from being noticed. Deciding on a refreshing shower before dinner, she intended to make a bee line directly to the master bath. But to her surprise, Kelly was already awake. Melinda quickly acted as if she had something in her eye, and placed her index finger in the corner of her right eye, letting her hair fall over her face.

"Did you have a nice nap?" She looked at Kelly, continuing her rush towards the bath.

"Melinda, nice does not begin to describe how wonderful my nap was. Wait until you crawl between those heavenly sheets tonight! Did you have a good time while I was asleep?"

"Yes, the lake is beautiful, and I met one of Jessica's sons there." Melinda said this from the other room, now safely out of sight, while looking in the mirror at the red lines still formed around her mouth and eyes from crying.

Over the last years she had become an artist in covering up sadness with makeup. She felt all she needed was some time, a hot shower, and a bit of good foundation cream and eye drops. By dinner, no one would be the wiser.

"Jessica said something about her sons being here this weekend. Was he nice?" Kelly asked this, trying to keep her sister engaged in a conversation.

"He was very nice, and his name is Chase." *Different, but nice*, she thought.

"I think he is a few years younger than I am, but when he talks, you would never guess he is in his twenties."

"How do you mean?" Kelly asked.

"I'm not sure, just the way he talks, I guess. Anyway, I'm going to take a shower before dinner, so how about I meet you in the dining room at six o'clock?"

"Okay, enjoy the shower. The double shower heads make it almost as luxurious as the sheets," Kelly said as she headed out the door. Kelly knew her little sister all too well, and her heart ached as she left the room and headed toward the sitting room. She knew Melinda had been crying, but was unsure as how to respond to her. She could take offense easily in her sad mood.

Entering the sitting room, Kelly began to scan the wall of books, hoping one would call to her. There were many inspirational books and old classics to choose from.

"Do you think she has read all those books?" A spirited voice came from behind her. It was Kathryn entering the room.

"Sorry, I didn't mean to startle you. I'm Kathryn."

"Hi, my name is Kelly, and I wonder how she had time to read at all. I read some of her biography online after her book came out, and her life was an amazing story in itself. Did you know that Jessica, as a child, visualized living in a place just like this? I don't remember what I was doing last week, much less as a child," Kelly laughed.

"So true. I can't remember much as a child either, but my mother always told me that when I was a little girl, I loved to draw pictures of dresses and color them. She even kept a few of my drawings. *I wasn't half bad,* Kathryn smiled, as her thoughts wandered back a bit. She skimmed through a book she had pulled off the shelf. "Look; here's a classic by George Eliot."

Kelly took her hand and rubbed her stomach area, *"Well, maybe I'll start making notes about what my children like to do as youngsters,"* Kelly thought. Then she said, "George Eliot?"

"Yes, she was an author who used a man's name in order to be published, in the old days," Kathryn said.

"So, Kathryn, what do you do for a living?"

"I'm retired now, but I was a buyer for high-end department store clothing."

"Well, I guess you also visualized your future when you were a little girl." Kelly smiled at her.

"You know, you are right. I never thought of it that way, but yes, yes, I did." Kathryn, too, smiled at the irony.

Kathryn DuBois, who was living in remission with cancer, had quite a remarkable life story for herself. She may have started her stay at the Inn not wanting anyone to know about what she had been going through, but sometimes, what we think we don't want is exactly what we need.

*D*an was already setting the table when Aubrey arrived in the dining room. She was wearing a beautiful rust-colored dress. She walked into the room, and Dan did a double-take. He told her she looked amazing. Strawberry-blonde hair, cut short, and layered perfectly with red highlights, and hazel eyes outlined just right with eyeliner, completed the look she was going for tonight. Aubrey was petite and perky and didn't need much in the way of makeup to look like a million dollars. But she loved to play with make-up colors.

Aubrey did a three hundred and sixty degree turn and said, "Why, thank you, Mr. Romano, and, may I assist you with dinner?"

"That would be lovely, my dear," Dan said, as he offered his arm to escort Aubrey to the kitchen. They floated out of the room like Ginger Rogers and Fred Astaire. The two of them were so much in sync sometimes, that it made me a little jealous and lonely, to be honest. It was moments like that which I really missed. Were Jay and I in sync like that when we were together? I was sure that we were. However, Dan did have Aubrey on his hands then in the kitchen, the poor guy. Still, he appeared to really care for her, which warmed my heart.

I had returned to my own room after giving Tom the house tour. I decided, since it was a holiday, that I would wear my red dress for dinner tonight. I had purchased the dress over a year ago, but never felt it was the right occasion to wear it. I kept telling myself that I would wear it eventually, but tonight I looked at the dress hanging in my closet, seeing it with new feelings. I decided that tonight was as special as any.

Putting the finishing touches on my makeup, I looked at myself in the full length mirror. Clad in the v-neck red sleeveless dress, I admired my carefully made-up face and slim figure. My shining blonde hair fell down against my shoulders and I looked pretty, I thought. I paid careful attention to my eye makeup, for Aubrey and others always complemented me on my blue eyes and cheek-bones 'to die for.' I laughed to myself.

Opening my jewelry box, my eyes fell upon the bracelet that my Mom had given me so long ago. I have never worn the bracelet since that dreadful day when I found out that she had taken her own life. I looked away from it and reached over to pull out my favorite heart pendent necklace that Jay had given me after my heart surgery. Some simple gold hoop earrings were all that was needed. I felt as put together and attractive as possible. And that was pretty good.

It took me many years to be able to see that. As I gazed in the mirror, I suddenly wondered how closely I resembled my Mother. She died at the young age of thirty-four, and the only photos my father had kept were the ones of him and her before they married.

I really missed my father since his death in the summer of 2001. He and I had shared so many memories together. He never remarried. I was his one and only child. When I think back, there were things I regret now. There were times that I'm sure he worried about losing me to depression as well. I wish things could have been different. I wish I could have just understood the disorder better back in the day.

I tried to shake off my thoughts, as they were not easy to accept. I walked over to my closet and I slipped on my silver sandals. I looked back at my jewelry box, slowly approached it, and picked up the bracelet from my Mother. As I closed my eyes and thought of her with loving understanding, I placed it around my wrist and headed down to the dining room, with a peaceful heart.

Upon entering, I noticed that Aubrey was filling the water glasses.

"You look beautiful, Miss Jessica," Aubrey said as she saw me enter the room.

"Why thank you, Miss Aubrey, you are quite the looker yourself, tonight," I teased her.

Both of us smiled at each other. Dan entered the room dressed casually in jeans and a t-shirt, sporting his apron, and said, "I feel a bit underdressed, ladies."

"That's okay Dan, with Jessica in that red dress no one is going to notice your fashion statement of a designer apron anyway." Aubrey laughed heartily at her own joke.

"Okay Miss humor, you can make all the fun you like of my apron, but shortly you will be mesmerized by my shrimp dinner. As for you, Miss dazzling red dress; you may want to take some extra time enjoying your dinner tonight because remember...you do have a date with the dishes afterwards, and I'll loan you my apron if you wish."

"Not fair D'angelo! I did not make fun of your attire, and I can't help it if I look stunning tonight." I said this as I placed my hand on my hip and batted my eyelashes comically.

"Your date with the dishes is not because of the comments about my 'attire,' dear Jessica, which, by the way, I happen to think, is a very stylish piece of clothing. No, I recall a little game of pool that was played this afternoon, and a wager was made which you happened to lose," Dan replied smartly.

"Oh yes...that date. I may be fashionably late for that date," I said as I turned and took in the whole view of the table setting.

"The table looks so inviting. You two have outdone yourselves again. Does all this extra fuss have something to do with my surprise tonight?"

"What surprise?" Aubrey asked me, as she glared over at Dan.

Dan wiped his hands on the sides of his apron and said, "She may know a surprise is in the air, but don't let her fool you, Aubrey, because mums been the word from me." Dan was quick to defend himself.

"Nice try then, Jess; now could you put out those place cards, please?" Aubrey asked, as she believed Dan's version.

Aubrey's way of changing the subject was to put me to work.

I started my way around the table, putting out the place cards in order of seating: Jessica, Trey, Chase, Melinda, Kelly, Kathryn, Tom,

Jack, Rosemary and Aubrey. We had stopped adding Dan's name to the place cards since he insisted that he do all the serving of his creations. He would eat later. He may be soft-spoken, but he was very serious about his presentation of food.

Jack and Rosemary arrived in the dining room just as Chase and Trey were sitting down at the table. Soon the other guests arrived and everyone found their places. I insisted that Aubrey sit and enjoy the company of our guests while I took everyone's drink order and filled it from the beverage bar. The only guests yet to arrive to dinner were Kathryn and Tom.

Tom had been walking back from the sitting room with a small book, since he had decided to skip dinner and just commence with some private time in his suite, getting this ludicrous weekend over with as soon as possible. When he turned the corner to see that someone was obviously running a little fashionably late for dinner, he did a double take, or maybe a triple take.

'Dressed for success,' in her black heels, Kathryn was retrieving her dropped earring from the floor, when Tom almost stumbled into her.

Kathryn did not have to wait long for her impromptu introduction to Tom. She glanced up to meet him eye to eye, and saw a tall, somewhat adventurous looking man with a nice physique, though a little ragged around the edges. Nice brown eyes and good hair, she noted automatically, but those clothes…and boots!

Little did she know, but Tom was using all of his gumption just to get up the nerve to introduce himself to her.

Though a successful businessman, he was a little socially inept, which was why he kept himself 'up there' at work while the underlings did the 'people' work. But he was downright lonely now, and so he worked up the courage, that which had gotten him through many a tough situation.

Ellie, his daughter, had been aware of a change in her father since his tumultuous divorce. Though at first licking her own wounds, she began to see her dear father underneath the gruff, anti-social mumbling and temper tantrums. She knew this weekend would be good for him.

Tom said to Kathryn, hand extended, "well hello, darlin,' I'm Tom Hanley, and you look like you belong right well in these surroundings." Not a loquacious man, Tom did his best, though.

Damn, he had to stop talking like a country cowboy! he thought, looking down at his own attire, and feeling slightly out of place.

Kathryn glanced up at him with disdain, after spying the cowboy boots as her first impression.

Kathryn had been a beauty in her youth, and still was certainly a very classy woman. Long and lean, with dark, glossy shoulder-length hair, she was dressed in New York's Fifth Avenue's finest. Black and white were her minimalist colors, with silver bangles and hoop earrings. No cowboy talk or boots for her.

Tom muttered, "I mean to say, you are one lovely lady, with a friendly look about you to boot."

Kathryn almost thought she had heard all of this wrong, shaking her head, as if to remove foreign objects from her ears.

"Pardon me?" she asked with astonishment that someone could actually be so crude.

Tom was really dumbfounded now, as his hearty Texas greeting was met with a frown and totally rebuffed.

He stumbled around verbally, trying to think of something better to try in the way of introductions. After all, this lady was too lovely to just give up on.

Kathryn resignedly decided to give this obvious country shit-kicker the decency of a real reply. She put a limp hand out, shook his 'paw' (it felt like), and started with: "Ah, Mr. Hanley, how nice to meet you. I trust that you are making your way to the dining room, but have taken a wrong turn."

This was said with the attitude of royalty, confronted by peasants. Kathryn knew her way around awkward situations, and this was one.

Tom, becoming more rapidly red in his face, was also not one to suffer indignities directed at him in silence. And by now, his face was the color of a ripe tomato, perfectly matching his Ralph Lauren polo shirt. Now is perhaps the time to mention his chic khaki Bermuda shorts and argyle socks worn with his manly cowboy boots. He silently spewed out a torrent of words, just under the zone of hearing, though not without effect. *Well, Ms. La De Da, for your information, I happen to be Tom Hanley, owner of Hanley's Hogs Custom Motorcycles in Dallas, Texas. And if I so desired, I could buy a fleet of vehicles better than that sweet, little, current model vette parked outside, with Texas plates 'LVITUP,' that is undoubtedly yours!*

Of course, Tom did not actually say this out loud to Kathryn, but he sure as heck felt like it. Kathryn took a step backwards. It must have had some effect.

Just then, Jessica came around the corner and said, "Oh there you two are. I'm just getting everyone some beverages for dinner. Have you two been formally introduced?"

Tom discreetly disposed of the book into the conveniently placed corner planter beside him.

"Yes, ma'am, we have, and I was just about to ask this lovely lady if she would be so gracious as to let me escort her to the dining room." Tom said this as he gave Kathryn the best phony smile he had ever pulled off, and offered his arm.

As Tom and Kathryn entered the dining room, both simultaneously rolled their eyes as Aubrey, the good hostess as always, was quick to guide them to their seats. Right next to each other. And, she proceeded to introduce them as a couple to the others at the table.

After delivering the beverages, I returned to my seat at the table, and waited for the perfect moment to lift my glass and suggest a toast.

When there was a lull in the conversation, I lifted my glass and said, "I would like to propose a toast." Everyone lifted a glass. I continued with the following:

"To all of you, may you enjoy a beautiful, relaxing Fourth of July weekend. We're so happy you could all join us." I then extended my glass towards the middle of the table.

With the clinking of glasses around the table, the conversations began to commence again, as we awaited Dan's first course. Melinda was introducing Kelly to Chase, and Chase was introducing Trey to the sisters, in return.

Jack had started up a conversation with Tom about the type of business he was in, which Kathryn was coolly listening in on, all the while complementing Rosemary on her diamond earrings. Multitasking was a talent of Miss Kathryn's.

"So Tom, what business are you in?" Jack asked this, for he had overheard that Tom owned a business.

"Hanley's Hogs. We sell Harley Davidson motorcycles," Tom answered, with an explanation on how his daughter Ellie would probably take over someday. Also, Tom told Jack about some of the trips he had taken with his buddy Ralph to West Texas, and elsewhere. This brought Jack and Tom together, for Jack could easily imagine himself with them on their adventures. Tom was perfectly well aware of Kathryn listening in.

Kathryn, now eager to engage Tom in a more private conversation, out of hearing range of the others at the table, leaned in closer to Tom, and softy said: "Well Mr. Hanley, I couldn't help but hear that you are in the motorcycle business. Please tell me a little about this. I would greatly enjoy it," Kathryn suggested, with her best behavior on.

Tom could not help but smirk a little at her extreme politeness.

"Well now, Miss Dubois, and you can call me Tom, by the way, it is a great business to be in. Hanley's Hogs was started by my late father Jim. I was old enough to take over when he passed away, thankfully. Our main shop, and most business is done in Dallas. However, we also have shops in Austin, OK City, Albuquerque, L.A., Denver, and San Diego." He took a deep breath and a sip of water.

"My goodness," Kathryn exclaimed, "you do have a good head for business if you can keep all of those sites going!" The southern belle in her came out now and then.

Kathryn was impressed, and she knew it showed. She said, "Well, Tom, you may call me Kathryn."

Tom continued: "Miss Dubois, I mean Kathryn, I graduated with honors from Texas A&M. My daughter, Ellie, will follow in my footsteps, I reckon. Now, my dear, it's your turn, I believe," he joked.

"Well," Kathryn said, with a bit of her own drawl, "I'm from Richmond, Virginia and attended the Fashion Institute of Technology in New York. I became a buyer for several chain department stores and boutiques. I worked out of the Houston division until I recently retired.

Tom smiled and asked, "So did I pass the test?"

Kathryn frowned and said, "Test? What test? I'm just trying to be civil and make small talk, Mr. Hanley. It's not my fault I was seated next to you," she continued, with venom dripping from her voice. She did tend to take offence easily. This cowboy may make money, but did NOT possess social skills, she was convinced.

Tom laughed and said, "hold on there, Miss Kathryn, I was only making a joke. I didn't ask to be seated here, either. But I'm not sorry, ma'am."

Kathryn was a bit flustered now. "Well then, maybe we should talk about something neutral, Tom." She tried to smile.

"Do you ride any of those hogs?" She asked.

Tom was passionate about riding and said so. Kathryn soon became enthralled with more stories of Tom's trips with his buddy Ralph, which Kathryn secretly envied.

"Do you think I could learn to ride one," she asked, earnest now.

"Why, there's nothing to it, my dear. I could easily have you riding with the wind in your hair if you came up to Dallas," Tom flirted a bit. Tom had actually had a recurring dream in which an unknown female companion's long scarf whips around and accidently blinds him. He had to quickly put that image aside.

"I might just take you up on that, Tom." Kathryn smiled.

When the dinner was over that evening, it was almost too soon for the two of them, it seemed.

Aubrey had retreated to the kitchen to help Dan with serving dinner, while I was listening to everyone and thinking to myself how amazing it was when perfect strangers came together in the right atmosphere and instantly began to form relationships.

Laughter soon filled the room, as Jack told us all a story about one of his fishing excursions in Cozumel, Mexico. It entailed the ocean, a fishing boat, one six-foot marlin, and Jack losing his pole after a two hour fight, which the marlin won. Jack was a born storyteller, and had us all in stitches. No one but Rosemary noticed how she had been left out of the story. *It had been their anniversary and he seemed then and now to care more about the damn fishing*! Rosemary thought to herself.

Aubrey and Dan entered the room serving us all a divine salad, followed by Dan's incredibly scrumptious dinner creations. When it came time for desert, I was surprised to see Aubrey lower the lights as Dan came out with my special lemon cake.

With a lit candle on top of the cake, Aubrey offered a few words:

"To Jessica Aries; congratulations on another Independence Day weekend celebration here at *Luna's Hope.*"

"To Jessica," Dan added as he lifted a glass higher, and everyone toasted together.

"Go ahead Jess, make a special wish and blow out your candle, so we can all eat that yummy cake of yours," Aubrey exclaimed, her sweet tooth kicking in.

"Thank you for this," I replied, then made my wish and blew out the candle. I couldn't believe it had already been an entire year.

*I*t was almost eight o'clock when dinner wrapped up. Wishing my guests a good night, I retreated to the kitchen for my date with the dishes. I was pleasantly surprised to see that Trey had already begun cleaning up the kitchen.

"Well, this is a surprise, Trey," I said as I walked up to him, picked up a towel on the counter, and joined him.

"Hi Mom, did you enjoy your dinner tonight?"

"Absolutely, and the best part is that you and your brother were here with me. Speaking of your brother, he was quieter at dinner tonight than usual. Is everything okay with him?"

"Yes, he's fine Mom, it's just that he and I had a talk earlier and he is probably just processing it. I was kind of hoping maybe I could talk to you about something, too."

Trey looked over at me with his beautiful, gentle smile. I couldn't help but feel so proud of him. My youngest son, so tall and strong. It seemed like just yesterday that he was learning to ride a bike with his little helmet and knee pads. I suddenly remembered taking him to school for the first time, watching him go up the flight of stairs with his teenage mutant ninja turtle backpack. He never knew it, but it was that particular day that I went back to my car and cried like a baby. He was always so quiet, and I worried that he wouldn't tell me if something went wrong at school. Now I look at him and I see a man.

"Sweetheart, you can talk to me anywhere and anytime," I said with a loving smile as I leaned my head onto his shoulder.

"Well Mom, I talked to Chase last night about something very important to me, and I've been doing a lot of thinking about it lately. I have an opportunity to do something and I want to take it, but it's not a decision I am making lightly, because it will affect more than just me."

Trey talked as he continued to wash the dishes, and I didn't want to control the conversation, so I kept drying and listened.

73

"Mom, all my life, I have known that I wanted to help people and to do something good. I love the speaking engagements that Chase and I do, and I want to continue to do them when I can, but I have so many ideas going on in my mind when it comes to architecture."

I was listening intently, as I dried the same dish over and over.

"Well Mom, I've been reading a lot about a non-profit organization, which my friend's uncle heads up. He's been a priest here in the states for many years."

Trey then turned and looked at me, holding a dish in his hand and said, "Mom, they help farm, build homes, schools, and shelters for the Mangyans in the Philippines. It's a mountainous area and they need more people with skills like mine to help."

He stared at me, as if waiting for my response. In my mind and in a split second, I had so many thoughts forming at once. That's across the world, overseas, dangerous situations, not seeing him for months or longer, him being alone; the flashback again of that first day I had to leave him at school, the thought of the day he was born, and the fact that he and his older brother had always been so inseparable. With all of these thoughts forming, I somehow simply replied,

"Trey, I've always told you that you could do anything you put your mind to, and if this is what you want, you have my support."

I was fighting back the tears that were making their way from my thoughts to my throat. I had to use every ounce of control I could muster, so that I could listen to him with an open mind and focus on what he was trying to tell me, and not what my own personal wants and needs were.

"I contacted them, Mom, and told them where I work and what some of my training has been. I actually had a phone meeting a few days ago with one of the team leaders, and I'm considering going abroad with my friend before the end of the year and devoting my life to volunteering. I have a calling, Mom, and I think this will be a good start...an adventure."

Abroad! That word did it. The tears pushed their way through my throat and up into my eyes. My son was telling me that he wanted to devote his life to helping others in need, and that he was going to use his talents and gifts to take him wherever he needed to go. But I couldn't help but feel a sense of loss.

"Mom, please don't cry," he said, as he put the dish down and hugged me.

"Honey, I'm just so proud of you, but I'm selfish too; and I will miss you."

Trey took a step back and placed his hands on my shoulders. Looking down into my tear-filled eyes, he said: "Mom, you have inspired me to live my dreams, and I will be taking you with me in my heart wherever I go, with every place I help build, and with every person I meet. I'll know that everything I do is because you always told me I could do anything I put my mind to. Besides, I do get to come home sometimes!" He smiled down at me.

He was strong and determined, and I knew Trey well enough to know that he did not make decisions lightly. Everything he has done in his life has been well thought out. He was really going to leave and take this leap into a new journey.

"Was Chase supportive when you told him?" I asked.

Trey turned to the sink and picked up another dish, placed it into the soapy water and replied, "He wants me to consider everything that it will entail before I make such a big change, but he thinks this is a great opportunity, too."

I had dried my eyes, put away the last dish, and looked at my son with admiration.

"Well then, tell me about this non-profit group. And how do you pronounce that name again?" I smiled, but it was difficult.

Trey and I both pulled out two stools around the kitchen island and he explained the mission of this amazing group.

As he talked about the organization, a light shined so bright inside of him that it radiated from him through his words and enthusiasm. He spoke with such excitement that I temporally forgot about the pain I would endure seeing him off when the time came.

Trey and I were talking in a way that we seldom did. He has always been the 'quiet' one (he didn't even say his first word until the age of three, and that word was 'brother,') so long conversations with Trey and I didn't happen often. When they did, however, they were heartfelt.

"I look up to you, Mom, and I love you so very much. I could admire the times you would take us along to do volunteer work when we were younger, but sometimes, back then, I was sad too, and I'm sorry for that."

"Honey, why did you feel sad about my volunteer work? I thought you enjoyed going with me to the events for the Humane Society, animal rescues, and the times we went to the assisted living home and passed out wreaths every Christmas? Why didn't you ever tell me how you felt?" I asked lovingly.

"I didn't understand things back then like I do now, Mom. You used to sleep a lot during the day when we were kids and when dad was home from work. I thought that you were sleeping so much because you were unhappy with me. The only times you didn't sleep much during the day was when you were doing the volunteer work, so I thought that the work made you happy, but that I didn't." Trey looked down as he told me this, as if I would be upset with him for saying this to me.

"Oh, Trey, sweetheart! I'm the one who should be apologizing. You always made me happy. From the moment I knew I was pregnant with you, I knew that you were special. I have suffered bouts of depression, on and off, throughout my life, honey, and there really was not anything anyone could do to help me, at times. When the depression would temporally lift, I would feel so full of life that I'd want to give back by volunteering, and to include you boys so we could do something special as a family."

I tried not to look disappointed in myself, but I was. Trey reached over, hugged me, and said, "Mom, it's okay, because I know that now. That is why I wanted to tell you that what you did for me when you had those moments of light in your life, was so beautiful, and is the main reason I feel so strong about giving back, too."

Now we both had tears in our eyes, and as we wiped our eyes and looked at each other, we started laughing together, and began talking more about the mission work he would be doing in the Philippines. I felt yet another turning point in my life, but this time, it felt like a positive one.

6

Shooting Stars

While Trey and I had been talking, Chase decided that a night swim would be perfect, since it was still ninety degrees out at the pool.

Kelly and Melinda had returned to their room together after dinner.

"Melinda, I'm so happy that you could join me this weekend."

"I'm glad we could spend time together, too," Melinda replied as she sat on the bed and took off her heels from dinner.

"Tomorrow, you and I will do some real catching up," Kelly said as she took the oddly fluffy white robe out of the closet and made her way to the bathroom. She looked at the robe again, then shook her head and continued the conversation. Melinda was talking, and she paid attention again. (It was just something about that robe…)

"That sounds perfect, Sis. I know you are feeling tired, so I might take a quick swim at the pool to wind down the night, if you don't mind," Melinda replied. Then she looked up at Kelly and screamed: "What is that thing on you?" Kelly had inspected the odd, furry robe before, so she was not as alarmed at this outburst. She managed to calm Melinda down by letting her feel the robe. Our conversation was back to swimming in no time.

"Okay, I'll see you in the morning, hon…and Melinda…," Kelly said as she peeked around the corner with a washcloth in her hand.

"Yeah," Melinda replied, not realizing Kelly was standing right behind her now. "I love you," Kelly said.

Melinda turned around and saw her sister standing there, looking so angelic, and replied…"I love you, too, Sis, but I still hate that robe," she grinned, and walked over and gave Kelly a hug. She knew that she had loved her sister all her life, but saying the words, "I love you," did not come easily for Melinda since Keith's death.

As Kelly finished prepping for bed, Melinda changed into her swimsuit and made her way to the pool.

Melinda looked out the French doors to the swimming area. She could see that Chase was swimming laps. Walking through the doors, she waited until Chase came up for air.

"If you would like to swim alone, I can come back?" Melinda hesitated, as she watched Chase wipe the water from his eyes.

"Hello, Melinda. Are you kidding, jump in!" Chase invited.

"The water looks so refreshing, and I never get to see stars like this in California," Melinda mentioned as she put her towel across the chair and kicked her sandals off.

Chase thought to himself how stunning Melinda looked in her two-piece swimsuit. She had long, beautiful legs and long, blonde hair, flowing to one side. She didn't appear to wear, or need, makeup. Her natural beauty was apparent even from a distance.

Taking three steps down into the water, she began to swim gracefully to the other side of the pool.

The stars were abundant in the night sky, and a glimpse of a new moon was apparent above. Chase and Melinda had the pool to themselves.

Chase couldn't help but notice that Melinda's hair looked like spun silk in the reflection bouncing off of the pool lights.

"So Melinda, are you a night owl, or just taking this opportunity to do some stargazing?"

"Actually, I thought a swim would be a nice way to clear my head before I crawl between those luxurious sheets your mom put on our beds."

"Ah, yes...the famous sheets. Trey and I asked her where we could get a few sets of those sheets, but she refused to tell us. She said they are the real reason we come to visit her so often, so she's not telling," Chase replied with a grin.

"That's funny. Kelly was going to ask her where she got them too." Melinda half-smiled back.

Melinda was obviously feeling a little more at ease tonight than she was on the lake earlier. The glass of wine she had at dinner must have been quite relaxing.

"Good luck on getting my Mom to give up the secret of those sheets," Chase said before he reached toward the side of the pool and took a sip of his ice water.

"It's her coveted secret, and I don't think even Dan or Aubrey knows the source of the sheets," he laughed as he put his glass back down and relaxed against the side of the pool. "By the way, I enjoyed meeting your sister tonight at dinner," he said.

"She enjoyed meeting you two, as well," she called out as she swam towards the deeper end of the pool. Chase dunked himself under the water and came up near Melinda.

Both treading water and looking up at the stars, Chase asked,

"Have you ever seen a shooting star?"

"Once, when I was very young, I saw one. My Dad tried to explain what a shooting star really was, but my sister Kelly always told me to just make a wish, and it would come true."

Chase just smiled as he looked up in the sky, and said, "Yeah, my Dad told us that seeing a shooting star meant that we were going to have good luck the next day."

"Does your Dad live here in Texas, too, Chase?"

Both Chase and Trey had become distant from their father. Chase had not seen his dad in over four years. His father had moved out of state for a new job a few years after the divorce, and although his dad had tried to keep in touch with him, it was Chase who decided to stay absent from the relationship.

"No…I'm not exactly sure where he is living right now," hesitated Chase.

"I'm sorry. I didn't mean to…I mean… it wasn't my place to ask," Melinda said in a soft tone.

"Remember when we were talking about hurdles this afternoon, Melinda?" Chase asked.

"Yes," Melinda answered, feeling a little badly about being rude earlier at the lake.

"Well, my relationship with my Dad is my tallest hurdle, so I don't talk about him much. It's not that I don't want to talk about him, it's just…"

79

"It's okay Chase, I'm kind of facing something similar. I'm here with my sister to reunite after not seeing each other in five years."

"Five years, that's a long time," Chase observed.

"Yeah, she and I were always very close, but then..."

Melinda hesitated. Chase quickly looked at her, and said with all sincerity, "it's okay; you can trust me, Melinda..."

"Well, I have a pretty tall hurdle myself. I was engaged to be married once, almost three years ago. My fiancé was killed in an auto accident, by a drunk driver."

Under the stars, with this person she had only met hours ago, Melinda opened up her heart, and told Chase about her tallest hurdle.

"I'm sorry about your loss, Melinda," Chase said whole- heartedly, while trying to keep his thoughts about her beauty out of it. *God, she was so gorgeous!*

"I'm sorry about you and your dad. Does he even know what wonderful things you and your brother are doing?"

"Who knows...maybe he has heard," Chase replied vaguely, unsure.

Chase had not been able to talk to anyone about his father in years.

When anyone would ask if he had heard from his dad, Chase would always reply with something like: "I live my life, and he lives his."

"I do wonder sometimes how my dad is, or if he thinks about me and my brother. Before the divorce we were pretty close. But that was then, and people change."

"Chase, do you ever think about contacting him?"

Melinda was slightly fearful that she might have overstepped her boundaries a bit with her question, but just waited for his reply, if any.

Chase was in unfamiliar territory now. He was being asked questions, and his answers were opening up doors that he had not gone through in a long time.

"I have thought about it, but it just seems like it is pointless. If he wanted to talk to me, he would have called me by now." Chase was now the one shrugging his shoulders. He felt oddly vague...almost floundering. However, Melinda did not seem to notice.

"After you left the lake earlier, today, Chase, I went for a walk and I thought about my fiancés' death being one of those hurdles you spoke of. I really want to know how to learn to jump it, so I can move on with my life. My heart hurts so much when I see couples holding hands, or when

I watch a movie where a loving couple is getting married. It almost feels like a knife to my very soul."

"Yeah, I didn't lose a fiancé like you did, but I can understand having a hard time seeing couples and wedding movies. I haven't been too sure about the whole marriage thing since my parents divorced."

"My parents are still married," Melinda said, "but they did fight a lot when we were kids. I really believed that Keith, my fiancé, and I were going to be happily married forever. He was my first real love."

"Does your sister know how hard this has been for you?" Chase asked, as his eyes met Melinda's.

"Not really. Believe it or not, I have not talked to anyone about my real feelings until now. I think I know why you may be so good at speaking to crowds. You sure are easy to talk to." Melinda looked away for second.

"You are pretty easy to talk to as well. Actually, you're the first person I told about my feelings towards my dad. I don't even open up to Trey, and he is my best friend, as well as my brother."

"How about your mom, does she know how much you have hurt over the divorce?"

"Well, that's another story, I guess. My mom has had enough stuff happen to her over the last few years. Besides I'm fine now," he commented shortly, again somewhat unsure of himself. Melinda seemed to have a way of naturally bringing out his vague feelings and purposeful elusiveness! She did not even realize that she possessed these 'powers' over him, yet.

Melinda wished she could look Chase in the eyes and say the same for herself, but she wasn't fine, and the thoughts of leaving this cruel world still plagued her every day—mostly when she was alone.

Melinda then yawned, and began to feel tired. She turned and faced Chase, and said, "Well, Mr. Aires, in the words of a very well-spoken young man: live to love...love to live, right?"

Chase turned, faced Melinda, and nodded. "Very nicely put, Miss Embers."

And just as if something almost magical had told them both to look towards the moon at the same moment, a shooting star blazed its way across the sky.

Melinda quickly closed her eyes and made a wish.

Opening her eyes, Melinda said to Chase: "Okay, your turn now, make a wish."

Chase closed his eyes for a second and thought to himself: *"I wish for the happiness back into Melinda's eyes."*

Chase and Melinda said goodnight to one another, left the pool, and headed back towards their respective suites.

Kelly was already sleeping, so Melinda quietly changed, and crawled between the comfortable sheets that her sister Kelly had been raving about. Lying there, she looked over at her beautiful, pregnant sister, and thought about the conversations she had had with Chase today. Melinda then did something she had not done in years. She put her hands together and began to pray.

"Dear God, I know it's been a while since I've talked to you. I have been very angry with you for taking Keith from my life. I don't know if I'm ready to say much more to you right now, but I have heard that you have your reasons. I may never accept them, or understand them, but if I'm supposed to be able to move on and get stronger, could you please help me? Show me a sign. Because I'm not really feeling ANY good reasons for being here in this life.

With that, Melinda hugged her pillow, closed her eyes, and slept a typically fitful night, with many awakenings and strange dreams.

Back in his suite, Tom had attempted to settle in for the night and do some reading, but his mind was restless as he thought about the woman, Kathryn, he had met earlier. She was intriguing to him, yet frustrating.

"Why in the hell should I care what she thinks about me?" he asked himself. Looking over at the desk, he saw his cell phone sitting there. He gave into the temptation and decided to turn it back on and check for messages from work. The only message on the phone was from his good friend, Ralph.

"Hey buddy, so how's the retreat going?" laughed Ralph on the voicemail. "I still can't believe that Ellie got you away from work to go sit at some spa or *Luna's Hope!* If you are going crazy, man, just call me back and I'll send Life Flight over. You and I could be having drinks on Sixth Street in Austin, by midnight! By the way, are you wearing one of those sissified white, fluffy robes from Madison Avenue?"

Tom laughed to himself as he dialed back Ralph's number and waited for him to answer.

"Hey man, what's up? You ready for me to dispatch the troops to rescue your sorry ass?" laughed Ralph, as he took Tom's call.

"Very funny. So how's Virginia treating you anyways?" Tom replied, with feigned interest.

Ralph, Tom's old pal for adventures, recently was transferred to Newport News, Virginia, from Dallas. He was an electrical engineer. Not really a ladies' man, Ralph was more adept at these affairs of the heart than Tom, though.

"Ralph, I met a woman. She really intrigues me. How can I get her to give me a second look? I need advice, man."

"Tom, just try not to irritate her too much with your shit-kicking, cowboy one-liners." Ralph laughed hard at his own joke.

Tom, a bit irate at this advice, snapped back with "having the typical electrical engineer's humor is definitely not my idea of talent with women."

Ralph realized that his good friend had a real interest in this woman. He only wondered whether helping Tom would be for his own good. Tom could be so naïve, in some ways. Ralph remembered how busted up Tom was when Nancy, his Ex, left him for her hairdresser. Tom just never seemed to get over this humiliation, and became even more closed off to other people. Though highly educated, and owning his own company, Tom questioned his self-worth after the divorce. His confidence had plummeted, leaving one bitter and sarcastic man behind. Ralph knew from Tom's voice that he was very into this woman, and no matter what Ralph said, Tom was going to go after her, past be damned.

Tom, more frustrated by Ralph's sarcasm by the moment, told Ralph, "Listen, I have to go man. I'll call you back."

Tom was going crazy pacing in the room, not even able to resort back to his usual way of occupying his thoughts by burying himself in work. He just lay there in bed, tossing and turning for hours, full of anxiety, until he was plum-tuckered out. He had a restless night, to be sure.

"*H*ey Trey, I didn't think you'd still be up, bro," Chase commented as he walked into their room, returning from the pool.

"Yeah bro, I'm into this project. How was your swim?"

"It was good." Chase said this with a smile that his brother didn't notice, since he was busy working on some new sketches.

"I'm working on this new idea for the Mason Structure that Henry put me on at work. It's crazy bro, I look at the plans, and I see ways to enhance them. The people I work with have been doing this for years, and they are asking me what I think! I'm not even sure how I understand all this stuff. I just do."

"Yeah Trey, I remember when Henry asked me how we could get you to relax at the meetings, so that you would chill out and share those brilliant ideas of yours. Remember the meeting that everyone came to wearing bandanas on their heads? My idea, little bro; and it worked. You haven't stopped talking since!"

"That's cool," Trey replied as he lifted his head for a moment, flashing his brother a smile.

"Heck yeah, I always told you how smart you were when it came to buildings and architectural design. You have a gift, Trey. If those stuffed shirts wearing bandana headbands to one meeting helped bring you out of your shell, so be it," Chase said, as he walked past Trey, pulling off Trey's green and blue headband. Henry also had made sure that Trey had gotten the educational credentials he needed through his internship.

"You never answered me...how was your swim, dude?" Trey asked.

"It was good," Chase repeated, since it was obvious Trey didn't hear him the first time.

"Melinda came to the pool, and we had a good talk," Chase added.

"Rad, that's twice in one day that you two hung out. She must be pretty patient to sit and listen to your philosophical babbling for hours," Trey said jokingly, as he was totally well aware of his brother's vociferous nature. He had been the recipient of Chase's rather long lectures on life... many, many times.

"We talked about our hurdles. She has a huge one, and after talking to her, I think I do, too," Chase said, as he grabbed a fuzzy white robe from the closet and said, "what's this?!"

Trey said, "How should I know; it looks to me like a giant bunny rabbit had to give its poor life for fashion."

"No bro, it's says it's 100% polyester, and I'm wearin' it!" Chase replied, as he slipped it on.

"Is there one in there for me, too?" Trey added. Chase took out the other robe and threw it at his brother.

"Are you talking about Dad when you say 'hurdle'?" Trey asked, as he ducked instinctively when the robe landed on him.

"Yeah, I guess," Chase replied in a tone of finality.

Trey didn't say any more about it to Chase. He knew it was a touchy subject.

"Hey bro, I'm pretty tired. How about shutting that project down so we get some sleep?" Chase asked sternly, while walking towards the bathroom, looking like he had been sprayed with cotton balls.

"Yep, my eyes are tired, too." Trey agreed, as he stretched and pushed the drawing aside.

Trey turned off the lamp on the desk and crawled into his bed.

Chase had been in the bathroom washing up, and soon came out with his toothbrush in his hand and asked, with a mouthful of toothpaste, and a body covered in fluff...

"Do you still have Dad's phone number?"

7

Peace and Grace

*I*t was early Friday morning, and Jack awoke before dawn. Being quiet, so as not to awaken his wife, or anyone in the house, he walked to the kitchen to make some coffee. To his surprise, his coffee was made, and set out next to a newspaper. It was the fishing pole and tackle box, next to the table with a note that had Jack as giddy as a young boy on Christmas morning: *"Enjoy your morning at the lake, Mr. Hastings. I'll be sleeping soundly until your return. Love always, Mrs. Hastings."*

Jack smiled, as he realized that Rosemary must have gone to the kitchen after he went to sleep. He proceeded to pack his coffee, newspaper, and fishing gear in his bag, and headed to the lake, thinking of how Rosemary was always one step ahead of him.

I woke up before Aubrey, and went to check out the breeze from my bedroom porch. I could see that someone was spending an early morning on the lake, and I had a hunch that it was Jack.

Today was going to be the day that Rosemary was going to get a surprise from Jack.

Aubrey had confided in Dan and me about the surprise, before the Hastings even arrived. It was going to take place after dinner tonight, and before dessert.

I quietly changed into my morning walking clothes, and headed down to the kitchen. Looking at the clock, I saw it was only six o'clock in the morning. I thought Jack must have really been looking forward to some fishing time on the lake to get up this early while on vacation.

I stopped in the kitchen to fill my mug with coffee, and I headed out to the walking trails. I usually liked to walk by the lake, but this morning I figured I'd leave Jack and the lake alone. I decided on a long walk this morning to visit with Peace.

I started to think about the things Aubrey and I discussed over tea last night. *Luna's Hope* was booked for two weekends each month for the next seven months, and there wouldn't be a break until we closed for the entire month of February. Last night, as Aubrey and I talked, we discussed what we were planning to do as far as vacations. That's when she told me that Dan was going to take a trip to Colorado for that month and had asked Aubrey to join him.

Aubrey and Dan had hit it off from the very beginning. As a matter a fact, Aubrey was the reason that Head Chef D'angelo Romano, personally waited on our table the night we first met him. He had taken one look at Aubrey, and knew he had to at least meet her.

Aubrey and I frequented that restaurant quite often after that first night. One night we went in and asked if he might want to have dinner with us sometime. He obliged, and we all went out for Italian. That night, Aubrey and I told Dan about our plans for *Luna's Hope*. We asked him if he would possibly want to join us in our new venture, and become part of the endeavor. It didn't take Dan long, after the estate was finished, to call us with enthusiasm and ideas. He soon pulled up in his little RV, and the rest is history.

As far as Aubrey goes, he has had a crush on her since the moment he first set eyes on her. The two of them have become good friends over the last year. Last night, when Aubrey asked what I thought about her and Dan taking a vacation together, I told her I always knew the two of them had a special connection. I was very happy to hear they were going to travel together.

As for my vacation plans…I would be writing my novel, "Moonlight Wishes," and taking my morning walks as usual. Having the place all to myself would be a first, but I had Henry and Felix to bug if being alone got to be too annoying.

Henry was scheduled to arrive sometime Sunday afternoon for the big barbeque and fireworks display. He told Chase and Trey that he needed to discuss a project at work while he was here. Then he confided in me that Chase was actually going to be promoted, and Henry wanted to surprise him with the news. I decided it was best to let Trey inform Henry about his plans to work abroad when Trey felt it was the right time.

Henry loved this place as much as I always did. One day, about a year ago, when the estate was finished and opened for business, he finally told me why he took the time that day to invite me to lunch, and also listen to my ideas on building the house, and making it a perfect place for others to come and rejuvenate their spirits.

Henry explained to me about a man, William, aka Will, whose memory inspired him to listen to me that day. Will and Henry had become life partners after their days in the service. When they first met in Norfolk, Virginia, it seemed as though they had always been friends.

Both leaned towards music, art, and fine literature, rather than wild nights on the town. What really got them together, though, was Will's volunteer work with the Animal Rescue in Norfolk, whenever they got back to town. He had always been a volunteer wherever he lived, or was stationed. One day in 2006, Henry was looking for a pet for his young niece, Angela, when Will introduced him to Felix. But Henry fell in love with Felix, and that was that.

Will, on the other hand, became ill with pancreatic cancer in 2008. It struck him down, fast and furious, despite treatment. Henry and Felix were by his side when he made Henry promise to do something that would ultimately change my life, too. Though Will tried to hang on, and Henry made a great nurse, Will passed away less than a year after his diagnosis. Thankfully, Henry had Felix and his work to keep him busy. It was just a pretense though, for until Henry and I actually met over the phone, he was adrift.

Will had told Henry that he had to promise something to him, one night, as they listened to some music and talked. Henry said "of course Will, anything you want. You know that I will do anything for you."

Will said Henry must promise to go somewhere beautiful and meaningful, to work off some of his grief, and especially, as Will put it, "to rejuvenate himself."

Henry was a little puzzled, but promised this to Will. Will thanked Henry for doing his best to let him go home when the time was right. They only had to exchange looks, and both knew it was okay.

Needless to say, I never questioned Henry's motivation for financing and building the Inn with me, but it all became clear after he explained his moving story to me. Henry David had granted the dying wishes of his closest friend, and had become a part of building a special place where he could always come to cheer his spirits. Henry began thinking of me as a daughter, and we became close friends, sharing many good and sad moments, often in confidence.

The Inn was perfect for Henry. He had excellent taste in décor and fashion. He was a strong business man in the home building industry, but still knew his way around a sewing machine, thanks to his seamstress mother, who took the time to teach him as a boy. Aubrey and I could not say the same for ourselves. Until Henry, we couldn't even thread a needle. Heck, Aubrey didn't even know what threading a needle meant! Henry's late mother was a quiet, intellectual woman with many talents. While working from home, Mrs. David was able to home school young Henry until college. She also taught him the arts, and the finest of literature.

We loved to go with Henry to the fabric shops, and revel in the newest silks and chiffons. To be honest, it was Henry that taught me about fashion and good taste. The Inn would not be as elegant if it were not for the gifted Henry David and his magic touch! Henry was not above picking up a paint brush and re-doing a room, if he felt it needed it. He often came over after shopping at his favorite shops in Boerne, bringing back new pillows, drapes, you name it. Nothing was too good for his favorite, beloved estate.

Henry also had a way of getting Aubrey, Dan, and me to pitch in and help on a big project. He seemed to know who would be good at what.

Henry spent a great deal of time turning his large RV into his own special home, and unless you really knew Henry, it was sometimes hard to pin him down just by looking at the inside of his RV. A sewing machine was in one corner, while sports memorabilia took up another corner. Drapes and coverlets were magenta velvet, with a rich, creamy, off-white contrast in the sheets, lamp shades, etc. And of course, a dog's bed, which matched Henry's. Carpeting was magenta, too, and I loved visiting him in his RV, because it always made me feel as if I were inside the genie bottle on "I dream of Jeannie."

*A*fter walking for about twenty minutes, I came upon my beautiful little tree, Peace.

"Good morning," I said, as I approached the little tree. I've heard that when trees are planted with love, that they grow very strong and healthy. She was certainly a testament to that theory.

While I was there, looking around at the nature that was now an everyday part of my life, I thought back to my childhood. It's crazy how much time it has taken, and what I had to go through to have enough courage to get here. I may never understand who I was, but I'm finally beginning to see who I am, and who I want to become. My life's purpose was still a partial mystery, but maybe it was always meant to remain a mystery. After spending some time enjoying the peacefulness, I headed back towards the house.

Upon arriving back, I entered through the foyer and made my wish at the fountain. It was the same wish I made each morning: "show me my true purpose."

I then walked back to the kitchen to drop off my coffee mug, and saw that Dan was there making a shopping list.

"Morning, Dan."

"Good morning, Jessica, how was your walk?" asked the typically, but sometimes annoyingly, chipper Dan.

"It was nice. I skipped the lake this morning, since Jack is enjoying some quiet fishing time. I went to see Peace, instead."

"I saw her the other day. She looks great," Dan replied, as he chewed on the tip of the pencil eraser pensively.

"So, what's on the shopping list? Something special for me, I hope," I joked, as I put my mug into the dishwasher.

"It's a list for the barbeque on Sunday. Aubrey and I are stopping to get the gift for Jack; the one he is giving to his wife tonight at dinner. Then it's on to the grocery store. Saturday will be too crazy at the stores, and besides, you know I like to be prepared in advance."

"I think that's a terrific idea. Oh and by the way…" I asked Dan in a nonchalant tone of voice, when actually I had been waiting to tease him all morning. "Aubrey talked to me last night about you going to Colorado in February. She said that you asked her to go along," I said, with an added inquisitive smile.

"Yes I did. I thought she might like to see the sights. Have you ever seen the Continental Divide, Jessica? Quite majestic, to say the least," Dan replied with a pinkish tint creeping up his face and neck.

"Why D'angelo, I do think that you may be blushing."

"Nonsense, I've never blushed a day in my life!" Dan replied, trying to keep a straight face.

"Well then, maybe you should go see a doctor, because you might have a fever starting. Your face and neck just turned a hot shade of pink," I laughed.

"Very funny, Jessica; you know you are welcome to come along as well," he stood his ground.

"And besides, even if I did have a fever coming on, you know I am just as stubborn as Henry when it comes to going to the doctor. Nope, no doctors or hospitals for me, either. Henry was right when he said that he would have to be 'gagged and dragged' before he went to any doctor, and I'm with him!"

Dan was trying to change the subject, but I put us right back on it, replying, "As inviting as going to freezing Colorado in February sounds to me, I'll have a novel to write, so I'll be fine right here, spending winter in my shorts and t-shirt. But, enough about vacation. I'm going to whip up some breakfast tacos, Dan. Would you like a few?" I asked, as I reached over and took his apron from the hook and put it over my head and tied it around my waist.

"Yes, bacon, egg, and cheese on flour?" Dan asked, instantly diverted.

"You are the chef, my dear D'angelo. I only make one type of taco...a gluten-free potato, egg, and cheese on a corn tortilla, so how many would you like?" I smiled at him as I walked over and took the eggs out from the refrigerator.

"I don't know about him, but I'll take two," came from a sleepy, but partially awake, Trey, walking into the kitchen in a certain white, fluffy wrap.

Dan did a double-take and choked on his coffee, spitting it out in the sink.

"Trey, I know the current culture of ambiguity as far as gender fashion goes swings widely, but isn't this going a bit far?" He looked directly at Trey's furry wrap. Just then, Chase arrived to the kitchen sporting the same type of robe. Dan slapped his forehead exclaiming: "Madre de Dios! Who is responsible for these 'things?!' AUBREY!!"

I quickly said, "Calm down Dan. Aubrey saw these in one of her fashion catalogs, and thought it would be a good idea for all of the guests to have courtesy robes in their suites in case they forgot to bring one of their own; for comfort. Many travelers do forget their robes, Dan, and I have been asked if we sold them."

"Well," Dan said, cooling off a bit. "I'll have to re-order some unisex, white, terry cloth robes. We can just tell Aubrey that there was some sort of recall on hers, as they are known to come to life and devour the poor soul wearing it!"

"Good morning sons. Don't listen to him; I think you guys look very comfortable, and besides, real men look good wearing anything," I declared, defending my sons.

Both of my sons just looked at each other, shrugged, and said, "whatever" in unison. Trey added, "Dude, they are soft; and besides, let's eat."

I had to quickly contain a giggle as I suddenly had my own secret visualization of Tom Hanley walking into the kitchen wearing his cowboy boots and one of those goofy, fluffy robes! I'd have fallen over in laughter if my eyes were ever privy to that kind of scene.

"How about I make a bunch of tacos, and maybe, as the delicious aroma travels through the vents of the house, more of our guests will wander in to eat some with us," I said, as I was now in this for the long haul. I felt good about cooking this particular meal, even though I was by far not the best cook in the house. Although, I was definitely not the worst. I believe she was still sleeping.

"If the guests don't show up, Mom, I know Chase and I will be happy to help you eat them all," Trey said.

The cooking began, and just as I had hoped, one by one, some of our guests began to join us in the kitchen.

Chase, Trey, and I settled down at the garden table, near the Koi pond, to have our breakfast. Even Kelly was up bright and early and joined us.

Dan ate a couple of tacos quickly, but Aubrey decided to skip breakfast since as she had slept in that morning. She grabbed an apple on the way out, as they both went to do some shopping together.

Soon Kathryn and Tom came out to the front to enjoy their breakfast, amidst company. Thank goodness, no white robes.

Kathryn and Tom soon became engaged in a friendly, but somewhat heated, conversation; the subject of which was hummingbirds.

It turned out that each of them had been a secret admirer of the vital energy and pure joy of the little bird and its nesting and feeding habits.

Each of them knew facts about these birds that would surprise most people, especially to hear them coming from Kathryn and Tom. They both owned at least one book on the subject.

"Why Tom, then you should know that with over three hundred and twenty different species, still only twelve species breed in North America," was overheard.

Tom: "Yes; most do breed in South America. However, we do have Anna's, the Ruby Throated, and the Rufous. And their plumage is basically green; or the lighting makes them appear green."

That was his answer to Kathryn's statement that one could catch the colors of red, ruby, deep violet, metallic greens and blues, shimmering bronzes, and golden-yellow, shifting with their every movement. The excitement each felt about this subject was enough to get others to stop what they were doing and start sending covert glances over their way.

Neither Tom nor Kathryn noticed.

"Tom, I bought a new book about hummingbirds recently, and I happened to bring it along with me. I'd like to show it to you."

As Kathryn was about to go get the book from her room, Tom offered, "I'd like to see that book, and I make a mean Bloody Mary, Kathryn. Would you like one?"

"Of course; I'd love one," Kathryn called back as she went to get the book.

Kathryn came back, flipping the pages of her new book, anxious to show Tom what she had found.

As Tom handed her the drink, she said "thanks, darling," without even thinking.

Both of them, red-faced at that, smiled nervously at each other.

"To Vincent Van Gogh." Tom toasted the great painter and lover of nature. This relaxed Kathryn, and she settled back in her chair as they both sipped their drinks. Kathryn read more obscure facts from her book as Tom leaned back and drank in her sweet voice and her beauty.

How could he not have noticed how gorgeous her deep brown eyes were before? Hungry for all that the world offered. Why, she was just as adventurous as he was, in her own way. He realized he was attracted to Kathryn in a fast and furious way. But he couldn't seem to help it.

As the others started to make their way back into the house after finishing their breakfasts, Tom quickly met Kathryn's eye, and just as she was about to get up, too, Tom shakily asked, "have you ever ridden, Kathryn?"

"Ridden?" she questioned; not getting it at first.

"I'm an idiot," Tom secretly scolded himself. *Is that the best I have!* Now feeling his face begin to flush, something inside of him wanted to keep her there with him longer. *Could he be actually engaging in a real life conversation with a woman, more than just yes and no?!*

As Kathryn returned to a seating position, she continued, "you mean, ridden a motorcycle? No, I've been a passenger on one a few times, but no, I never had the chance to learn to ride. Are you an avid biker, Tom, or do you just sell them?"

Tom, now feeling a bit more at ease, replied:

"Actually, I love to ride. I own a beautiful custom built chopper, but it has sat in my game room, looking more like a statue, for almost two years."

"Is there any particular reason why you haven't ridden for two years, Tom?" Kathryn asked curiously.

"No reason good enough, that's for sure," Tom laughed. Tom had visions suddenly of Kathryn hanging on to him for dear life, her long scarf whipping around his face, blinding him to the highway, possibly causing a motor vehicle accident! His recurring dream! He was determined to lose that nightmare once and for all.

"I've always wanted to learn to ride," Kathryn expressed again, surprising herself.

Tom quickly quashed his vision from Hell and answered, "Well darlin' if you are ever in the Dallas area, come on over and I'll dust off the one I'm showcasing to the four walls in my game room. I'll teach little ol'you how to ride in style." Tom was starting to loosen up and see that he had been missing out on a few of the things he used to enjoy so much.

The motorcycle business was his career, but riding had been a passion since he was a boy. Somehow, over time, his career found a way to overshadow that passion.

Tom was proud of his interaction with Kathryn. The conversation was going well. Maybe his old friend Ralph was right. You had to get out there and live the life that you wanted.

As for Kathryn, she felt renewed by Tom's interest, able to start letting go of just being a cancer survivor. She was still a lovely woman, with all that entailed. Finding out that Tom loved hummingbirds, too, only led her to want to get to know his other interests, like riding.

"Have you stayed here before?" Kathryn asked Tom.

"No, I won this stay in a silent auction. I was going to give this four-day weekend to one of the associates at my company, but shoot, my darlin' daughter Ellie insisted that I use it myself to kick back a little."

"Sounds to me like you have quite the brilliant daughter, Tom, and personally, I believe relaxing is way under-rated," chuckled Kathryn.

"I don't even remember the last time I relaxed," said Tom, with some wonder in his voice.

"Got news for you my friend, you are doing it right now," replied Kathryn with another smile and a wink.

"Why yes, maybe I am. I'm oddly not worried about work, or anything else right now. I'm actually just thinking about my motorcycle, and how great it's going to be to take it out for a much needed ride when I get back home."

"That's the spirit, Tom. Trust me, enjoy life each day, and never take a living moment for granted," Kathryn said as she gathered up their plates.

"Oh please, Kathryn, it would be my honor to take those dishes in for you," Tom quickly offered. Tom wondered to himself if he had suddenly lost his mind, as those words had never been uttered by him before.

"Why, thank you very much," Kathryn said with sincerity, as she handed them to him, adding, "I've enjoyed having breakfast with you, and if you feel up to playing one of the board games by the pool later, I'm up for the challenge. But I must forewarn you that I play a mean game of chess."

"That's sounds like a great idea, Kathryn. Maybe we can meet there this afternoon, after lunch; say two o'clock?"

"It's a date, then," replied Kathryn.

It's a date, then! Are you kidding me! I play a mean game of chess? I haven't played that game since I was fifteen! Kathryn was replaying the conversation in her mind as she walked back to her room, and couldn't help but laugh at herself. She also replayed Tom's offer to take the dishes in and thought, *'honor?' What the hell did he mean by that? Does this man think I'm royalty?! Perhaps I should watch him more carefully.*

After taking the dishes in, Tom went back out and sat by the pond a little while longer. Taking mental notes, he decided that he would like to set up a similar pond at his home in Dallas, and put up a few more hummingbird feeders. Maybe some native plants for them, too. Then he thought, *shit, I really need to call Ralph, I can't seem to control the words that are coming out of my mouth when I'm near this woman... 'honor?!'*

After cleaning the kitchen from breakfast, I saw Kelly in the sitting room. I walked up to her with a stack of magazines I meant to put out.

"Hello Kelly, mind if I join you?" I asked, since I had some free time and I hadn't really had a conversation with her, yet.

"Not at all; I would consider it a pleasure to sit with a gifted writer amongst all of her favorite books," Kelly replied eagerly.

"Thank you," I said, as I made my way over to the corner where the fish tank stood. Taking out some flaked food and sprinkling it around in the tank, I commented back to Kelly, "I am the one who feels fortunate this weekend."

"You do?" Kelly asked curiously.

"Yes, you could have chosen any place to go and meet your sister for this extremely special occasion, and you chose to come here. I feel special," I repeated simply.

"Jessica, words cannot begin to explain the level of comfort I feel here, and I'm sure my sister feels the same way," said Kelly.

"I'm so glad. We enjoy meeting new people, hearing new stories, and sharing the beauty that surrounds this property with others," I said.

Sitting down near Kelly, I asked which book she chose to read.

"*Emma.* Written by Jane Austen," Kelly replied. "I heard great things about this old classic."

"Yes, I have read that book three times. It's a great short classic, and each time I read it, I like the story better," I commented.

Kelly placed the book on her lap and took a deep breath.

"Jessica, to tell you the truth...I'm a little nervous about talking with Melinda today. I want to ask her to move back to San Antonio and stay with me and my family, but I don't know how she might take it."

"Kelly, I've learned over the years that it's best to just say what's on your mind. Maybe pack a picnic lunch, take my little golf cart out to the picnic table you passed on the way up the driveway when you arrived. Talking over food is a great icebreaker. It always works for Aubrey and me," I said, with a reassuring smile.

"I want to say so many things to her, but I'm afraid I'll say something that will upset her even more. How will I know when I've said too much, or not enough?" Kelly said with obvious frustration.

"Here is a little clue I learned from watching my sons when speaking to someone about a touchy subject. Talk from your heart, and don't push the other person. Try not to answer for them, and if they are quiet and don't respond to you…honor that. If they do, then earnestly and honestly listen and just care. No judging or predicting their feelings. Just honor their feelings…always."

"Jessica, you open your home and your heart, to so many people, including myself. I don't mean to get personal, but I read your bio, and you went from working retail six days a week and living in a tiny apartment, until you went into heart failure, then on to becoming a bestselling author and opening this incredible place. It seems so amazing and almost surreal. How did you do it?" Kelly asked, with admiration in her voice.

"Well, when I was writing *"Finding Grace in Pennies,"* I told everyone I knew that my book would be published someday, even if I published it myself, just for family and friends. After my heart failure, I thought of death a lot. It took me time, but I did start to see things in my life differently than I did prior. I decided that I wanted to leave something behind when I did pass on. I wanted to leave a legacy," I said.

"That is something I'd like to do as well," Kelly responded back.

"Would you like to hear how I knew it was time for me to take a leap of faith with my first novel?" I asked.

"Yes, absolutely," Kelly replied as she sat up in her chair and listened to me tell one of my favorite stories.

"One day, I was taking a little walk outside my apartment in my old historic district neighborhood, when I passed a woman sitting on her porch. She was crying. I stopped, and asked if there was anything I could do to help her. She asked me if I ever prayed. I told her I did. Then she asked if I would pray for her dad, who was in the hospital and very ill. I asked what his name was, and I said I would pray right then, right there. I sat with her and we prayed for his health together. She then thanked me for showing *grace* by taking a second of my time to see what I could do for a total stranger.

Honestly, Kelly; that was the first time I had prayed in many years.

That's when I knew that Grace's story was ready to be shared.

I, like some people, do believe that there are not really entire coincidences, and I took that day as a sign to get things started. I wrote and sent out query emails to every publisher I could find. Like most aspiring novelists, I had my share of rejection letters, but I continued to imagine what I'd do when one of them said yes, and I became published. Again, I became impervious to rejection.

I decided I would build a large home around nature, and open a type of retreat where others could come and revitalize, or *rejuvenate,* their spirits with me. This was the home I visualized in my mind. Kelly, I could see it as clearly as you can see it sitting here. It's as if I took the idea from my mind, dared to share it with others, and like finding a penny and making a wish…here we are."

Kelly listened in awe, and then asked, "Is that why you have your very own wishing fountain?"

"You've got it. And, many people who have been here actually tell me that their wishes come true."

"That is a beautiful story, Jessica, and I thank you for sharing it with me. It makes me believe that anything is possible, if we just believe it to be. Jessica, I brought along my own copy of your book. I was wondering if you would mind signing it while I'm here."

"I would be happy to sign your copy, Kelly. Just bring it to me anytime while you are here, and honey, don't worry about the talk you are going to have with Melinda. It is often said that things happens for a reason, and the words will come to you, I promise." With that, I respectfully excused myself, and left Kelly to her reading pleasure. I made my way to the kitchen for a refreshing drink.

It was after I went to make myself a glass of iced tea that I decided to go to my office to check for any phone messages on the house phone. As I approached the door to my office, I heard my son Chase on the phone…

"Hi Dad, it's me, Chase. I wanted to wish you a happy Fourth of July. Hope you are doing well."

I was so surprised at what I was hearing; Chase making a call to his Dad.

"Dad, I'll leave my phone number so that if you get this message and want to call me back, that would be cool with me."

I turned and headed back to the kitchen so as to not let him know that I heard him on the phone.

As I heard him coming down the stairs, I took a spoon and started stirring my tea, pretending to be busy.

Chase passed through the kitchen by me, simply saying "love you, Mom." He continued on to wherever it was he was heading.

"Love you too, Chase," I said lovingly, but as nonchalantly as I could, making my way back up the stairs with a smile on my face.

I'd heard people say: There are really no coincidences. I recalled just saying that phrase to Kelly, and here I ended up hearing my son leaving a message for his father, who he hasn't spoken to in years. I never pushed the subject of their 'father' with my sons after they stopped speaking to him. I had to admit, I felt good knowing that Chase was reaching out to him.

I looked over at the house phone, saw that there were no messages, and decided to take out my laptop.

Aubrey and Dan were busy shopping yet, so I began re-reading all that I had written in my latest chapter.

*M*eanwhile, Jack had returned to his wife after fishing. She had already been awake and relaxing, when Jack greeted her with details of the lake. He also brought her a cup of coffee.

Then Rosemary greeted him back with: "Hon, there is one little thing I really need to discuss with you."

Jack, noting Rosemary's somewhat serious tone, and the slight change in her typically pleasant demeanor, decided to get comfortable and changed out of his fishing attire before sitting down next to her. Jack patted her hand nervously, as he wondered if this was going to be about his greatest fear, her internet 'friend.'

Jack asked: "What's up, honey?"

Rosemary felt that over time, their marriage had taken on a life of its own, as most marriages might be said to do. She had gradually given up some of her hobbies and minor interests to be with Jack, but the one big thing that Jack did not share with her was her passion for her photography.

She was extremely skilled at photography, and always tried to keep up with what was new, and all that entailed, by reading the industry magazines and ducking into camera shops here and there in her very limited free time. Jack never expressed jealousy over her talent, but his interests were more into sports and a little side gaming. They traveled together, and alone, a lot, worked hard at their jobs; so where was this "free time" anyways? Rosemary had made up her mind that this was the perfect time to approach Jack with her ideas, and her need to go back to her 'first love.'

"Jack darling, what would you say if I quit my job? I've been thinking of this for ages, it seems, but now I know that this is something I need to do. I need more "free time" to pursue my real passions.

Jack was certainly taken aback. He said "Rose, what would you do? I thought you loved your job, and worked so long and hard for this ability to have the freedom to do, and, yes, buy, everything we could ever need or want? Besides, Rosemary, is this 'free time' what you think you need in order to spend more time with your internet *friend*?!"

Rosemary was dismayed. "What! Have you totally lost your mind? What are you talking about?"

Pacing the room, Jack blurted out: "Maybe I am losing my mind, but what does it matter if I'm losing you, too!" Jack kicked the chair in frustration. His anxieties were showing big time.

"Whoa baby, slow down, this is NOT like you. I'm confused; tell me what the hell you're talking about, Jack."

"You know better than I do, hon! What about Mr. Mitch McCoy, and his dinner invitations in your email!"

"Jack, I don't know whether to be more concerned about explaining dinner invites that went unaccepted, or the fact that you must not trust me, because you have reduced yourself to snooping through my emails."

"Rose, you have turned away from me so often that I couldn't help but be nosey." His voice was so unusually loud that she feared others may have heard him.

Trembling, she replied, "Jack, lower your voice, everyone will hear you."

"I don't give a damn who hears. You are my wife; I love you. And, I damn well am not going to share you with some pencil-neck geek who owns a café and gets hyped up on caffeine, and hitting on beautiful women!"

"Really Jack, is that what you think?"

"Yes, I have this guy pegged!" was Jack's rebuttal.

"No! I mean, really Jack, do you think I'm beautiful?" she shouted, almost.

A few guests heard shouting coming from Jack and Rosemary's room, and it took us all by surprise, for they seemed such a nice couple. It was normally the policy at *Luna's Hope* to live and let live. However, there could be no assaults or any such mayhem allowed. I was in my office, which was over Jack and Rosemary's suite, when I heard what appeared to be loud talking and some 'thumps.' I quickly went to the Hastings' room to nip any trouble in the bud. Knocking on the Hastings' door brought Rosemary, in a satin nightgown, looking a bit disheveled. I asked Rosemary, "Is everything all right?" Rosemary blushed, and brushed a tear away from one eye. Jack appeared, assuring me that all was well. I managed to keep things quiet, so the other guests would not be upset. Only Tom and Kathryn really heard anything, and they kept it to themselves. When they were alone though, Kathryn asked, "Tom, what if he hit her?" Tom could barely believe that Jack was the type who could do such a deed. "If he did, he deserves a whack himself, I reckon! Hittin' women, children, or animals is not allowed under any circumstances," Tom replied with seriousness.

Meanwhile, Rosemary said to Jack, "He is just a friend, Jack. How could you get so upset over a few stupid emails?"

Jack answered by kicking an ottoman. "Hell, Rosemary, I just thought he was trying to take you away. I couldn't live with that! I've been holding these thoughts in for far too long, and I'm tired of it."

Rosemary pleaded, "Please stop the noise, Jack, or they will hear again!" Jack said he would pay for anything he wrecked. Rosemary sighed, and said, "If it makes you happy, I'll tell him I can't spend any time with him anymore."

Rosemary had become friendly with Mitch McCoy over at the book store/café near her work. They carried the latest photography magazines and books. That's how she liked to keep up with all the latest camera and accessories news. Mitch, the owner, was knowledgeable on the subject, also, and liked to sit and have coffee with Rosemary, now and then.

Yes, it was possible that Mitch, if you really asked him, would admit to having at least a crush on Rosemary. However, they had never been inappropriate. Mitch was twenty eight, medium height; usually with a day old beard. He favored plaid flannel shirts and jeans. Most would call him quite handsome. It is true that Rosemary loved to hear his compliments, and also, to be fair, his photography experience was what really hooked her on his friendship. They had so much in common. Rosemary admitted that Jack was not one to complement her, except at special times, like now, when he was confronted.

Mitch always told her how lovely she looked, how her eyes sparkled, etc. "This is important to a woman", Rosemary told Jack. Not to having to drag it out! "Sometimes I feel that you don't see me as the same woman you married."

Jack stopped his abhorrent behavior, and really listened to Rosemary, for a change. After all, this was that special weekend. He kept his temper, and made himself settle down. He knew his marriage could be on the line.

Rosemary continued, "Mitch understands that I have little free time, so he picks out special books or articles for me on photography that I can quickly read and absorb. Jack, you just can't get too far behind in that business. Yes, he sometimes compliments me, and I eat that up, I admit. But Jack, you know me better than that…I'd never be unfaithful to you!"

Jack, after settling down and really hearing Rosemary, realized that he had been amiss with not telling Rosemary how beautiful she looked, how smart she was, and what a wonderful wife she really was. And, did he take the time to really listen to her?

Rosemary looked at Jack, and said slowly, "Honey, you know you mean everything to me, and are the love of my life, right?" She added, "I only mentioned quitting my job because I know of a way to still earn income, but actually enjoy my career. Besides, we have way more money than we ever expected to have. Look at the attorney's salary you alone bring home. Jack, please, I need to go back to my photography, full time. Believe in me Jack; it's so important to me." Something in Rosemary's voice and eyes went straight through him. "And Jack, our marriage can be even better."

Jack, when hit by this explanation of Rosemary's, no longer thought of money or Mitch McCoy. He slapped his hand to his forehead and cried, "I've been an idiot! Of course you love taking pictures. You are so talented at it, too! Baby, don't worry about the money. Quit Monday. All I want is your happiness and love. And a puppy, of course…you know I've always pined away for a dog…" Jack added jubilantly, since he knew Rosemary had always wanted to rescue a dog, too.

Surprised by Jack's reaction, Rosemary looked at the boyish look on his face now, and she was instantly reminded of the old charm which made her fall in love with him so easily, and so fast and furiously.

"Yes, Jack, we will finally be able to get that puppy we have always talked about, and that we have pined for, for many years."

Rosemary cradled Jacks head, and looked deeply into his eyes. "Honey, I'm very competitive; my art is important to me, but I intend to make money at it, too." She looked at him with a new energy shining in her eyes. He was going to accept her in all ways! Jack said, "Baby, let's go into the city and buy you all of the latest equipment you need." He was serious and turned on by this new Rosemary. She was so smart, and yet she could always handle her man with honesty. Not for her the 'baby voice' and 'negligee act" to get something from him. Rosemary was a genuine class act, and she still wound him around her little finger. And he loved it! Rosemary was naturally elegant in her taste, and in her manners; and that included her love for him, he realized with a slight scare. He could have lost her, it suddenly hit him.

She laughed and said, "Okay, on Saturday we can go into Boerne and hit the camera shop. But it's a new world out there, honey. You have a digital camera on your phone now! Film and 35mm are a thing of the past, I'm afraid," she shook her head a little sadly. But she was excited now, too, and she took Jack back into her arms.

"Honey, isn't it a bit hot in all those clothes?" She looked pointedly at Jack's shorts and sport shirt. "C'mon Jack, we don't have to wait until Saturday to get some things done," she winked at him and took down her beautiful hair at the same time. Mitch McCoy was completely forgotten.

Kelly had spent most of the morning talking with me in the sitting room and reading. She had returned to her room around eleven that morning and was brushing her hair and putting it up in a ponytail, when she saw that Melinda was finally waking up after sleeping nearly eleven hours.

"Good morning, sleepyhead," Kelly teased.

Stretching, in her six hundred thread count sheets, Melinda yawned and asked, "What time is it, Sis?"

"More like; what day is it," Kelly laughed at her little joke.

"What!" Melinda sat up in confusion.

"You, my sweet little sister, are still so gullible." Kelly smiled and shook her head teasingly.

"Not funny...now really, what time is it? Did I miss breakfast?" Melinda asked, as she felt a true shadow of a smile flicker in her face.

"Yes, sleepyhead, you did; but it's okay, because we have plenty of time for lunch," Kelly replied.

"I am feeling hungry," Melinda said, as she stood up and made her way to the shower.

From the shower, Melinda called out to Kelly, asking her what she wanted to do today.

"I know we were going to check out the lake, but I saw a picnic table when I was driving in yesterday. How about we pack a lunch and have an outing like we used to do as kids. We could chat and catch up," Kelly replied, hoping that this would be a perfect opportunity for her to try to get Melinda to open up to her.

Yelling back from the shower, Melinda replied, "Sounds good; I'll be ready soon, I promise."

Kelly left the suite, and made her way over to the kitchen, where she saw that Kathryn was pouring an ice cold glass of sweet tea.

Kathryn looked up and smiled.

"Well hello, Kelly. How is our glowing 'mama to be' today? I meant to ask you yesterday. Is this going to be your first child?"

"Nope, he will be our third child, but he will be our first son. I'm planning on telling my sister today that I'm having a boy," Kelly replied with a big smile, as she rubbed her belly in a circular motion.

"How exciting, your first boy! Wonderful things in your future, little one," Kathryn said, leaning down towards Kelly's belly. Kathryn then looked at Kelly and added, "Well, sweetie...I wish you and your family all the blessings in the world. Enjoy your lunch. I have some journaling to do this afternoon." She looked pointedly at her new white journal on the counter.

"Thank you Kathryn," Kelly said as she waved goodbye, and proceeded to pack the delicious picnic lunch. Melinda weighing heavily on her mind.

Melinda had showered, and felt more awake and refreshed than she had in years. She dressed more carefully, too. She was sitting at the vanity putting on her makeup, when she started to reminisce about her and Kelly as young girls. She laughed to herself as she remembered the time when she and Kelly had their first picnic together. They packed a couple of sandwiches, chips, and iced tea. With a table cloth and a few pillows from the family couch, they had made their way out to their back yard and pretended they were on vacation in some far off land. They had attempted to talk to one another in British accents too, like, "*Oh yes, that would be brilliant*, and *please pass me some more chips, luv.*" They had so much fun as kids. Melinda missed those 'young at heart' days with her sister.

When Melinda arrived in the kitchen, she saw Kelly putting the napkins in the picnic basket and closing the lid.

"Perfect timing, little Sis. Jessica said that I could feel free to use the golf cart in the driveway to make my way around the property whenever I felt like exploring, so let's take it for a spin and go have ourselves a picnic."

"*That would be the bee's knees,*" Melinda replied in her best British accent.

Kelly laughed heartily, and came back with, "Well, then my darling Sister, *let's chivvy along.*"

Arriving at the picnic table, Melinda and Kelly were surrounded by trees, and the enchanting sound of the mourning doves cooing from the branches above.

Unpacking the picnic basket, Melinda began to put out the plates as Kelly poured the freshly squeezed lemonade.

"I'm so happy to see you Melinda; you look so beautiful."

"You do too, Kelly. You are glowing, just the way you were when you were pregnant with the girls."

"Well, maybe just a little different glow," Kelly said with a coy smile.

"A different glow; how do you mean?" Melinda asked with curiosity.

"Well, maybe a kind of bluish glow?" Kelly implied impishly.

"You are having a boy, aren't you?!" Melinda exclaimed, as she went to hug her sister in congratulations. It was so rare that Melinda had bouts of excitement anymore. She was genuinely happy for her sister, yet the feeling didn't last very long.

"Yes…you are going to have a nephew!" Kelly burst out with delight.

"That is wonderful news, Kelly. Ben must be so excited that you two are having a son. Have you talked about any names yet? And to have a nephew will be so cool…"

"We do toss some names around, almost all of the time. The one we keep going back to is, Jonathon."

"That sounds like a perfect name for him. Have you shared the good news with Mom yet?" Melinda asked. Melinda felt nervous bringing their Mother into the conversation. Melinda had been very close to her Mom when she was younger. The last few years, she pushed most of the family away, using the excuse of being busy at work.

"I've talked to her about names, but no; I haven't officially told her yet. You're the first," Kelly smiled, adding: "Ben and I wanted to ask you something, Melinda."

"Sure, go ahead," Melinda replied with curiosity, and a bit of anxiety.

"Well, do you remember how our property is also commercially zoned, in San Antonio?"

"Yes, the one where you have your house and then the cottage attached where you sell your crafts. I do remember, and I really like your place," replied Melinda.

"Well Sis, I won't have time for selling crafts anymore, and that lovely cottage would be big enough for you to have your flower shop in. You could stay upstairs above it, in the apartment. Ben and I finished renovating it, and it's lovely. All ready to be rented. And, the kids would love to have you so close. What do you think?" Kelly looked at her, eyes full of hope and expectancy.

"Kelly Embers McFarlane! Sounds like you and Ben have been very busy." Melinda knew that her sister was offering a very generous proposal. She didn't want to sound ungrateful, but she did ask, "What about our shop in California?"

Kelly was quick to catch *our* in Melinda's question, and felt a sudden, sinking sadness. She didn't want Melinda to sense it, so Kelly acted as if she didn't notice.

"Ben knows people who sell commercial property like yours. Yours is a turnkey business; you'd be set to go once you sell. The family is willing to help you set everything up by us, if you would choose to come back and take our offer."

"Keith left the floral shop to me, so that I could continue on with our dreams," Melinda replied, as she struggled to keep her shifting emotions in check.

"Maybe, Melinda, Keith wanted you to move on with what you loved to do, and he made it possible for you to do that, no matter where you chose to live." Kelly was trying so hard to remember the words Jessica had spoken to her about 'letting the words come to her.'

"That cottage is perfect for a flower shop, Kelly. The only thing is that Keith is in California. How will I visit him?" Melinda was feeling the familiar and heavy sadness settle in again.

"Melinda, you don't need to make this decision right this moment. Think about it, please, and keep it in your mind and heart that Keith is always with you. His spirit is limitless…he is everywhere we can't be, and everywhere we are."

"I think the offer you are giving me is incredible, and I will think about it, Sis; thank you again," Melinda replied, somewhat overwhelmed. She was also thinking to herself: *"How does she know where Keith is now?!"*

"So, how's that peanut butter-marshmallow sandwich I made for you?" Kelly asked, as she took a bite of her own sandwich.

"Delicious. And your sandwich. Well, it looks interesting, to say the least." Melinda said this with a bit of confusion in her face, looking at Kelly's sandwich.

Swallowing her bite, and washing it down with a gulp of lemonade, Kelly cleared her throat and proclaimed: "Melinda, when you get a craving, you get a craving, and you just have to go with it."

Kelly then took another giant bite of her peanut butter and pickle sandwich.

Melinda shook her head as she looked at her big sister enjoying something as simple as a sandwich. It reminded Melinda of when they were kids, and the good memories. That was before tragedy entered her life.

Aubrey and Dan were shopping at the local nursery, looking for the perfect young tree which was to be part of Jack's surprise for Rosemary that night at dinner.

"Aubrey, how about this tree; it's a nice one, don't you think?" Dan approached her with a young magnolia tree. "Oh, it's perfect," Aubrey replied, as she inspected it. Then she took the young tree and placed it in the shopping cart. "Only, we'll have to plant it in a sheltered area, and water it well. Magnolias are not native to this part of Texas."

"Rosemary is going to be excited tonight when Jack gives her this surprise," Aubrey softly spoke, almost as if to herself.

"Aubrey, every time you help someone plan a surprise, it always works out. You have a special gift, you know." Dan said this in a gentle voice, with admiration for her talents.

"Thanks Dan, you're going to make me blush..."

Dan thought to himself...*You wouldn't be the first person to blush today...darn that Jessica!*

"We'd better wrap it up here, Dan, and get to the grocery store. Any hint on what you are preparing for dinner?" Aubrey asked.

"Well, I thought I would serve a tomato-roasted pasta dish, and recreate one of the meals I made for you and Jessica the night you first came into the restaurant, years ago."

"You still remember what we ordered?" Aubrey asked in amazement.

"I remember very well," Dan replied. "It was the first night I saw the two most beautiful women in the world."

"Thanks, Dan," Aubrey said, as she leaned over and gave him a gentle kiss on the cheek.

Aubrey had always been an affectionate person. Hugging Dan, and the occasional kiss on the cheek, were not unusual acts by her, but at that moment, in that nursery, a spark had flickered between them. Although it couldn't be seen, Dan and Aubrey both felt it. Their relationship seemed to climb to a new level that day.

Meanwhile, Kathryn had decided to retreat back to the personal patio, just outside her suite. Once there, she placed her glass of tea on the table, got comfortable in the lounge chair, and took out her reading glasses.

Opening the journal that Aubrey and I had given her, she put her glasses on, and titled her first page...

"Friday, July 1st 2011- *Luna's Hope.*

I arrived at *Luna's Hope* yesterday afternoon, met by Miss Jessica Aries, author of one of my favorite novels, *Finding Grace in Pennies*, and Aubrey Saunders, one of the nicest people on earth.

I have been looking forward to this stay for almost six months. Being here in person is more remarkable than I could have imagined. The house is splendid, but tasteful, and the property is breathtaking. But, it's the energy here that is beyond words.

Only a few people here know about my medical situation. I actually feel like I left my cancer behind. It's just me, here alone, for a few days.

That's the way I would explain living with cancer. It's like you took on a bad roommate in your body, one you didn't invite, and it was going to be a heck of a fight to get them evicted.

Here, however, I feel like I'm free, with no bad roommate, no hospitals, no phones or internet, no work, and no questions. Just other people like me, who are experiencing, for the first time in a long time, what it feels like to relax and spend some time with their own thoughts.

What a concept. Taking time to listen to your own thoughts! Kathryn thought.

*T*om had been spending the morning walking the grounds of the property, taking in all of the sounds and beauty of nature. As he arrived by the lake, he noticed that Chase and Trey were getting connected with their own inner children. There was a huge oak tree that had a rope fashioned to it, and the two brothers were taking turns swinging from it and landing in the water.

The first thought that came to Tom's mind was that he wished his daughter, Ellie, could have been here with him. When Ellie was twelve, Tom had taken her to a friend's lake house for a weekend, and there was a similar tree there, as well. Ellie had spent the entire weekend swimming like a fish, and swinging from that tree into the lake. *How important a part trees play in our lives*, Tom thought, *and how fast time flies!* It seemed like yesterday that he and his daughter were inseparable, a team of two, flying kites, fishing trips, and even the occasional Sunday afternoon tea party, together. Lately, it seemed the two only met for the occasional dinner meeting, to discuss work. Or, maybe a phone call about work. How did this happen...when did our lives together get put on pause. Our careers got the fast-forward button pushed on, permanently. Tom tried to remember the last time the two of them spent quality time together. *I don't even know if she has a special someone in her life,* Tom thought, with some alarm.

He hadn't realized how long he had been walking when he noticed the time on his watch. It was already one o'clock, and he had made plans earlier to meet Kathryn at two o'clock by the pool. He didn't want to be late.

As he continued down the paved trail towards the house, he could hear one of the brothers yell out as they dropped into the water: "Cannonball!"

Chase let go of the rope in midair, folded his knees in, wrapped his arms around them, and dropped into the cool waters of the lake. Coming up for air, he yelled out to Trey: "Now *that's* a Cannonball, Bro!"

"Hey Chase, remember when Mom first brought us out here to see this property?"

"Yeah, that was almost two years ago. You didn't believe her, Trey. That she was going to buy it." Chase laughed as he stepped out of the lake and dried off with a towel.

"Well, you have to admit, Chase, that Mom always had ideas and dreams. But money was not something she had much of, after the divorce." Trey said this as he tried to skip a rock across the water.

"Goes to show you that dreams are worth more than any amount of money on the planet," said Chase, dreamily.

"I agree bro, but she has come so far since we were young. Just look at this place. Do you remember how she would sleep so much, when we were kids?" Trey asked.

"Yeah dude, I remember. But she is not like that anymore. I can't even remember the last time I saw her take a nap," Chase added, as he skipped another rock.

For some reason, Trey couldn't get the whole rock skipping thing down. Chase told him it was because his hands were too huge.

"Remember that little two-bedroom, one-bathroom apartment that Mom rented for us three, after the divorce?" Trey asked.

"I remember," Chase replied, as he began gathering his things together.

"I've been doing some thinking. I'm going to give Henry my ideas about developing some apartment complexes that would cater to families with financial needs, like we once had, back in the day. But change it up a little. I'd like to create more space out of the traditional small apartment layouts. I have some ideas that I think will work. I took the layout of the old apartment we lived in with Mom, and with a few changes, we could have had two bathrooms, instead of only one."

"Trey, little brother, when it comes to your mind, anything is possible. You could find a way to change a shed into a condo," he laughed. "Let's get going back to the house, bro," Chase suggested.

"Wait up Chase. Not to change the subject, but last night I gave you Dad's phone number. Are you planning on calling him? It's the last number I had for him; so it may not be current." Trey was stalling for time, for a second.

"I did call him, and it was his voice on the voicemail," Chase replied nonchalantly.

"Did you leave a message?" Trey asked, as he was trying not to show his surprise.

"Yeah, I just wished them a happy Fourth, that's all."

"Sounds good. Maybe I'll send him a text on Monday at that number and say '*hello*,' too," Trey said, as he turned and started walking back towards the house behind his brother.

Life Angels

"**W**ell hello, Tom, are you ready to take on a three-time chess champion," Kathryn asked Tom, as he approached the table near the pool. She had the game all set up and ready for play.

"I'm not sure if I'm a worthy opponent, but I'll give it my best." Tom smiled as he sat down and pretended to push up his nonexistent sleeves.

Melinda and Kelly had returned from their picnic and were just arriving at the pool. Kelly carefully stepped onto the first step in the pool, and Melinda followed.

Aubrey and Dan had returned from shopping, and were unpacking in the kitchen. This was almost a daily ritual for them.

Trey and Chase were down at the lake, and I was completing a chapter in my book. I closed my laptop, and sat back in my chair, thinking about all the nice things Kelly had said to me in the sitting room earlier. I thought to myself, *It's true; so many different things that I experienced over the years have taught me so much. It's the sum of all my experiences that have made me the woman I am today. What or who will I be twenty years from now?*

My characters and their experiences are but a reflection of my own life. Hum...*I should write that down*, I thought, as I grabbed a pencil.

I could hear faint giggling and laughter coming from downstairs, in the kitchen. It was time to go see what my two friends were up to. When I got to the kitchen, Aubrey saw me, and quickly hid something behind her back. She looked away as if I didn't notice, and started whistling; a sure sign of something going on with her.

"Very funny…what do you have behind your back?" I asked, as I tried to circle around her to see.

"Should I give it to her, Dan?" Aubrey smiled mischievously.

"Might as well; she is going to get it from you eventually…she can smell gluten-free chocolate a mile away!" Dan laughed.

"You brought me that chocolate from the market that I love so much, didn't you?" I asked, as I took a step closer. The pleading was now being heard in my voice.

"Yes, we did. You know we love you, Jess!"

Handing me the candy bar, I smiled with satisfaction and said, "thank you."

When I was diagnosed with celiac disease after my heart surgery, I thought that my days of enjoying food were over. I spent months wandering aimlessly through grocery stores, looking for the words "gluten-free" to be listed on a label. It was difficult at first, but knowing what was causing my painful stomachaches after every meal was half the battle to wellness. I read every book I could find on the disease, and learned how to shop and cook in a whole new way. Soon, I was able to enjoy food more than I did in my entire life.

I used to eat so quickly, without a single thought of what it was that I was putting into my body. The majority of my meals were ordered through a loud speaker, and consumed behind the wheel of my car in thirty minutes or less. Now, I have to think about every single thing I eat: what's in it, and what else was made in the same vicinity, possibly causing 'cross-contamination.' I actually felt better than I ever had, and my energy level was good most days, except for the occasional bout of depression that I worked very hard at keeping at bay.

To see Kelly relaxing in the pool, with her oversized T-shirt and round belly, brought an instant smile to my face.

"How's the water?" I called out to the sisters.

"Hi Jessica, wow…its perfect. Would you like to join us?" Kelly yelled back.

"Thanks anyway, but I'm curious to see who our reigning chess champion is over here," I replied, as I walked towards where Tom and Kathryn were seated.

Walking up to Kathryn and Tom, it was obvious that this was a serious game of chess. Tom was deep in thought and rubbing his chin, contemplating his next move.

"She's got me in a corner, Jessica. I'm thinkin' she may be keeping her title today," Tom commented, as he made his move.

Just then, Kathryn made a stunning move, and said: "Check-Mate!" It was a sight to behold. Tom maintained his game face, as Kathryn jumped up and did a little dance of victory.

I pulled up a lounge chair and watched as Kathryn won the game. Tom looked over at me and asked if I would like to take on the champ.

Laughing, I graciously declined to take on the victor. I noticed that my sons were arriving for a swim.

I was so impressed when my sons respectfully asked Kelly and Melinda if they could join them for a swim, before they entered the pool.

"Of course, come on in," Kelly replied.

Melinda looked at Chase, and nodded with a shy smile, saying, "wow, the water's nice."

Aubrey and Dan soon walked out the French doors together, each holding a tray filled with ice cold glasses of lemonade. The temperature outside was around ninety-five degrees, but the pool was refreshing, with a shaded veranda on each side. Everyone except Jack and Rosemary were here, cooling off poolside. They were enjoying their newfound friendships, and, Rosemary started her book of short stories and soon was hooked.

I'm not all too sure how the conversation got started that day at the pool, but it was, by far, not one I had seen coming.

With everyone sitting around drinking lemonade and having fun playing games or swimming, I brought up the fact that there was going to be a fireworks display the day after tomorrow. Then, Kathryn began telling us all about her favorite Fourth of July memories…

"As a young girl, I remember looking forward to my parents making popcorn and packing a cooler of snacks and root beer, so we could drive down to the state fair grounds and see the fireworks with thousands of others. My little brother and I would be in our pajamas, and we would meet up with our neighbors and friends and have a party under the moon."

Tom then told us what he and Ellie would do on the Fourth of July. "Yeah, Ellie and I would pack up our hiking gear and climb to the top of

'Timberland Hill.' We would bring along some bottle rockets of our own, and light them up while we waited for the big show. Gosh, it's been nine years already, since my daughter and I first saw fireworks together. For some reason, those nights on the hill were some of my fondest memories as a father. I didn't realize until recently just how much I missed those times with my daughter. Lately it seems like all we talk about is business."

Trey looked at Tom and said, "Yep, those sound like good times."

"Mom, remember when Dad took Chase and me out to the country that one year, and we helped his friend run the fireworks stand?"

"Yes, Trey, I remember very well. Wasn't that the time you drove your dad's car, without permission, on that farmer's property in the country?" I commented with a smirk.

"Yeah, those were good times," Trey answered, with a smile of innocence.

"Well," Kelly said, speaking up for herself and Melinda… "I'll never forget the first time my little sister here, saw and heard fireworks." Looking back at Melinda, she continued…

"You were about four years old, Melinda, and we walked down a few blocks to the neighborhood park. We set out our blankets and pillows while the adults were setting up their lawn chairs."

Turning her look toward the rest of us, Kelly continued. "We had these things called sparklers, and Melinda just loved them. She would dance around with her sparkler like she was a ballerina, putting on a show. When the first firework went off in the sky, she threw her sparkler in the air and came diving under the blankets by me. I lifted the blanket and assured her that they were way up in the sky, and I would hold my hands over her ears so she could watch all their pretty colors."

Melinda then commented, "Kelly, I remember that."

Kelly smiled and said, "I told her that there was going to be a big green one that was special, just for her, and she should watch for it with me.

She sat on my lap, with my hands covering her ears for the entire show. I knew that there was always a big green one every year, because that was my favorite color.

Sure enough, it showed, and then she turned around and said to me…"

"Was that one mine?" Both Kelly and Melinda said the words out loud at the same time.

"You do remember," Kelly said to Melinda.

"Aubrey, what about you? Any favorite fouth of July stories?" Dan asked.

"Let's see," Aubrey said as she looked up towards the sky.

"There is one special one that comes to mind." In a brave move, Aubrey shared a story I had never heard before.

"I was in my twenties, and in college in Nashville. A bunch of us from school were dedicated cave spelunkers, and we wanted to see the caves in New Mexico. I invited my best friend, Elizabeth, and after some coaxing, she reluctantly agreed to join us for the trip. We all had a fabulous time in the caves, and watching fireworks that night, I thought. Yet at this time, my friend Elizabeth was suffering from depression, and never let on how serious it was, even to me. She took her own life within months of that trip. I will never forget her, or get over not guessing that something was really wrong."

Raising her glass, she toasted to the 'good memories.' "To my dear friend, Elizabeth, watching over us now, like a bright, beautiful firework in the sky." Aubrey smiled through some stray tears.

Dan quickly put an arm around her and pulled her close. "Let's toast to her again," he suggested. "Some stories are bound to be sad." Then he toasted: "To Elizabeth, may your life now be happier, and may we all meet again." Everyone toasted to that. Chase noticed Melinda's head droop down a bit, after this story of Aubrey's. He decided to keep more of an eye on her than before.

Aubrey wiped her eyes, looked over at me, and said, "Any special Fourth of July memories, Jess?"

"I've been listening to all of your wonderful stories, both happy and sad, and yes, I do have one that is probably the most memorable," I said as I walked around filling everyone's glass with more lemonade.

My favorite Independence Day celebration was some years back. I was visiting family and friends in Wisconsin and I was invited to the house of an old friend of mine. We hadn't seen each other in almost eighteen years. We had been friends since we were fifteen years old. The last Fourth of July we spent together, we were around the age of seventeen and were typical teenagers. Quietly climbing out of the second story window of the house, onto the unstable old patio roof, without any parental knowledge, we waited to watch the skies light up.

Eighteen years later, to the date, my friend and I looked at each other, and I asked, "So, do you think we could still fit out your upstairs window?"

My friend smiled back and said, "how about you get the blanket and pillows, and I'll get the bug spray!"

This was Wisconsin, after all, and in July the mosquitoes are relentless and huge!

Looking at one another, and the window, which was considerably smaller than we recalled it being in our youth, I volunteered to take the first approach to the roof. As I lifted my left leg out of the window, I realized that getting the first leg out was the easy part. But I had another leg, which now felt like a thousand pounds, hanging inside the house.

My arms were clinging on to each side of the window ledge, and all I could see was my friend, falling down in laughter watching me. "What... I've got this...no problem; could you just maybe lift my leg over, please?" I asked my friend, who was now in tears from laughing so hard.

"I would, Jess, but I have to get my camera, because this is too priceless not to share at our next reunion." I screamed, "Don't you dare!" as I almost fell out of the window.

After clumsily climbing out the window and onto the creaky roof, we carefully set out the blanket, sprayed some bug spray on, and relaxed back on our pillows. As the fireworks began to go off in the sky above us, we looked at each other, and I said, "How did we just travel through time and end up here eighteen years later?"

My friend replied, "I don't know Jess, but, damn, we look good!"

"That night I learned a few things. One, is that windows and houses do shrink as we get older. Two, the fireworks displays lasted nowhere near the time they did when we were kids, and, lastly, time travel is not only possible...it's an incredible feeling," I said, with a grin.

"Awesome story, Mom," Chase replied. Then he added, "How about you, Dan; any stories?"

"Ah, yes, the Fourth of July!" Dan began to tell us his tale...

"As you may have guessed, from my accent, I am not originally from this country. We moved to America from Milan, Italy, when I was fourteen years old. My soon-to-be stepfather was an Irish/American in the United States Military, who fell in love with and married my Mother, a beautiful Italian seamstress. Mi Madre; she was an incredible cook, too. She taught me everything I know. May she rest in peace, Mi Madre. Well, we moved to the States to be with her husband, my stepfather, and have been here ever since. That year, when I was just fourteen, we had our first Fourth of July celebration.

We lived in the city, near downtown Boston, and we took the Metro for miles to join others for the show at the harbor. There were families grilling food and fun parties all along the waterfront, with music and dancing. It was a wonderful night. It is my favorite holiday now, and this Sunday, I will cook a feast. And we shall dance, eat, and celebrate, and toast Boston and Milan!"

Dan than stood up, took a drink of his Mike's Hard Lemonade, and extended his other hand out to Aubrey.

Aubrey then put her hand into his, and he announced, "We are off to create another dinner to remember."

Aubrey stood, with her hand still sitting in Dan's hand, and looked at our guests, saying, "Yes, I shall assist in making 'a dinner to remember' because, as I recall, the assistant always gets to taste test." Smiling toward one another, Dan and Aubrey retreated off to the kitchen. Dan turned around with a playful wink at me. I had to think again, "Those two were joined at the hip, or *somewhere*." Of course, Aubrey was nowhere near the chef that Dan was, although she did get an 'A' for effort, I had to reluctantly admit. After all, I was no Julia Child.

Kelly had come out of the pool to dry off, and announced that she was in need of a little nap time. She covered up in her soft, fluffy robe. Oddly enough, most of our guests seemed to really enjoy those robes. I still had to laugh at Dan's first reaction to them.

Kelly slid on her sandals and told us that she would see us all at dinner. Tom had also decided that a nap was a pretty good idea, and so he left shortly after Kelly.

Melinda, Chase, and Trey stayed in the cool swimming pool, while Kathryn and I made ourselves comfortable on the couch, under the veranda.

"Such terrific stories, Jessica, don't you think?" Kathryn asked.

"Yes, they are. It's the one holiday that you don't have to get dressed up for, you don't have to feel like you have to have a date for, and you know that it's going to go out with a bang!" I replied.

So Kathryn, are you enjoying your stay so far?" I asked.

"Oh yes, I'm delighted to be here. This house and the property are exquisite. I can't thank you enough for my journal and the plant you left for me in my suite," Kathryn said, while placing her hand across her heart.

Once again, I took notice that when some people are really sincere about what they are saying, they place their hands instinctively across their hearts, as they speak.

"I'm so happy you like it, Kathryn. I know that you chose not to bring up your health conditions in front of the other guests, but may I just say one thing to you…you are an inspiration to me. I have been looking forward to meeting you since the day we spoke on the phone."

"You have been looking forward to meeting me?? I have been looking forward to chatting with you!" Kathryn replied with fervor.

"Well, just jump right in, Kathryn, for I love nothing more than a good chat."

"I confided in you about my medical problems, but what's on my mind, you see, is that I have never felt that I was ever able to grieve properly for my late husband, Blake. With my cancer treatments, and Blake dying in the midst of the treatments, I still feel somewhat empty inside. I miss him so much, Jessica. My heart is still alone, I'm afraid. Yes, he may have been an intellectual snob at times; in fact, sometimes he made me feel like the recalcitrant child."

"Well, Kathryn, that does surprise me. However, it makes perfect sense, too. Perhaps you have two things to grieve for: Blake's death, and your cancer. Could it be that you are still grieving for both?"

Kathryn wondered aloud whether that could be a reason for her sardonic sense of humor, bordering on snide meanness, sometimes. She thought of Tom, and how she had misjudged him, at first. She had lost a few old friends this way, too.

"Grief may turn to anger, at one stage, I think I remembered reading," Kathryn continued. "You know, Jessica, it does the heart good to talk with someone as sweet as you, without the overly saccharine approach of some of my friends, back home."

Kathryn actually felt good about confessing her dislikes for some of her friends' approaches when it came to comforting her emotionally.

"Jessica, you are a born healer, but then, you already knew that," Kathryn smiled, with a genuine, good-natured nod to me.

"Well, I said, sometimes it just happens, and you don't know how it does. Other times, you have to push here, and shove there, without anyone even knowing. I wish I had known a long time ago, what I know now, but then again; where would all the lessons be, right?"

"Well said, Jessica; I agree." Kathryn smiled, and continued the conversation with, "so, tell me about the support group you started after your heart surgery."

"Sure; I named the support group: 'A Heart to Heart.'

It's a way for those who have gone through heart surgery, or are close to someone who has gone through it, to share their inspirational stories.

Some of the people that come to the meetings are scheduled to have surgery, soon, and others have just had surgery. Still others, like myself, have celebrated many years out since surgery."

"I've been to a support group a time or two, as you have probably guessed, and they are helpful," Kathryn said, as she nodded her head in agreement.

"The stories are incredible, aren't they; from everyday people just like us. Some, just like myself, woke up after surgery, and had to go through stages of depression, frustration, and pure exhaustion before their new outlook on life took hold. Then, there are stories of the famous light and tunnel, with the flashing of an entire life passing before their eyes," I said, with excitement.

"I've never had any sort of near-death experience, per say, but I know what it is like to wake up one morning, after finding out you have cancer, and not know where to turn, or who to tell. The support groups can be lifesavers in many ways, and I wish there were more," she commented.

"It definitely helped in saving my life. On this very veranda, right here, where we are sitting, there have been children, teens, adults and the elderly, all supporting each other. Some of their stories involved patients helping patients to get through the recovery process, and some people came just to vent out their fears and frustrations. I sometimes used my own story as an example. It was just people helping people. It's so simple when you really think about it," I replied.

"I would love to hear your story; about what you felt after your surgery, if you wouldn't mind," Kathryn persuaded.

"Well, Kathryn, the day I went from the ICU recovery to an intermediate care unit, a man showed up in the doorway of my room with his walker. He was standing there in his hospital gown and robe, and introduced himself to me as 'Kenneth.' I wasn't quite sure what to make of him at the time, so I said 'hello,' and told him my name was Jessica. I asked him if he was lost."

"What did he say?" asked Kathryn.

"He pushed his green metal walker, the kind with squeaky wheels, right into my room, next to my bed, and to my complete surprise, said: 'Ok, youngster. It's time for you to get up out of that bed and do some laps with me.'

"Laps…now?! They ripped open my chest and spread it like a turkey, holding my heart in their very hands!" I angrily told this determined stranger."

"Maybe he was missing from the psych floor." Kathryn joked.

"Then this strange man said to me: 'I know you hurt, little lady. I was in that ICU the same time you were. I may look pretty darn good for my age, but I have many years on you. If I can do this, you can do it better! Up, Up, Up.'

"Kathryn, I actually shouted, "No Way! Get OUT of my room. I am not getting up!'"

"Oh Jessica, that sounds like an awful experience," Kathryn chimed in with empathy.

"It was at first, but then Kenneth saw the fear in my eyes, and he gently pushed his walker in front of my legs. He helped me place my hands on the hand rails, and he said: 'No worries, little lady, take it slow, but I promise you, you will be doing circles around the rest of us oldies by later this week.' Then he leaned over closer to me, and whispered: 'besides, I've got five dollars bet on you with old Myrtle in room 21B, that you can outpace us all by the end of the week, and I'm not about to lose five dollars to Myrtle!'

"I looked at him with wild and frightened eyes. Let's just say I didn't want to get out of that bed. Just as I was about to start ranting, Kenneth said: 'It's not every day we get a youngster like you to give us a real challenge.' And then this strange man, named Kenneth, winked at me!"

"Winked? Like he was flirting with you, or something?" Kathryn asked, surprised.

"I'm not really sure, but you have to give him an 'A' for effort!" I joked. "But seriously, I slowly, with the help of my nurse, was able to get myself to a stable standing position next to him.

"He did not have the open heart surgery the same as I did. He had blocked arteries and had undergone surgery, but you'd never have known it. He was like a pillar of strength, and I couldn't understand how he was doing so well, so fast, at his age. He must have been about ninety years old; I swear it!"

"It sounds to me that he sure was determined to push your buttons," Kathryn said.

"That he was. It took me what seemed like forever to get from the bed to the doorway on that first trip into the hall. Once we got into the hall, I kid you not, what was probably only fifty feet, looked more like the length of two football fields to me. I just wanted to get to the end of the nurses' station."

"So, tell me, Jessica, what happened next?" Kathryn was genuinely intrigued by my story.

"Well, everyday Kenneth came and met me for a walk. He and I would exchange our stories in those hallways. Personal stories about our fears, our kids, our lives, basically.

We would always pass room 21B, but the door was always closed. He would comment that Myrtle must be sleeping again, but that he kept her posted on my progress, and that she was about to lose a bet.

By the end of the week, I was walking without the aid of the walker, and Kenneth and I even got permission to take an elevator ride down to the café to get a cup of coffee. Decaf, of course!"

"Could you have ever known how liberating it could be to take a simple elevator ride for a cup of coffee, before that experience, Jessica? I now know that feeling, too," Kathryn said.

"The day before I was to be sent home, Kathryn, Kenneth stopped by my room in his regular clothing. He looked at me, and said:"

"I'm heading out, little lady. I did my time here, and now I'm going to venture back into the world. You take care of that beautiful ticker of yours."

"Was that it? He left with just those words, never to be seen again?" Kathryn asked.

"No, I couldn't let him just leave like that, so I said: "Kenneth, I can't thank you enough for what you have done for me."

The tears were filling my eyes faster than I could control them, and I must have looked like a scared little girl to him. I didn't want him to leave me, Kathryn; he was my friend, and he understood the fear I was feeling inside. He knew what it felt like to be scared to sleep for fear that your heart was going to stop beating, and you wouldn't be able to wake up."

Kathryn now listened with tears in her eyes, and I knew she must have experienced similar fears and questions during her cancer treatments.

"Before he left, Kathryn, which was the last time I ever saw him again, he said: 'don't cry, Miss Jessica; you did something to help me as well,' and with that, he took out a five dollar bill and said, "thanks to how well you did, I'm getting a free lunch from Myrtle today!"

I knew he was trying to make me laugh instead of cry, but I started to cry even harder. Kenneth walked over to me and stood next to my hospital bed. He reached for my hand and said, 'everything happens for a reason, little lady; so keep your eyes open, and you will be shown the way.'

Kathryn, a life angel is what I call people like Kenneth. They appear when you need them the most, and then they are off to help someone else."

"Yeah...and they work for only five bucks! What a deal," Kathryn both laughed and cried with the emotion.

And she and I started laughing together with our tear-filled eyes.

"There's one more thing that proves to me that Mr. Kenneth was a life angel, Kathryn."

"What's that, Jessica?" she asked, as she wiped her eyes with a tissue.

"I was released the day after Kenneth left the hospital, and as Jay and I were leaving, we stopped at room 21B to meet Myrtle, since her door was finally opened. When I walked into the room, a nurse was getting the room ready for a new patient, and I saw the name of the previous patient who had stayed in that room: *Kenneth Bartle*."

"There never was a *Myrtle*, was there Jessica?"

"Nope, just a wonderful and smart angel, disguised as a grey haired, elderly gentleman, who found a way to help a very scared 'little lady' get through the toughest time of her life," I answered Kathryn.

"Jessica, I believe I had one of those life angels the first year I was diagnosed with cancer. I completely understand, and I believe in them with my entire heart!" She emphasized this with a hand over her heart again.

"I have enjoyed this talk so much, Kathryn, and I think you are a very special 'little lady,' yourself!"

"I have enjoyed it, too," Kathryn replied softly, as she was still filled with emotion.

Looking up towards the sky, I could see that some clouds were rolling in.

"I heard on the radio that we might get some sprinkles of rain tonight," I said to Kathryn, as I stood up.

"That would be lovely. I love the rain," she replied, wiping the last of her tears away.

"Well, I must excuse myself now; to check on dinner and to see if Dan or Aubrey might need any assistance from me, though I very much doubt it! I will see you at dinner, Kathryn."

"I look forward to it," Kathryn replied.

I left the veranda while Kathryn stayed and enjoyed the fresh air.

A Leap of Faith

*E*ntering the house, I could already smell something delectable coming from the kitchen, so I made my way there to lend a hand, or, should I say, "maybe be another taste tester."

"Need any assistance in here, you two?" I asked, as I entered the kitchen where Dan was preparing a feast, with Aubrey assisting the best she could.

"Nope, you just go and enjoy yourself. Aubrey and I have this all covered, but thank you," Dan replied, as if shooing me away like a fly.

"Well then, it looks like rain might be coming soon, so I may just take a quick little walk down to the lake before getting ready for dinner, if you two don't mind," I called out as I slipped toward the doorway.

"Not at all, enjoy your walk, and we will see you at dinner," Aubrey called back, as though she were shooing a child out to play.

I left the house feeling a little like a third wheel, in the kitchen, anyway, and started walking down the path. I have a favorite bench near the lake, and thought maybe I could clear my head in the fresh air for a while.

As I approached the bench and sat down, a familiar feeling came across me. There was something about today—my mind was filled with thoughts of Jay.

I could smell the rain coming, and it reminded me of a night that he and I spent together during a thunderstorm. It's amazing how a certain scent can take you back in time.

It had been a July evening, some years back, when the sky began to darken and the wind picked up with a fury.

In this part of Texas, storms can be few and far between, so an excitement fills the air when one is coming through.

Jay and I had been stargazing when the weather began to change. We had just started to move our chairs into the house when the skies opened up on us.

His favorite, goofy hat was blown off the top of his head, and took flight as if it had been a feather in a breeze. The hat and wind toyed with us as we attempted to chase that thing down the driveway.

We were laughing so hard, that by the time he finally caught it, you would have thought we were a couple of kids, just playing in the rain.

We hurried into the house where we began to feel the chill of the air conditioner on our rain-soaked bodies, so we quickly changed out of our wet attire and spent that night caught up in each other's arms. How we enjoyed the romance of the storm under the covers.

Memories of the times that Jay and I shared made me smile, but at the same time, they pulled at my heart strings for I was still very much in love with him.

I was sitting there with my thoughts on my favorite wooden bench near the lake, when I saw Rosemary walking down the path. I smiled at her as she came near, and asked, "Can you smell the rain coming, Rosemary?"

"Yes, it's getting closer. I can feel the temperature dropping, too," she replied. She was dressed in a gauze, pale aqua, long dress and looked stunning, as usual.

"We probably don't have long before we get a good soaking out here," I said jokingly. "Are you warm enough, Rosemary?"

"Oh my, yes. But I'm not sure I'll ever get used to the quick changes in the weather down here. And Jessica, I know we have only just met recently, but would it be too much for me to ask if I could confide in you about something?" Rosemary's smile began to fade.

"I moved over on the wooden bench, and motioned with a pat of my hand to the space next to me, for her to have a seat.

"Is everything okay with your stay?" I asked in a soft tone.

"It's amazing; perfect, actually. Everything about your home is perfect, Jessica." She said this as she looked down toward her sandals. Then she looked over at me, and continued...

"Jessica, everything here is so perfect. It's my life back home that I'm rethinking. I'm suddenly full of questions on what really makes me happy. I told Jack about it earlier, and he was so supportive and kind, after the stink he first raised; and, by the way, I'm sorry…but a part of him knew I needed to speak to a woman, too.

He even suggested that maybe I could talk with you, because you might understand what I am going through, as far as my career and needing a change."

"There couldn't be a more perfect time for us to talk, Rosemary. I'm here, I have nowhere to be, and I believe we have some time to chat before the storm makes its appearance," I replied with a smile. "And please, don't worry about that little tiff."

"When Jack and I first arrived here, all I could think about was work, and all the things that could pile up while I was away. I worried about it the entire trip here. Should I really be going away for a few days?? Why did I promise Jack that he could have my cell phone for four entire days?

Every time I had asked Jack…what should I bring to wear, or what kind of excursions were we going to go on…he would simply reply with: just bring something comfortable, and we would just spend some quality time leaving all of our worries behind us.

"Comfortable clothing and no planning; are you kidding me!" I thought. The not having to think about planning our short vacation was even more stressful to me, Jessica," Rosemary replied with a slight laugh.

"Rosemary, it is hard to stop the clock of repetition once it takes on a life of its own. I've been there, myself," I said.

"That is a perfect way to put it, Jessica. It is like a clock of repetition that just keeps on ticking. My life has become that clock, and when Jack told me about this little getaway, he was essentially going to stop that clock for four entire days. For him to suggest for me to bring comfortable clothing, and have no cell phone…I didn't know what to do with that! She said this with her hands flying up into the air. "And then he accused me of having an affair!"

Rosemary continued: "Jessica, I began to think about my life the day I filled out your questionnaire. It really made me think, and then the moment Jack and I entered our beautiful suite, I let myself actually relax. Jack and I spent time laughing at the pool our first day here, and then we talked for over two hours after dinner. The morning Jack came back from the lake, I found myself asking him if I was the same woman he had married. Am I going crazy, Jessica…has this happened to other guests who have stayed here?" she asked. "And the fight?"

"Rosemary, you're not crazy; and believe me, I do understand, because I've been where you are right now: questioning where your life is, how it got there, where is it going. And then the typical 'seven year-itch fight,' too."

"Honestly, Jessica, I think I'm going through some kind of withdrawals, because I feel like I am an emotional train wreck waiting to happen," she replied, as she laughed and cried at the same time. It seemed to be happening a lot, lately; this emotion.

"Rosemary, you are not a wreck. What you are feeling is that part of your spirit that has been waiting for the right time to remind you that you are human, and that life is more than just the ticking of a clock. Have you ever thought about what you loved to do as a child?" I asked.

"Jessica, I loved photography. Ever since I had a Brownie camera when I was little. I still have it, if you can believe that."

Rosemary then looked out towards the lake and said, "I miss my husband, and I miss being at home more. Is it selfish of me to miss my house? I want to spend more time decorating our home, and to try cooking again. I also wouldn't mind taking every clock in our house and tossing them out!"

I laughed at Rosemary's comment about throwing the clocks out, and asked her, "Have you noticed there are no clocks here, except the ones on the nightstands in the rooms?"

"I hadn't noticed, but I think that's a great idea," she replied.

"The only reason anyone needs a clock at all here, is to make sure not to miss Dan's six o'clock dinners," I smiled.

"Jessica, do you think I've been feeling this way for a long time, but chose to ignore it? I think I feared making a change, but I couldn't for the life of me figure out why."

"That is so completely normal, Rosemary. We have all been taught *how to fear* in many different forms since we were born. Try taking the *fear* out of the decisions in your life, and you will see that *fear* gets far more attention than it deserves."

"Why did I ignore my happiness for so long?" she questioned herself. *Was it to please Jack?*

"That's the funny thing about life, Rosemary, you can try to ignore what really makes you happy, but the minute you get to spend some quality time alone with your real love, real interest, or thoughts of them, then it happens; your spirit makes its appearance, loud and clear. Rosemary, that's why I chose to build this place and share it with others. My spirit found a way to show me what was going to keep my life full. I call it rejuvenating the spirit, and now you, my dear, are rejuvenating your spirit, too," I said with a big smile.

"Jessica, you are a real life hero for people like me, who want to follow their dreams, but are *fearful* they will fail. Look at where believing in yourself has gotten you. I mean, this place is amazing."

"Why thank you, Rosemary, that is very nice of you to say, but I can't take all the credit; and besides, I still have work to do on my spirit, too. It is an ongoing process, that's for sure," I said and laughed heartily.

"So, that's the key, isn't it, just have hope, and take *fear* out of the equation." Rosemary added, "And Jack does seem to understand."

"Yes, I do believe that is the key, and just to let you in on a little secret: it's quite contagious, so you may want to keep an eye on Jack.

"On Jack, how do you mean?" Rosemary smiled, confused.

"I'm pretty sure that if Jack doesn't *fear* that I will notice, he may try to take this lake home with you two on Sunday night," I whispered.

"I'll check his suitcase before we leave," Rosemary whispered back, as we began to laugh together.

"Speaking of Jack, I believe that is your husband coming up the path right now," I said, as I waved toward Jack.

Rosemary smiled in Jack's direction, and then looked over at me; and with a soft and sincere voice, she said, "Thank you, Jessica, you have no idea how much talking to you has helped me."

Jack greeted us back with a wave, and met his wife with an extended hand as she stood up from the bench.

"Isn't that lake beautiful today, ladies," Jack commented.

"Yes, honey, it is," Rosemary replied, as she turned towards me and winked.

"I'll see you two at the house," I said, as they walked off down the path, hand in hand.

The talk that Rosemary and I had just shared meant as much to me as it did to her. It reminded me that although I was fulfilling my dreams, and I was happy with myself, that life always finds a way to bring even more happiness, somehow, someway, if you let it.

I kept that in mind as I felt the first rain drops come down on me. I stood up from the bench, looked up at the sky, and quietly said, "Thank you, God." Then I walked quickly back to the house, thinking I had better practice what I preached!

Walking back into the house, I made my way up the stairs into my room and decided on a nice hot shower before dinner. All the talking had tired me out a bit, too. I needed to wake up for tonight.

*D*an was in the kitchen, putting the finishing touches on the salads when Aubrey walked into the room. She had excused herself about an hour earlier to change and to get Rosemary's gift ready for Jack's big surprise.

As Aubrey walked back into the kitchen, Dan couldn't help but notice how beautiful she looked. Aubrey was one of those people who made even a warmup suit look fashionable, so when she walked in wearing a colorful lace top and a black flowing skirt, he was awestruck.

"As always, Miss Saunders, you look beautiful this evening," Dan said, looking at Aubrey from across the kitchen. She never failed to amaze him with her loveliness, and the kindness she possessed.

"This old thing," Aubrey replied jokingly, as she did a little spin.

"Dinner smells incredible, Dan," Aubrey said, as she looked out the window above the sink and noticed the rain coming down.

"The rain is lovely, isn't it," she commented with excitement making her cheeks pink, and in the process, making her look even lovelier, if that was even possible.

"Yes, it is, and all the flowers that you and Jessica planted around the pond last month love every drop," Dan replied, as he put the salads in the refrigerator.

Stepping over to the sink near Aubrey, Dan rinsed his hands off and joined her in watching the rain.

"Dinner is in the oven for another hour... would you like to accompany me to the veranda for a glass of wine and some rain watching?" Dan asked Aubrey, as he put a hand lightly on her shoulder.

"I would love to," Aubrey replied, turning towards him.

Aubrey chose a bottle of red wine, and Dan gathered a couple of wine glasses and a cork screw. Making their way out to the covered veranda, Dan held open one of the large glass French doors for Aubrey. They soon settled in on the outdoor sofa, overlooking the tranquil landscaping of the property.

Popping out the cork, Dan poured them each a glass. Sitting back, next to one another and looking out at the rain, all seemed so natural to the two of them. They were happy and content whether talking, laughing, cooking, or just sitting there, watching the drops come down.

Dan started to think how amazing it was to be able to just sit with someone and do absolutely nothing but enjoy the moment. He realized more than ever that he was in love with this woman by his side. She was the woman he had always hoped to meet, and when he wasn't looking... she stepped into his life.

Unbeknownst to Dan, Aubrey was starting to realize that she had feelings for Dan, too. There were days when she was unable to come out to the Inn because she was needed in the city, and those days she found herself thinking about Dan, and missing him.

"Did you get everything together for Jack that you were working on?" Dan asked.

"Yes, he is going to be so happy!" Aubrey said, "and Rosemary, too!"

"You are quite the romantic, Miss Saunders," Dan replied.

"Me? How about you...you were the one who said dinner had to be perfect for Jack's special surprise," Aubrey said, as she turned her attention to Dan, and took a sip of her wine.

"Okay, I admit it...I'm a hopeless romantic, too. I think what Jack is doing tonight is great," Dan smiled again.

In Dan's mind, he was thinking about the romantic dinner he would love to cook just for Aubrey.

That's when I showed up on the veranda.

"Hey, you two...got room for one more on that sofa?" I asked (Okay, so not my best timing...)

Aubrey moved closer to Dan, and made room for me next to her. The rain was letting up, and the three of us went over the plan for Jack's surprise.

It was a few minutes before six o'clock, and everyone was arriving in the dining room for dinner. Like clockwork, everyone sat in the same seats as the night before.

Tonight, Chase did the honors and took everyone's beverage requests. Dan had already placed a delicious salad at each one of our places.

The conversations around the table were flowing naturally, and we were all enjoying ourselves. The topic of Chase and Trey, and their speaking engagements, came up as Melinda asked the two when their next engagement would be.

Kathryn, listening in, decided to ask a few questions herself.

"So, you two young men are speakers?" she asked.

"Yes ma'am, we have done some speaking around Texas," Trey proudly answered.

"I'm so impressed. May I ask what topics you speak about?" Kathryn asked.

"Well actually, we have a speaking engagement set next month at the children's hospital. We are going to be talking to kids about the fears of living with, and fighting cancer," Chase replied.

"Yes," Trey added… "Our youth group leader is looking around for some inspiring guest speakers to join us. Maybe a doctor or two who can answer some of the medical questions that are sure to come up."

Kathryn knew that this subject was very near and dear to her heart, and she wanted to offer to join them at their speaking engagement; but she wasn't sure if she should bring up her personal experience with cancer.

The other guests all commented on how impressed they were that the two young men donated their time to help others.

Jack chimed in, and told Chase and Trey that he was friends with a few doctors who specialized in oncology, and he would be happy to make a few calls to them. Then Jack mentioned that maybe Chase and Trey could find a cancer survivor that wanted to share his/her positive thoughts with the kids and their parents.

Kathryn debated whether to tell them that she was a cancer survivor. She went back and forth in her mind: "should I?" Tom was sitting there, too, and she wondered if he might just pity her, then. "If I don't, maybe he will think later that I was hiding something from him." But she had to tell him about her struggle with ovarian cancer; it's only fair! Kathryn felt she had an uplifting story to share, but was not quite secure enough to share it at that moment. She did however say, "I know someone that you two may want to talk with. She is a cancer survivor and would love an opportunity to share her uplifting story."

Aubrey and I instantly knew that Kathryn was referring to herself, but it was not our place to say anything. If Kathryn wanted to share her story, it was hers, and hers alone, to share with whomever, and whenever, she chose. Chase told Kathryn that it would be great if they could get more info after dinner, and thanked everyone at the table for their support and ideas.

The salad plates were cleared, and I helped Dan deliver a delicious dinner. We talked Dan into joining us, and made room for him at the table. The laughter and conversations were abundant tonight. Dan and Aubrey had excused themselves from the table in order to get dessert ready, while I cleared the dinner plates and dimmed the lights. Aubrey turned on some after dinner music that happened to be one of the songs that Jack and Rosemary had played for their wedding dance. It was *Elvis Presley* singing *"Only Fools Rush In."* As Rosemary announced... "Honey, this is our song!" to her husband, Dan. Aubrey, and I took our seats.

Jack then stood up from his chair and knelt down on one knee next to his wife. He took out a small, red jewelry box and looked deeply into Rosemary's eyes, saying...

"Rosemary, you have been my best friend, my wife, and my whole heart for almost eight years, and I love you even more today than I did yesterday; and I'll love you more tomorrow than I do today. I want to spend the rest of my life with you, and I want you to know, without a shadow of a doubt, that you are the same woman I married, and I would marry you all over again, if you would have me."

With that, Jack opened the little box, and there was a beautiful emerald ring shining up at her. Rosemary's eyes were filled with tears as she placed one hand on her heart, and the other covering her mouth. She tried to speak, but her voice was cracking. She cleared her throat and said,

"Oh Jack, yes, I'll marry you again, and again, and again. I love you, honey!"

Jack stood up, and so did Rosemary, as they embraced in a hug while everyone at the table clapped. Then the song, *"Only Fools Rush In,"* was replayed, so they could finish enjoying the music.

Aubrey then stood up and said that she had an announcement to make, too. As she went around the corner to get the little tree, Dan retreated to the kitchen to get dessert ready. Aubrey came back with the little tree, and held it up for Jack and Rosemary to see.

"This little tree is a symbol of the strength and love that your marriage holds. Rosemary, your husband has asked that we plant this tree for you both, and for your growing love and devotion of one another. Every time you come back to visit here, you will be reminded of how beautiful what you have together really is. If it's okay with both of you, we'd like to name it *Hope*.

"I don't even know what to say…I'm so happy to be here, and I would be grateful to have the little tree…*Hope,* planted here," Rosemary replied, as she gave Jack a very private *look.*

Dan then returned to the table with dessert, and we all enjoyed the perfect ending to a perfect dinner.

Tonight, the men had a surprise for us girls, as well. As I stood to start clearing the table, they told me that tonight they would be doing the dishes, and that the girls could just sit and relax.

Needless to say, there were no arguments, as the girls made their way to the great room near the piano. Trey came over to select some jazz music to play on the player system attached to the baby grand piano, and asked if he could bring us anything to drink. It was wonderful, to say the least. The baby grand was not something I had ever learned to play, but Henry was quite good at it, and graced us with a tune, now and then. Any guests that wished to play a tune were encouraged to play, as one of my favorite enjoyments was to listen to live music.

Soon the guys joined us, and we all enjoyed some more after dinner music and drinks. Then Jack reached out his hand and asked Rosemary to dance to some mellow music. They both stood and started to slow dance. Tom, surprisingly, also enjoyed the music, and asked Kathryn if she would join him in a dance, to which she happily obliged. Then, to my amazement, my son Chase asked Melinda if she would like to take a spin, and they joined the other two couples. They then played *"Twist and*

Shout," song by *The Beatles*, and everyone joined in on that one; including Aubrey and Dan.

Trey and Kelly were still seated near me, deep in conversation about possible plans to change her cottage in San Antonio into a flower shop for Melinda. Kelly was excited to hear all of Trey's ideas.

Watching my guests dance, I have to admit that I wished I could be out there dancing, too. Just at that moment…a voice from behind me whispered… "May I have this dance, Miss Jessica?"

I knew that soft voice…I turned around with a big smile, and said, "Yes, Mr. David, I'd love to."

Taking Henry's hand, and being lead to the middle of the room, I asked him when he and Felix got back.

"You surprised me…I thought you weren't coming in until Sunday?"

"Felix and I got back to town early, and we thought a surprise entrance would be grand," Henry replied, as he spun me around.

Chase was trying his best to act as if he was a natural at slow dancing, but the truth was that he had only danced a few times in his life; but he didn't want to pass up an opportunity to spend more time getting closer to Melinda.

Moving closer to Chase, Melinda looked at him and said, "Thank you."

"Thank you?" Chase questioned.

"Dancing; it always makes me feel a lot better," she answered.

"Well then, Melinda…dancing is what we shall do," and he dipped Melinda, and made her laugh. It was the first time he heard her beautiful, sparkling laugh.

The song ended, and we all returned to sitting again, as I introduced Henry to our other guests. They were more than excited to let him know how impressed they were with *Luna's Hope*.

The night was getting late and I was feeling tired, so I said my goodnights, and politely excused myself.

Melinda turned in early, as well. Her emotions had been wreaking havoc on her the last few days, and she needed to rest.

Kelly, on the other hand, needed no excuse or arm twisting to turn in early, and crawled in between those luxurious sheets.

Henry, Kathryn, Tom, Chase and Trey were the night owls on this unseasonably cool evening. They moved to the veranda, where Trey kept an outdoor fire burning as the night came close to midnight. Dan and Aubrey slipped away for a late evening walk and some more wine.

Henry was telling Kathryn and Tom about his friend passing away from cancer, while Trey and Chase listened intently.

Kathryn was debating whether to tell them that she was a cancer survivor. She was going back and forth in her mind. Especially since Tom was there; she wondered if he would just pity her, or what he would think.

If I don't tell him now, he may think later that I was hiding something from him, she thought again.

But she had to tell him someday about her ovarian cancer, if she was going to get to know that man better. "It's only fair!" she concluded. Kathryn, very touched by Henry's story about Will, offered her sincere condolences to him.

Kathryn then felt there was no better time than the present to bring up a subject from earlier with Chase and Trey.

With a leap of faith, she looked at Tom first, and then focused on Trey and Chase.

"You two gentleman have shown much maturity in the speaking engagements that you hold. Earlier tonight, when we were talking at dinner about you having a possible cancer survivor speak next month with you; well, I was wondering if you might be interested in having me speak at your event." Kathryn stunned everyone, it seemed.

Henry looked at Kathryn with understanding eyes, and Chase quickly replied, "Yes, Ma'am, we would love that. I didn't know you were a cancer survivor. You have obviously endured a battle and won, and we would love to have your positive light shine on some very special kids and parents."

"Yes, absolutely, we would love for you to come talk," Trey added.

"Then, it's a date, gentlemen. Just let me know the time and place, and I'll attend with you," Kathryn said with a smile, before she turned towards Henry, conveniently avoiding Tom's eyes.

"Henry, it has been a joy meeting you, and I look forward to seeing you over the next few days. I think it's time for this old bird to hit the nest," Kathryn said, as she stood up.

Tom, still in a bit of shock at what he had just learned about Kathryn, didn't know what to say.

And, as southern gentleman do in these parts...all of the men stood as they said goodnight to Kathryn.

As she was about to walk away, Tom did not return to a seated position, but instead chimed in and said, "umm, Kathryn, would you mind if I walked with you, since I'm about to turn in myself."

"That would be nice, Tom," she replied and they gave their goodnights to the remaining night owls.

Kathryn was walking, head down, next to Tom, thinking: "what do I say now?"

As they turned the corner and were alone in the hall, Tom blurted out in a loud whisper: "Cancer!" Are you....are you...over it?"

Kathryn: "What! Do you think it's contagious or something, Cowboy?"

Tom: "You want to talk about contagious! Girl, I had scabies when I was in college. It damned near killed my social life for the next two years! Everybody knew!" He turned bright red in his face and neck. Then he said, "God, Kathryn, can you ever forgive me? It just came out...please, honey; I'm so sorry."

Hearing how much this incident had affected Tom, and what a shock her announcement must have been to him, Kathryn's face betrayed her lack of tact and empathy, at first. She turned beet red, herself, then; and tears came to her eyes, out of nowhere, it seemed.

"Tom, I'm so sorry, it's just that sometimes people treat me like I'm too fragile now to do anything. Others can't get away fast enough. Sometimes it is all about me. And I'm sorry I didn't tell you about the cancer before."

Tom put on his exceptionally winning smile. "It's okay, Kathryn; others might give you the exit plan, but I'll never do that. You must know that about me, by now."

Kathryn said, "well, aren't we a pair. But I'd rather be a pair with you, than anyone else, Tom."

This brought the flush to Kathryn's face again, but she just burst out with, "I would like to visit you in Dallas, and do all that we talked about."

Tom suddenly had an epiphany. This was the lady he had fallen for, after all.

"Kathryn, are you assuming that I would just throw you under the bus? Over a little thing called cancer? And after we just found each other?"

"Well, Kathryn answered, hand on hip, and taking a step backward, "are YOU still contagious, or what?"

"No Kathryn, its terminal," Tom answered, with some of his old sarcasm.

Kathryn stared at him, and suddenly broke out in a loud, raucous laugh. Tom started laughing, too. They ended in a big hug.

After leaving Kathryn with a smile at the door of her suite, Tom was full of energy, and needed to sort all of these new feelings out. He knew exactly what he needed to do, and it didn't matter what time it was. He was going to sneak a cell phone call to his buddy, Ralph, and hopefully, get some advice.

"Ralph, man, are you there? Pick up, man." Tom's voice sounded so urgent that Ralph, watching reruns of games on the NFL Network, had to pick up.

"Tom, what the hell is wrong with you, you sound like you owe a cool million to the damn Mexican mafia. You ARE calling from Vegas, aren't you? Or what, is it Reno, ha-ha...! C'mon man, fill me in..."

Tom, laughing at Ralph's antics, couldn't help but calm down a little, then. He said, "Ralph, this is it. This is the woman for me. There is no holding back, now. What do I do? Where do I go? What do I say? Help me, pal; you know all of those damn things. Hell, you've been married four times!"

Tom ended with exasperation. Sometimes Ralph could act so dense. Yet, he held a PhD from Texas A&M.

"Tom," Ralph said with a grin, "will you sit your sorry ass down and shut up for a second. YOU *know* what to do! You are just too damn stubborn to admit it, or to do it. If this is it, go for it, man; live it, man! You've got to capture her heart like a little bird in your big ass hand...I don't know if I've ever seen hands so big, they're more like paws; hell I..."

"Damn, Ralph. Shut up," Tom thought, but did not say.

"Okay," Ralph finally let out a long breath. "Do your music thing, my man. No woman of class could resist your voice, and you mentioned a piano, right? Maybe those lessons at Julliard will finally pay off! Just live that life like you mean it. You've got to show her, tell her, and sing to her. Women love that shit! Live like Hanley's Hogs!"

138

Tom knew immediately what he had to do, period. Ellie had gone to see *Michael Buble* recently, and simply swooned over his music and performance.

Tom went out and purchased the sheet music for a few of *Michael Buble's* songs. His favorite song to perform for Ellie was the song *"Lost,"* as it had such a mellow melody. Ellie teased her dad for sounding so romantic, and said he would be much sought after by the ladies, if he'd only get out of the house or office long enough to display his true talents. The Hanley house was filled with this famous artist's music, thanks to Ellie and Tom. Tom suddenly was struck with an idea that he hoped would be perfect for knocking Kathryn out of the ball park, or he wasn't Tom Hanley of Hanley's Hogs!

With his heart full of resolve, Tom was finally able to sleep like a baby. As he drifted off to sleep, he heard *Dwight Yoakam's* song *"Fast as You"* somewhere in his brain.

It was certainly a complicated game; this new competition called *Love*.

*M*eanwhile, Dan and Aubrey had ended up walking back to Dan's RV for another bottle of Merlot. Like a couple of teenagers, they stepped into Dan's RV gingerly, as if they were afraid of being caught in a compromising position. Aubrey, after a bit of Merlot, bravely teased Dan about their 'cooking partnership,' and how everyone knew the truth. Dan, red faced, said "Honey, don't put yourself down. You're a talented, beautiful, woman full of love. And your story about Elizabeth was so moving, I almost cried myself."

Aubrey, touched by this, put her hand on Dan's chest. As if feeling for his heart, she left it there. Dan immediately felt lightning strike. He reached for, and held Aubrey's face in his hands, as if handling fine porcelain. His emotions nearly overcame him, as his hands slid gently down to her shoulders. Aubrey melted into his arms, and both searched for each other's lips at the same instant. The kiss was hungry and deep, each of them searching for the other's inner soul. Somehow, they ended up among tangled sheets, clothing strewn all over Dan's RV. Upon awakening from a quick nap, it was already three-thirty in the morning. Dan helped Aubrey find her items of clothing, and she got herself together. He had asked her to stay with him, but she preferred to wake up in the house in the morning, so as not to be put on the spot with questions from Jessica.

Dan again pulled her close, and whispered, "I am so happy, Bree, and I'm in love with you."

She put her finger to his lips. "Dan, don't say anything more. I am trying to digest this all. I'm so happy, too," she summed it all up with her huge, cute smile.

As Aubrey started on her way back to the main house, she heard a couple of hoot owls in the distance. Then she was so startled by the sudden sound of someone's cough that her heart nearly jumped out of her chest. "So hon, out for an insomniac's walk?" Henry asked evenly, with his kindly manner, as he took a puff from his pipe.

"Oh Henry, you scared me!" Aubrey cried softly. *So am I caught*, she wondered?

"Darling, I'm just out for some fresh air myself. I've been working on this little gift for Jessica, and I'm just about finished with it. Would you happen to have one of those little, fancy bags from that antique store that I could use for this gift?"

"Sure thing, Henry. I'll bring it to you later today." Aubrey said this in a light tone of voice, as if passing by Henry's RV in the middle of the night was the norm.

"Thanks dear, and no worries…your secret's safe with me, and the hoot owls." He laughed quietly.

She felt so relieved, she could have hugged that big, bear of a man.

10

Queen of Hearts

"**W**ell, good morning, Sunshine," I said to Aubrey, who had opened her eyes around eight o'clock, just enough to get a glimpse of the time on the clock beside her bed, and groan. "Did you have a late night last night?" I asked, with a smile.

"Yes, Dan and I, umm…ate too much of the leftover dessert, and after getting a super sugar high, we went for a long walk."

"Like a couple of teenagers," I remarked.

Aubrey smiled back, and said, "One more hour, Jess." Then, she buried herself under her covers and went back to sleep.

I had gotten up early today, took a hot shower, and worked on my novel for about an hour. I was heading down to the kitchen for a cup of coffee, when I saw Jack and Rosemary buttering some toast. "Good morning, Jessica," Rosemary said, rather spritely.

"Good morning, you two," I replied.

"We are going to venture out to the city for a few hours and do some shopping. Kathryn mentioned she might be going there today, as well."

"That sounds great. Be sure to stop by the antique shop on Main Street; it's full of treasures," I said with a smile.

I poured myself a hot cup of coffee, and then walked into the main sitting room to feed the fish, when I saw Kathryn looking curiously at the shelf near the window.

"Good morning, Jessica," Kathryn said.

"I've been meaning to ask you where you got this exquisite, decorative egg. I think it is so charming, and it has an air of 'antique-vintage' about it. I guess I'm suggesting that it must be old," she laughed.

I smiled as I tried to cool my coffee, and said "I got the egg at my friend Martha's antique shop in Boerne. Coincidently, I just told Jack and Rosemary they might want to visit it today, when they go into town. You must go see her shop if you have an interest in vintage items. She must have one of everything on earth." I joined in laughter with Kathryn.

Kathryn said, "that's incredible, Jessica; it's not often you find this color. I do a little painting, and this color is called robin's egg blue. It happens to be my most favorite color in the spectrum, or color wheel, or, even all of nature, she enthusiastically pointed out.

"That's great that you are an artist. What do you paint?" I asked, now even more interested in Kathryn.

"I like nature, of course; flowers, birds, you know…fields of Texas bluebonnets, Indian Blankets, interesting trees, and you name it," Kathryn replied.

"I would really love to see some of your work sometime," I said sincerely.

"Well, that's a go," Kathryn smiled, adding…"My next visit, I shall bring a few of my paintings along with me to show you."

"What's all this about nature?" Henry walked in, and asked with an air of expectancy. "I adore nature and the outdoors," he commented, before he took a sip of his steaming morning coffee.

"Well then, you are going to have to go with us to Boerne today, so we can go for a walk at Boerne's Cibolo Creek Nature Center."

Kathryn said this with a grin, because she had not even asked Tom to go yet, but she had decided to take a chance and invite him.

I said, "Yes, Henry, you should go and have fun. I'll watch Felix. He can keep me company as I work."

"Okay-y." Henry was eager to get out and explore a little.

Kathryn went to knock on Tom's door, in hopes that he would already be up and about. Kathryn knew that Tom was somewhat of an "adventurer," so she decided to find out for herself just "what was what," in that department.

As she approached his door, Tom was walking out of his suite.

"Oh, Tom, I was just coming to ask if you might be up for some walking at the Cibolo Nature Center with us today."

Tom, a little caught by surprise at the invitation, said, "why yes, Kathryn." I don't know the place, but a little walking out in the woods sounds like something I could use."

As they walked down the hall together toward the kitchen, they ran into Aubrey, who was walking toward them. Aubrey overheard them, and chimed in: "I've always wanted to see the huge, cypress trees there along the river. Mind if Dan and I join you for a hike?"

"Why, not at all," Kathryn replied. It would be great if you guys joined us."

Tom shrugged, and said, "You got it, darlin."

Aubrey had already made plans to go to town with Dan, so this would be a perfect excursion, she thought.

A short time later, after working out the details as to who would drive with whom, they waited as Henry ran to his RV to grab something.

"Okay all, I'm ready for an adventure." Henry spoke up as he walked back in the side door where everyone was waiting.

Henry produced his little Canon Rebel, and said, "just might need a memory card, or two."

Rosemary said, "Henry, what kind of camera do you think I should get, Nikon or Canon?"

Jack and Rosemary were going to a camera shop in town because of their little talk.

Henry said, "I've always been a Canon man, but it is the eternal question: Canon or Nikon?"

Jack said, "So, Henry, since you will be riding with us, maybe you could share your experiences with the two brands, before we choose one today."

"Sure, sure...of course," Henry happily replied.

With most everyone now pulling out of the driveway, and heading to a day's adventure in the city, I decided to take a walk with Felix to visit *Peace*, before I returned to the house to do some more writing.

It was a beautiful cool morning. The sun was out and felt great. *Peace* was looking lovely, and I enjoyed spending my morning with the birds and butterflies. I was thinking about tomorrow's festivities, and how nice it was going to be.

Returning back to the house, my sons were in the kitchen with their skateboards in hand. They had been skating as a hobby since they were toddlers, it seems.

"Hey guys, how about spending some time with your old Mom today?"

"For sure, Mom... after we do some skating, we will come back and have a late lunch with you. Sound good?"

"Yep, sounds great. Don't get hurt, you two...you are not as young as you used to be," I laughed.

"Peace, Mom, we love you," Trey said, as they hugged me goodbye.

Kelly and Melinda had also decided to venture out into town, so I happily gave them the use of my Nissan. Since they both had arrived by taxi, they did not have a vehicle here of their own.

I haven't had a Saturday afternoon alone in over a year. What would I do with myself? I thought, maybe, work on my novel...or take a long hot bath...wait, how about a swim in the pool? Maybe I should just take a nap, until my sons come back...ah, the decisions I was left with.

I decided to take out one of the rowboats and take Felix for a little boat ride on the lake. That little dog was so used to traveling, that the minute he got into the boat wearing his florescent green life vest, he just propped himself up on the bench seat in front of mine, as if he were my shipmate, ready to help me navigate the waters.

I, now wearing my pink and brown swimsuit, began rowing out to the middle of the lake. It wasn't but a few rows to get to the middle of the lake, but it reminded me quickly that I needed to keep working on my arm strength.

Once we reached the middle, I decided to prop up an extra life vest on the bench seat, and lay back facing the sun. I put my sunglasses on, and just rested there peacefully, doing absolutely nothing. It was so quiet that I could hear the soft pants coming from Felix, who was now keeping a steady watch. For pirates who might materialize out of nowhere, I guess.

I closed my eyes, and thought, *"Dear God, thank you for everything in my life, and especially for this peaceful time."*

A few minutes later, a splash came from the water, and startled my eyes wide open. I jumped off the seat and was taken aback by the beautiful pair of ducks that took a break in their flight to join us on the lake.

Felix was also amused by our feathered friends, and leaped into the water after them. Felix could not swim, but had no fear of the water, so it's a good thing that his little life vest did its job and kept him afloat until he tired, and I scooped him back out of the water and into the boat.

Making our way back, docking the boat, I looked over at the ducks swimming by. I glanced down at Felix and thought...

God sure knows how to make an entrance. Then I looked up towards the sky, and said *Thanks, again,* with a loving smile and vague wave at the sky.

Back at the house, I decided to make some lunch and listen to some music.

The house, without anyone else around was too quiet for my liking, anyway. So, I went to the great room and cranked up some good, old, classic rock and roll on the player system attached to the baby grand. I was singing along to an old *Foreigner* song, "Long, Long, Way From Home," as Felix began to howl, as if in pain. I couldn't help but associate his pitiful howl with the same moment I began singing along with the song. I felt chastised.

"What's wrong, boy, you don't like this song?" I asked him, as I made my way to the kitchen for a snack. The front gate buzzer rang and I almost tripped over Felix, who was now lying on the floor, paws covering his ears. I went to the intercom and answered, "Hello?"

A voice on the other end responded, "Hi Jessica, it is Sarah from up the road. I got a postcard addressed to you this morning by mistake, and I thought I'd drop it by."

"Oh, sure, Sarah, come on up," I replied, as I pushed the release button on the security pad that opened the electronic gate at the entrance.

Opening the door, I saw Sarah standing there; a real vision in a strange outfit. Sarah, always ready to tell you how many people have it worse than you do, was dressed in workout clothes. Though everyone knew that Sarah did not 'workout,' she also had a plaid muffler and leggings on, further confusing the viewer. I smiled in a bemused manner and said, "Hi Sarah."

Sarah quickly handed me the postcard, and seemed in a bit of a hurry to leave.

Maybe she had a hot date with the pro wrestler down the street, I laughed to myself.

Sarah was eccentric and sweet, but mostly misunderstood. She was an eternal optimist, so even if something was going wrong in my life, I'd stick to only the positives while in her presence. She had a way of unknowingly making a person feel guilty for complaining. If you were sick, she'd bring up someone who was dying. If you broke your foot, she would show you someone with no legs.

If you were the type of person that needed to vent to a friend, and get a good old fashioned southern reply of, "bless your heart, you poor old thing," then you might not want to pick Miss Sarah as your outlet!

However, Sarah was not here today to tell me how good I had it. She was just being a good neighbor, bringing me my mail. She couldn't stay, and just gave me a cordial hug after handing me the postcard, turned, and headed back to her car.

With Felix following at my heels, I looked at the return address on the postcard…and nearly fainted, dead to the world.

Jay Alvarez
721 Forest Lane
San Antonio, Texas

I reached behind me for the arm of the chair, and with a light head, I sat down and read the post card. It simply said, "Thinking of you, and, always, missing you."

I set the postcard down temporarily in my lap, and took a deep breath. *"Could this be, after all this time?"* I wondered.

With the tears now welling up in my eyes, and little Felix curled up in my lap, I asked myself, *"Could it really be him?*

I picked the postcard back up and read it over a few more times, rechecking the date. I needed to think this one over carefully. I knew the exact person I wanted to share this with, and that I trusted implicitly with my deepest feelings…Henry.

I somehow knew that he would have just the right advice for me.

*D*riving down the winding road from the Inn to get to the town of Boerne was lovely. All of the trees and wild cacti made for a postcard scene. As the two sisters turned onto the highway to catch the exit into downtown Boerne, Kelly said,

"It was really nice for Jessica to loan us her vehicle for the day." Melinda was staring out the passenger side window. She replied back, "yes, it was nice of her." Her mind was obviously straying elsewhere, momentarily. Melinda was thinking about Keith again, and how the two of them had planned to come to San Antonio to visit her family; a trip that was not destined to come to fruition.

"Oh, Melinda, I think this is the turn to get to the shops Jessica was talking about." Kelly then made a turn onto Main Street.

"Is everything okay, Sis?" Kelly asked, as they waited at a red light.

"Sure, everything is fine. I was just thinking about something. This is a nice little town, isn't it?" Melinda said, changing the subject.

"I can't believe all the years we have lived in Texas, and we have never ventured out here to Boerne, before," Kelly mused, as she continued to drive slowly down the street. She was admiring all the little shops and buildings, especially the vintage homes with gingerbread trim.

"Look Melinda! It's 'Market Days!' Let's park, and go take a look around. Maybe you will see something you like." Kelly turned the car around, and parallel parked in front of the Pub and Grille. She got out of the car and came around to Melinda's side. The two began walking along the sidewalk towards the park. Kelly was very intrigued by the window displays of the shops they passed. Melinda kept her focus straight ahead, but did take notice of an older couple holding hands as they crossed the street.

Kelly and Melinda meandered down Main Street in Boerne, until they came upon the craft fair taking place in the Market Square. A band was playing in the pagoda, and people were buying items, window shopping, or just making their way leisurely from one vendor to the next. Melinda's attention was caught by one tent, where she saw a painting of a nest of robin's eggs.

"Such a pure blue," she murmured. She sadly looked at Kelly, but perked up a little when the artist came over and talked with her. Then they moved on.

"Melinda, why did you look so sad when you were looking at that painting, just then?"

"I don't know, Kelly. Just the purity and innocence of those blue eggs. About a month ago I found some broken bird's eggs that very color."

"I know Jessica loves that color blue, and so does Kathryn. I overheard that." Kelly blushed a little, and added, "So, why don't we buy each of them a little memento in that color?"

Melinda did perk up more, and said, "Sure, Kelly, that's a great idea."

They went back and picked up some miniatures of the nest print for the ladies. As they walked on, a very tall man with a heavy German accent, tried to start a conversation with Melinda about taking photos. Melinda had a camera around her neck. The man's demeanor made the girls crack up with laughter over an old private joke they once shared, and now shared again. Kelly felt that she was succeeding in raising the spirits of her little sister, and that had her feeling very joyful.

Then Kelly pointed out some shorts that both girls liked. They each bought a pair, and gauzy peasant tops to match. Admiring the awesome old buildings in downtown Boerne, they made their way back to the Pub and Grille, where they were parked.

They both spotted some of the others from the Inn, sitting at a table in front of the window. "Wow, nice scene you guys make," laughed Kelly to Henry, as the sisters entered the little restaurant.

"Long time, no see," she continued, as Henry stood up to pull two chairs over for the girls to join them. A nice break was had for everyone, they all agreed. Then they ordered too much food and discussed what they were going to do next.

Loaded up, they made their separate ways onto their next destinations.

Kelly and Melinda started back, exploring Main Street again. They came to a quaint glass shop where Kelly noticed the horror-stricken face of the owner, as a customer let her children run rampant through the delicate shop. That was in spite of the sign, which was posted for all to be seen, on the entrance window: "UNATTENDED CHILDREN WILL BE SHIPPED AS CARGO!" as clear as can be. The mother appeared not to notice the children leaving their DNA, by way of runny noses and sticky little fingers, all over. The poor shop owner had just been polishing her glass pieces before they all came in. Obviously a pro at tuning out the clamor of her children, the mother finally turned toward them, when the distinct sound of glass shattering forced her attention back to them. The mother called out in a shrill voice: "Tommy, Sophie, you two okay?"

"Are THEY okay?!" the shop owner thought, with incredulous annoyance; barely able to contain her blazing irritation.

"Ma'am; that was one piece of a fine, antique china set. It is completely irreplaceable!"

"So, Ms. 'whatever,' do you know what; just put that on my account!" The mother angrily spat out the words. And, as she corralled her children, they left abruptly.

Kelly and Melinda looked at each other. Kelly whispered, "Don't you worry, Melinda, my kids will never run amok in your floral shop."

Melinda half-smiled back and touched her sister's arm, asking, "So, do you think we should go?"

Melinda didn't mention it to Kelly, but she was thinking that just last month, she had put a similar obnoxious sign in her floral shop about "unattended children." She was now wondering, *exactly when it was that kids became more of a liability to her than a source of joy.*

Melinda recalled when she had first started working at the shop with Keith. It was her idea to host floral arrangement classes on Saturday mornings, just for kids, and Keith loved the idea. Melinda had always loved children. When she was quite young, she had wanted to be a teacher or a pediatrician.

Had Keith's death been slowly stripping away her ability to love? Maybe Chase was right about that whole 'live to love- love to live' thing. Maybe Melinda didn't want to live because she couldn't love, anymore? She wondered about that, even as she tried not to let her grief become apparent to anyone.

Melinda was realizing just how ridiculous those types of signs must look to customers. She couldn't help but wonder what type of tragedy might have contributed to this shop owner's obvious frustration with children.

Kelly said, "Yes, we could leave, but I feel badly for the owner. She is noticeably upset. Let me first buy something to make up for that little incident."

Kelly picked up a vintage glass decanter with a matching drinking glass, and headed for the cash register. As they checked out, Kelly commented on how beautiful the shop was, in an attempt to minimize the previous encounter.

The woman's anxious face relaxed a little, and she said "thank you, so much girls; how kind of you."

They left the shop and drove along the river before heading back to the Inn. Kelly asked Melinda, "Did you have fun?" Melinda said "I always had fun with you. I really want you to know how wonderful a person you are. And, that you are a great mom, too, Kelly."

"Thank you," Kelly replied, while thinking about the wistfulness she thought she heard returning to Melinda's voice. And Kelly could have sworn that she heard Melinda say, *'always HAD fun with you...'* This was all very disheartening to her.

As they pulled in towards the gate and Kelly entered the code, each of them secretly thought of how difficult it would be to part at the end of this holiday. Kelly knew that she needed to try harder to get Melinda to open up, but she was still worried that if she pushed her too hard, Melinda might cut her off completely.

*M*eanwhile, back in Boerne, after lunch, Tom and Kathryn arrived first at Martha's antique shop. Then came Henry, with Jack and Rosemary. They were so excited at their purchases from the camera shop that it took them a minute or two to settle down.

Rosemary bought a Nikon D5200, with a new flash. She already had many of the lenses for Nikon cameras; her first being a Nikon 35mm. Henry, a Canon man, bought a new point and shoot, as his was getting pretty old. Plus the memory cards he had gone for, of course.

Tom and Kathryn were in high moods, since they had decided to go off to the Boerne Nature Center on their own, in a little while. Henry had begged off, realizing that they needed some private time.

Martha welcomed them all, and her shop was every bit as grand as Jessica had described. Splitting up to observe the incredible array of antiques, Tom and Kathryn first took a look at the jewelry case. Tom spied an old silver and turquoise ring. It was not in his size, though. Kathryn saw a garnet ring with diamond accents, and fell in love with it. She mentioned it, and Tom replied, "Try it on, by all means." This was said in as even a tone as he could manage, for he did not want to give away that he planned to surprise her by purchasing it for her.

"Look Tom, it fits perfectly!" Kathryn cried, like a child, with wonder in her voice. Tom smiled at her as she said, "I may think about it for a bit, though."

Martha served them tea in a grand, old, silver tea set.

"I feel like the Mad Hatter at the Tea Party," Henry joked, referring to the book *"Alice in Wonderland"* by *Lewis Carroll*.

"I guess that would make me the Dormouse," Jack laughed back.

"So, I'm Alice, and Rosemary is the Rabbit, and..."

Martha suddenly stopped and forgot what she was saying. "You know," she said, with embarrassment, "this happens so often, lately. Dear me," she said, as she took a sip of her tea.

"This is good," Rosemary said quickly, to lighten the mood again, adding, "What is it?"

Martha said she had made up the recipe herself, with herbs from her little garden in the back. Jack gave Tom a quick sidelong glance, but said nothing.

"Well, it is delicious." Kathryn said. "I'll have more."

As this was occurring, Aubrey and Dan walked in. Aubrey was sporting a new bracelet.

"Is that real opal?" Rosemary couldn't help herself. She loved jewelry, especially vintage or handmade.

"Yes," Aubrey said. "Dan bought it for me; I love it!" she exclaimed, smiling at Dan. "And, I picked up a beautiful pair of silver earrings with obsidian stones for Jessica," she added.

"By the way," Rosemary said, "If you love jewelry, take a look at Martha's goodies."

Rosemary had picked out a pair of amethyst earrings for herself, with Jack's hearty approval.

Martha was in a good mood after making a few sales. Tom had decided on the turquoise ring, and he would get it sized.

"Well Kathryn, what about the garnet ring?" Tom asked evenly.

Kathryn said with a grin, "I think I'll hold off a bit yet."

Martha brought out some exquisite old silk and lace linens to show the girls, who oohed and ahhed over them. Then she showed them her collection of vintage clothing, which everyone always liked.

Rosemary picked out a metallic, pearl-colored handbag, which she recognized was from the thirties.

Kathryn broke down over a jacket embroidered with butterflies and flowers. She didn't care when or where it was from. Aubrey saw a painting of the sea with a lone ship on the horizon. The frame looked ancient and nautical in some way. Aubrey decided it brought her a feeling of peace, so Dan bought it for her.

Everyone was having fun, it seemed, except for Jack, snoozing in the oversized chair. Every once in a while he snorted and mumbled.

"Jack!" Rosemary shouted. "Come look at these..."

151

"Honey," he said, as he jerked awake, "knock yourself out."

He went back to sleep. Rosemary found some old silver and enamel bangles which intrigued her. Kathryn kept looking for that robin's egg blue color; like the egg Jessica had. She finally happily settled on a forties tea set in nearly the same shade.

"Nice choice," Martha admired Kathryn's taste.

As Rosemary awakened Jack again, Kathryn and Tom said their goodbyes and caught a cab to the Nature Center.

*T*he trail following along the Cibolo Creek was full of huge Cypress trees. They stood underneath the tall and stately old trees, examining the incredible root system they had with wonder and excitement. The beauty was astounding, and they saw several bird species at the Nature Center, along with many swallowtail butterflies in the Prairie area.

As the couple walked, Tom thought about Kathryn. *She has been through a living hell and still sees the beauty in life. How wonderful and brave she is to be able to get through such of life's obstacles and still keep going like she does.*

He knew he could incorporate some of her lessons into his own private life. He would do it for her, he decided. No, wait. Kathryn would say this is something I had to do for myself, first. And she would be right.

Just then, Kathryn said, "Why Tom, a penny for your thoughts. Why are you so quiet?"

"Are you feeling ok?" she added.

Tom was serious. He replied, "Kathryn, I was just thinking. Would you really like to come out to Dallas to see Hanley's Hogs? We could even get in a bike ride or two. Why don't we plan a weekend before we leave here? Let's really do it."

He was at his most charming now, all enthusiasm and full of new confidence.

Tom remembered being this way years ago; before.

Kathryn was taken by surprise, but said, "yes, Tom, that would be fun. We can make plans for a weekend." She smiled a rather shy smile, but was so happy inside. Her heart now melted at the sound of Tom's voice.

*I*t was after four o'clock when my sons arrived back at the house; about the same time Kelly and Melinda had returned. I had taken a swim after reading the postcard, and no longer looked as if I had been crying. My eyes were red from the chlorine in the pool. At least, that was my story, and I was sticking to it.

"Hey Mom, how's your day going?" Trey asked as he came up and gave me a sweaty hug after skateboarding. Chase was standing by the kitchen island, leaning up against it with one arm, as if he was winded and holding up the island. I looked at him and couldn't help but smile and say, "Not as easy as it was when you were younger, huh, old man?" He just nodded his head and worked up enough energy to say, "You're not kidding, Mom."

After the boys went to wash up and change, we sat down to eat a late lunch together. I sat at the table listening to them, as they talked about the tricks they were teaching the youngsters down at the skate park, and I was thinking: *It feels like yesterday when they were the youngsters, first learning to skate.*

I heard a car pull into the drive, and I knew more of the guests were arriving back from their excursions. First, it was Aubrey and Dan walking through the front door, laughing and obviously having a great day.

Henry followed in after them, shaking a bag of some sort and yelling out, "Felix, boy…come and see what I brought you in this doggie bag." With a flash, little Felix jumped up, out of a sound sleep, and ran to Henry at lightning speed.

Henry leaned over with his arms open as Felix jumped right up into his hug.

"Okay, boy, okay, settle down, little guy; and have a sit. As Felix tried with all his might to keep both front paws planted in a sit position, Henry rewarded him with a delicious piece of leftover chicken. Felix did three spins and sat again, with his tail wagging for more.

"Was he a good boy for you, Jess?" Henry asked, as he gave the little guy another piece.

"Yes, and as always, we had a great time exploring today. But Henry, we really need to teach him to swim. He has no fear of water, and without that life vest he would sink like a rock; like last summer…remember?"

"Yes, I remember; and I promise Jess, I'm working on it. But you know the old saying…you can't teach an old dog new tricks!"

"Nonsense, Henry, you know that's just a silly old saying. Besides, I taught you how to play poker, didn't I," I joked.

"Yes, and that's real funny, Jessica. I don't want another scare, either, like last summer, when he dove in after that duck. I almost lost the little fellow."

As Henry lifted Felix into his arms and hugged him, I knew how much that dog meant to this man who had already endured the heavy pain of losing his partner to cancer.

Then I thought of Kathryn, and wondered how her day in town went.

"Did you guys see Kathryn and Tom in town?" I asked.

"As a matter a fact, we all had lunch together this afternoon. Those two wanted to go exploring the Nature Center for a while, and said they would bring a taxi back," Aubrey answered.

"That's good. I hope they are enjoying themselves," I said.

I turned to Dan and asked: "So, does that mean you won't be cooking tonight, if you all ate a big meal in town?"

"We talked about it at lunch, and we all thought if you were up for it, we could just order some pizzas tonight, and hang out by the pool. We're going to be grilling all day tomorrow, and so far everyone else is up for the idea," Dan said, as he unpacked some leftovers from the restaurant.

"We can order from the pizzeria that offers gluten-free pizza, Jess... remember how you liked it last time, yes?" Aubrey asked.

"Sounds great to me. I'm always up for their pizza," I said, half listening, for my mind was still on the postcard I had received earlier.

"So, how about it Trey, pizza sound good to you, too?" Henry asked, as he washed his hands at the kitchen sink and Trey took out a cold soda from the refrigerator.

"Absolutely," Trey replied.

Chase was outside, standing near the pool and looking at the water, so I walked out by him.

"Hey there, old man. I'll give you a dollar for your thoughts?" I looked up at my son.

"Oh, hi, Mom, I was just thinking...remember when you first told us that you were going to build this place, and we thought you were kidding?"

"Why yes, I do remember that."

"You are an amazing woman, Mom. I just want to say thank you, for showing me that anything is possible."

"Did you hit your head skating today, honey?" I laughed, as I reached over to feel the top of his head.

"No Mom, I'm just feeling grateful to you," Chase said, with a big smile on his face.

So many years I thought my oldest son was angry with me, and might never truly forgive me for all the things I put him through with the divorce. And here we stood, as I listened to him tell me how much he loved me, in his own words.

"Jess, what do you two want on your pizzas? I'm going to order them to be delivered at seven o'clock," Dan yelled through the French doors that lead out to the pool, where Chase and I were standing.

We both answered at the same time: "Cheese and sausage!" A rain cloud soon passed over the house and opened up, as it did unexpectedly around these parts, and the rain poured down as we ran back inside the house.

Rosemary and Jack were caught in the sudden downpour, out in the wooded area of the estate. Drenched to the bone, they eyed each other a little nervously, but then they laughed and embraced like in the old days. They came back to the Inn, flushed and soaked.

Rosemary had managed to keep her new photographic equipment dry with her jacket, and she was eager to show off what Jack had gotten her.

Jack asked, "has anyone seen Tom and Kathryn? Maybe they went back and got stuck in that strange antique shop we met up at."

Rosemary said, "It wasn't strange! Martha was just a bit eccentric. I thought she was charming. And, gosh, the beautiful jewelry she had was incredible."

"What was all that hocus-pocus and the sleepy-time tea? I'll bet she knocked us out!" Jack protested, with humor.

"Oh Jack, baby, you always were so skittish around 'different' people. Wait until I start shooting the homeless and toothless, with my new camera," she dared him to protest. He snarled kiddingly, but said nothing. He was proud of his *Roy Orbison "Pretty Woman"* imitation.

Just then, Tom and Kathryn burst in with all sorts of tales about *History in The Making*. Kathryn was enchanted by a vintage garnet ring, an old satin gown from the 40's, and a beaded bag from the flapper-era. Tom was taken by some old golf clubs from the 30's, and some old photos, postcards, and letters from years ago—*what were these people like*, he

155

wondered. He had always been enchanted by treasures of the past, even as a child. He had a cigar box of *treasures*. He had always felt the 'spirit of place,' (as *Frederick Turner* had put it, in his writings) wherever he had traveled or visited.

I left Chase and Trey in the kitchen where Henry had been and walked out into the hall and down to the great room. I stood looking out the window, and began thinking...

I was amused, but in awe of what was going on around me. My guests all seemed so special in their own ways. And some of them seemed to be especially getting on well with each other. I smiled at the thought of Kathryn and Tom. And Jack was so over the top in love with his wife Rosemary, he was now following her around with puppy-dog eyes. Henry, Aubrey, and Dan had been so good to me, and my sons were all grown up and full of life. I felt secure, even with strange and unexpected things happening. I was going to have to discuss the postcard with Henry, sooner than later. But did I really want to tempt fate?

Henry had watched me walk away from the kitchen, and must have read the look in my eyes. He instantly recognized a look that was all too familiar. He remembered how during the construction period, I had relapsed into a depressive state. Henry had noticed that I had a few crying spells, when I thought no one was looking. It was all I could do besides sleep during the day. I did not eat, and did not sleep at night. He almost thought they might lose me, at one point. Henry called my therapist, and personally dragged me to her. I seemed to be getting better, but there were times he had caught my eyes looking wistfully and sadly away, into the distance; like today. He and Felix had started keeping a close eye on me. Aubrey and Dan knew the drill, also. They all had my back, one might say. Henry had quickly become protective of me, like a father figure, and valued my friendship so much since his beloved William, 'Will,' had died.

Henry was in his early seventies when I first met him. Handsome, even in his grief; he had short grey hair, and a closely clipped beard, with sparkling grey eyes that crinkled when he laughed. At first, this was not often. But over time, he started to heal. *Luna's Hope* and I saw to that. And Felix, of course.

Looking out the window in the great room, I knew I had to share my news with Henry. I knew he would know the right words of advice to give me.

Henry walked up to Aubrey, back in the kitchen, and quietly whispered to her, "I think Miss Jessica might need a friend, right now." Aubrey didn't ask any questions; she just nodded politely, and walked to the great room where I was.

"Jess, are you up for a quick game of pool?" Aubrey asked, as she looked at me inquisitively. She knew I had something on my mind.

"Sure," I said, as I uncrossed my arms and walked over to the pool table. "But I'm not playing you for dishes, anymore." I added that to cover up my anxiety. I gave her a big smile, and grabbed a pool stick off the wall.

As she and I were in the midst of a game (which I was losing again, of course), Kathryn and Tom walked in with all of their bags, totally lost in conversation: "I'll never forget Jack falling asleep at Martha's, Tom. I swear, he acted like he thought Martha had poisoned him, or something," Kathryn laughed loudly.

Tom laughed too, and suggested that they save the story for everyone to have a laugh at later.

Melinda and Kelly decided to play a new CD, by *Leonard Cohen*, that they had bought in town for Trey and Chase. Chase was immediately interested, though Trey wasn't sure who *Leonard Cohen* was. "That man has flow!" Chase exclaimed. Kathryn and Tom overheard this, and just looked at each other.

By the time the pizza arrived, everyone was famished again and ready to eat. Trey and Chase ate a whole large pizza between them.

After dinner, everyone called it an evening, and made their ways to their suites. As the night brought peace and relaxation to most of the guests, there was one who was struggling with her thoughts.

Kathryn decided to try and relax and do some writing, using her new journal to explore her feelings about her new acquaintances.

"Jessica was certainly a sweetheart, plus intelligent and well-read. Henry and his little Felix were precious. Aubrey, a complex, yet interesting, character. Dan was a good guy, you had to say that. Jack was fun, she thought. She saved Tom for last: *He was still a mystery to her, and for that she was grateful!*

It was getting very late, so, she put the journal down on her stomach and had a final sip of water. Though she put her head down on the plush pillow, her fingers kept busy, drumming on the cover of the journal.

Though Kathryn meant to sleep, her body chose to fidget, and soon she was lost to her all too familiar insomnia. She threw the coverlet off, and stepped onto her patio to watch the stars and moon.

As she watched the heavens above, she remembered the book, *"Goodnight Moon"* by *Margaret Wise Brown*. She used to read it to Blake's little nephew when he was a child. *But what was the good in remembering sad thoughts*, she wondered. Blake had become so cruel and bitter from drinking, especially in his later years. He took a big chunk out of Kathryn's self-esteem for a while, that's for sure. She never realized that she was beautiful and intelligent while she was married to Blake. Only later, did she come into her own. Now she spoke up when she needed to, and drove a little, red Corvette. She dressed just as she liked, with no one to criticize her style. *Was she making a mistake, getting close to Tom*, she wondered. *But, NO! Stop it*, she scolded herself. She did not have to live like a recluse because of her past. For some reason, Tom Petty's song, *"Refugee*," had come blasting from her speakers when she first drove up to the Inn, she remembered, smiling to herself.

Most people assumed that Kathryn had always been a sharp dresser, with intelligence and style. Now, she intended to live her life as though that had always been the case. She had no intention of going back.

She heard someone walking outside. The unmistakable sound of cowboy boots!

Kathryn stood up and looked out her patio door. Sure enough, Tom was pacing back and forth, looking again like the cares of the world were on his shoulders. Kathryn cried out, softly: "Tom!"

"Tom, what are you doing out there? It's almost midnight." Then she laughed. What was she doing?

Tom almost jumped at Kathryn's interruption, but he was glad she was there.

"Kathryn, I can't sleep. I don't know if it's being out in the country, or what."

Kathryn felt sorry for Tom, so she said, "wait. I'll get a robe and join you."

As she made her way outside, as silently as she could, Tom welcomed her with, "I guess I can be a bit of a worry wart, sometimes.

Tom peered closer at Kathryn,

"Err, by the way, hon, what's that *thing* you're wearing over your pajamas? I'm sorry, but I've seen dead sheep look, ah, more lively than *that* thing."

Both nodded and laughed.

Kathryn said, "This is the courtesy robe they offer here, and you probably have one just like it in YOUR closet, too!"

"A courtesy robe…I don't have to take that thing home with me, do I? And Kathryn, I must ask you, since you are *a woman of class*; is it considered rude to leave it here, when I check out? Ralph would never let me live it down, if he saw that in my house!" Both laughed at the idea of that.

"Okay, seriously now, Kathryn," Tom went on, 'it's like life turns you inside out after a death or a divorce. I always intended to have a long talk with my daughter, Ellie, after Nancy left, but it just never seemed to be the right time."

Kathryn shook her head. She knew exactly what he meant, and said, "Tom, it's one of those giant obstacles in life that you just have to get through. Maybe you never get through it completely, but you navigate your way the best you can, and make it to safety, one way or the other."

Tom said, "For some reason, that reminds me of one day, years ago, when I found a dead hummingbird near one of the bushes that had been sprayed with insecticide a few days earlier. I was crushed. I vowed never to use harmful chemicals again on my land, and to use only natural means for insect control. Then, I read the book by *Rachel Carson*, called *"Silent Spring."*

Kathryn replied, "Tom, I read that, too. It made me really aware of how important our environment is. Sometimes, it's really sad to see the things that are going on. When problems, like pests, could actually be controlled naturally, with just a little bit of knowledge and care."

"Kathryn, I've never had someone like you to talk with like this. It feels good. I can't tell you."

"I know, Tom, me too. And, it does feel good."

"I never told anyone this, but I've always wanted to. I've not been able to trust a man since the end of my marriage, but you are different."

Kathryn found herself opening up to Tom about the abusive relationship she had had with Blake.

"It's not so much the physical pain that scars you; it's the emotional pain that Blake was so good at inflicting."

Tom was quiet, and a good listener. He nodded at her last statement, as if saying, "go on, I'm listening, girl."

"He died during my cancer treatments, and I barely grieved for him. He never even talked with me about them. Like, how were they, did I hurt, did losing my hair make me feel ugly; nothing."

Kathryn's tears were slowly making their way down her face, as if they were two, tiny, cascading waterfalls.

Tom surprised Kathryn and himself, by reaching out and touching her face, very gently. "Never you mind, little lady," he said softly.

"There is no way in this world that you could possibly be ugly, Kathryn. I would love and care for you, no matter what physical changes your body went through. Because, it would still be *you*."

Tom did not realize that he was capable of being this caring, especially with another woman. He himself had felt so empty of emotion, at times.

Kathryn was overwhelmed with Tom's kind words, and she smiled at him through her tears. "Okay, Tom, maybe I have my moments, but don't you think I'm easy, Cowboy."

She grinned broadly as she said this, and winked.

Kathryn felt so relieved at opening up to Tom about her thoughts and past hurt. She would not have believed this man was capable of so much empathy. She felt so badly for making fun of him, but he seemed to really like being called *Cowboy*. She smiled a charming smile at him, saying, "Tom, thanks so very much. You are a good listener and give great comfort."

Tom blushed, for he knew he had learned most of this from Ralph, his pal back home. But he really meant it, too!

"Kathryn, if there is ever a time you think I'm not listening to you, then you have my permission to bat me over the head. I have the bat at my place, so you will have to visit me in Dallas."

"Now it's nearly dawn already, Tom. And yes, I will visit you in Dallas. I really want that bike ride!"

"Let's try to sleep a little, before everyone wakes up, or we will look like something the cat dragged in. Tom nodded his head *good night*, almost as if he was tipping a cowboy hat.

They both returned to their respective suites, where Kathryn, feeling rather high from her rendezvous with Tom, had to write down a few notes in her journal before turning in. As Tom walked back to his room, he knew he would be making a call, first thing in the morning, to one Miss Martha, at *History in the Making*.

11

When One Door Closes...

*K*elly and Melinda were in their suite where Kelly was getting ready for the day. Melinda was quiet and full of thought. She wasn't in the mood to socialize or talk, so she tried to keep to herself, telling Kelly that she might just spend the day resting in their suite. She tried to give Kelly the excuse that she didn't feel well, but Kelly knew her little sister, and felt very strongly that Melinda was making up an excuse. She sat down and asked Melinda to have a seat, too. Melinda sat down. She understood her sister's tone all too well, and she was sure Kelly was about to ask her some questions that she did not want to answer. Not to anyone.

But, it was now time for the *mother* to come out in Kelly, and, she felt that she was running out of time to get Melinda to open up to her.

"Melinda, I love you, and no matter whatever happens in our lives, I will always love you."

Melinda nodded her head and said, "I know you do, Sis, and I love you too, and always will, no matter what."

"Melinda honey, its things you say like, 'no matter what,' that scare me. I know that Keith wouldn't want you to keep your pain hidden away, and be out there alone in California. And, I just want you to think about..."

Melinda stood up and interrupted her sister, blurting out: "How does everyone seem to know what Keith would have wanted, or *anything* about him, for that matter. I knew him best, and nothing anyone has said to me about his death makes *any* sense to me! It never has! I don't want a lecture right now, Kelly. I need to take a walk...I'm sorry!" and with that, Melinda left the room and stormed off, slamming the door behind her.

Melinda had hit her boiling point, and she was just beginning to *finally* release her steam.

Kelly sighed, as she knew she had pushed her sister too far. She had meant to show support and love, but it had backfired on her. She tried not to take it personally, because she knew it was her sister's pain talking. So, she made her way to the kitchen for a glass of water, trying not to cry. She thought: *I just have to get some help for her, but how?*

Chase was in the kitchen after eating a quick breakfast, when he saw Kelly walk in.

"Hey, Kelly, how's it going?" Chase asked.

"Well, hello Chase, how are you doing this morning?" Kelly replied, as she cleared her throat.

"I'm doing very well, thanks for asking. I was actually going to see if Melinda might want to take a walk with me on this awesome morning, before I start helping Dan with any food prep," Chase suggested.

Kelly knew that Melinda had left the house feeling frustrated at what Kelly had said to her. She was worried about her sister, and thought: *Chase just might be the person to get her to open up.*

"You just missed her. She said she was going out to do exactly that... take a walk. And, I think she was looking for you, too," Kelly replied, knowing full well that she had just lied to him, in desperation.

Chase had been the only person that Kelly knew of that Melinda had somewhat of a rapport with.

"She headed down the path, toward the lake. You should be able to catch up with her. She left here only ten minutes ago," Kelly added.

"Sounds good; I'll go see if she is up for some company," Chase said.

Kelly was wondering if it was wrong not to tell Chase that Melinda had left for the walk feeling upset. Or, that Melinda hadn't really been looking for him. But, she decided that Chase had a way of getting her little sister to communicate her feelings, and Kelly needed all the help she could get when it came to getting Melinda to talk. Kelly quickly said a prayer for her sister.

As Chase walked down the path near the lake, looking for Melinda, he heard a voice coming from a spot in between some trees.

Throwing rocks between the trees in a clearing, there stood Melinda, talking loudly to herself...

"He is in a better place, Melinda!

His spirit is always here with you, Melinda!

It was his time, Melinda!

Celebrate the life he had, Melinda!

Oh, and of course, my favorite...God must have needed more angels in heaven, Melinda!"

"And now, Kelly, with: Keith wouldn't want you to be out there alone, Melinda!"

"What's next?" Melinda yelled, loudly. "Maybe someone will tell me that it was just a part of a bigger plan in my life!"

With every sentence, she was throwing a rock further, and Chase sensed her anger. Then, he heard her yell out again...

"What about me? I needed him, God. I'm so trying to understand, but you have more than enough people and angels there with you already. Why take Keith away from me, damn it! He had so many wonderful things left to do in his life!" She was furious.

Her hair was wildly flying with the jerking movements of her head as she shouted and flung her arms and hands in her violent desperation. But to Chase, she looked more beautiful, if possible. She was so full of life, if only she could see it!

Chase was not sure if he should approach Melinda and let her know that he had seen and heard her. He was concerned for her. Should he leave her alone to release what was obviously some built up rage?

Deciding that he had to do something for her, he pushed past the branches of the trees and respectfully announced that he was there.

"Melinda, it's me, Chase...I come in peace, and from what I can see... you may still have another rock in your hand."

Melinda replied, "Chase, you might not want to see me right now."

"I know you are angry, Melinda...just let it out," Chase replied, encouragingly.

"Look, I'm not one of your stellar audience participants who know exactly how to feel after speaking with you."

Chase just stood there silently, as Melinda continued to unleash her pent-up sorrow...

"Yes, I'm angry. I'm very angry. No, I'm pissed off, Chase, and no disrespect; but I don't care who hears me anymore!" Melinda yelled it as she sent the rock sailing with all her force, through the trees.

Looking at Chase, she exploded with fury. "I've been thinking, Chase, and right now, I can't help but tell you that if you mention hurdles, and all that crap again, I swear I'll just puke. I tried to see things differently, like you talked about; I really tried, but I can't do it anymore," she continued on, mercilessly.

Chase had never had such a violent rebuke to his beliefs before. He had pretty much watched as Melinda tried to exorcise her resentment and despair by throwing rocks, and shouting at the water, trees, and the heavens above.

Once or twice, he interrupted her, but she went on with a torrent of insults toward Chase and hurdles.

"Whoa there, Miss Melinda," he quickly walked over to her as she finally seemed about to collapse from the extreme effort and emotion.

Chase caught her, as she did start to falter, for she was just a slim slip of a girl, worn out by life. He gently helped her to a big rock next to a grassy area, and guided her as she sat down.

"Melinda, I have heard some of these things before, believe me," Chase started, but Melinda cut him off.

"Yes, well, don't give me anymore about *hurdles*, and climbing over them, because I'm here to tell you that I'm living proof that hurdles do exist that can't be climbed. It's all mumbo jumbo to me. I'd just as soon not hear it, and I'd just as soon not be here, at all!"

"Well, Melinda, maybe you just have to try a different method for your grief. Perhaps, what you just did is a more helpful type of therapy for you."

"Why does it always have to be *therapy*?" Melinda pronounced the word with derision. "It's been three years since he died, Chase. I'm never going to get over it, and it's just too draining to go on, anymore."

"You can't just give up, Melinda. That's selfish of you," Chase remarked.

This comment startled Melinda, and she shook her head in disbelief at what he had just said. She stood up, and shouted: "Selfish! Are you kidding me! We had plans, Chase. He said he would love me forever, and never leave me! I was going to walk down the aisle with him, have children with him, and buy a big house, and get a dog, even if his family was against us from the start! *They* are the selfish ones."

Chase knew his 'selfish' comment had sounded cruel, but he had to say *something* to get her fighting for her life.

"There's more I haven't told you, Chase; Keith's family didn't even acknowledge me as being a part of his life. They even blamed *me* for his death. They said I took him away from them. I'm a good person, Chase, and they hated me, because I wasn't the type of woman they wanted for their son."

Tears began to stream from her eyes as she finally said what her heart had been holding in for so long. She said: "Chase, he was such a wonderful man, and I miss him so much. I miss calling him on his cell phone, whenever I want; I miss hearing his laugh, and I miss being in his arms, and feeling safe and loved! Chase, I kept the last messages he sent me on my phone, so I can hear his voice, at least. What will happen if my phone breaks? I just can't, Chase, I'm so sorry..."

Chase stepped closer to her with his arms open. She fell into his arms, and cried harder than she ever had. Chase held her tightly as she let out some very deep-rooted tears.

Chase then took Melinda's hand, and they walked to a bench that was right outside the trees, near the lake. He sat next to her and helped her wipe the tears from her eyes.

"So tell me, what was Keith like, to have won the heart of such a beautiful girl like you?" Chase asked with a smile.

Melinda let out a small smile through her tears and said, "He was super kind and loving, but his family did not see me as a beautiful girl, that's for sure. They were traditional Japanese, and Keith was all-American. His birth name was Keita, but he always went by Keith. They blamed me for stealing him from his family. They even said that the family name of Shoji would be despoiled if we got married. We talked about eloping to some tropical island, just the two of us, because his family made it so hard on him."

"It sounds like Keith loved you very much, Melinda," Chase said, as he continued to listen to her talk.

"We loved each other that much; more than I can even explain, but Keith's family tried to stop me from even attending his funeral. They cut me off completely, and we have no contact. I don't even know if they live in California anymore. Before Keith's death, his sister, Sumie, and I, were starting to get close. But after his death, she had to sneak over to see me, and now I don't have any contact with her, either. It's been lonely, running the flower shop out there alone, without him. The pain in my heart is unbearable, and I just don't want it, anymore."

"We never get over a death, Melinda; we only get through it," Chase replied.

Melinda just realized what she had all told Chase, and her face reddened.

Chase remained calm, but put a friendly hand over hers. She did not jump away, so he said, "Melinda, can I ask you something?"

"After the verbal assault I just gave you, Chase, yes, you can ask me anything," she replied, quietly.

"Have you talked to your sister about the loneliness and pain you feel inside? I don't want you to get upset at me, Melinda, but you said some things that worried me a few minutes ago; and I'm not sure you heard yourself say them."

"I didn't mean to alarm you, Chase. I did hear what I said, but I just don't know what to do to make the pain stop."

"There is a lot of help out there, Melinda; and if anyone deserves to be happy, again, it's you," Chase said, softly.

"My sister wants me to move back here, to San Antonio, and stay with them. I haven't given her an answer, yet. I'm not really sure what I want. Remember when you said, 'live to love-love to live,' the other day?

Chase nodded, "Yes."

"Well, I can't love anymore, and I feel numb," she cried.

"I understand...you can't feel love, so you don't feel life, right?' he asked, as he was all too familiar with depression, himself.

"Pretty much," Melinda replied. And that's about as open as she was going to get without saying the actual words: "Help me, please!"

"Have you told Kelly about not wanting to live anymore?" he asked.

"No; I have not told her how I really feel. I'm not sure why I told you everything I did. No offense, Chase, but I don't open up like this...ever."

"None taken; it's cool. But Melinda, it was time for you to tell someone, and I'm glad it was me. I'd like to suggest something, if you don't mind?"

"I know what you are going to say Chase; you think I should go talk to Kelly." Melinda looked at Chase, awaiting his reply, and then away again.

"Yes, I do, and I don't think you should go back to California without first having some kind of plan to get some help with your sadness and anger. You are probably in a depression, and that is a killer situation if you don't talk to a doctor. Personally, I want you to come to San Antonio, too, because I would like to spend some time with you, and hang out. I think you are amazing," Chase said, with sincerity. "But I'd be happy just knowing that you are able to feel 'life' again. Otherwise, the alternative is unalterable, and it will hurt a lot of people, including me."

"You mean I haven't scared you away, yet?" She asked this as she shook her head in embarrassment.

"I don't scare easily," Chase answered, with a smile.

"Well, I'm afraid to tell Kelly how I really feel. I don't know why; but I am. She would do anything for me, but I don't want to put any stress on her right now, in her condition, and also; what if they want to put me in a hospital, Chase?"

"Chase looked into Melinda's eyes and said, "Trust me, if you talk to her, you will be taking stress away from her. She is your sister, and please believe me when I say she wouldn't be here offering for you to come live with them, if she didn't already know the pain you're in."

"Would you go with me to talk to her, today?" Melinda boldly asked.

"Absolutely, yes, I will," Chase replied, much relieved inside of himself.

*R*osemary decided to take her new Nikon D5200 out for a spin. She started out with the garden of wildflowers near the house. There she found columbine in golden yellow, pink vinca, and purple, cone-shaped flowers that the hummingbirds and butterflies seemed to especially flock to. Then, she came upon the rose garden. Rosemary favored a coral, yellow, and red rose. It was amazing how it changed colors, as it blossomed from a bud to a full, blooming rose, just in the course of one day. She spied them yesterday, before heading out to town, and vowed to shoot some photos of them, later. She loved her new camera; and she was excited by the photos she would be showing off when she got back.

Just then, she spotted a doe on the grounds, and was able to get a few fast frames of the beautiful animal. *What a world of majesty and stupendous color we lived in! That was the reason she shot photographs.*

Rosemary was fond of photographing old, live-oak trees, for they grew into such amazing shapes. She knew she would have to go back to shoot the cypress trees along Cibolo Creek, too.

That old excitement came back to her; making her feel like a young girl again. She thought of Jack, and how lucky she was. She wanted to share all that she had seen, and headed back to the house.

As Rosemary walked up to the door, Henry was standing outside, enjoying his pipe, and said, "I see you have been busy with your new equipment."

"Yes, and I'm very excited to show Jack the photos I captured; this camera is amazing, Henry!" She said this with exuberance in her voice and a shining glow about her face.

"Well, last I saw him, he was sitting in the library," Henry smiled at her energy.

Rosemary thanked him again, and proceeded through the house to find her husband. Entering the library, she found Jack, holding a small box. He was seated in a big comfy chair, and he smiled broadly as he saw his beaming wife.

"Can you take one more gift from me, hon?" he asked, with a wink.

"Jack," she said with a touch of excitement in her voice. *What could it be*, she tentatively wondered, and said, "Of course, darling, but you've given me everything." She opened the wrap and box, and what she saw made her heart leap. "Oh Jack!! I love you, my dear, dear husband!" Inside the box was a book titled, *"Rescue Me,"* by *Bardi McLennan*. And, a dog collar and leash with little red hearts on them.

Rosemary started to cry, for she realized that Jack must have planned to surprise her with this before they had even arrived at the Inn. Jack had taken her every small wish and made it come true.

Jack laughed and said, "Baby we're going to rescue any big or little dog you pick out from the Animal Rescue. I even wrote down a website for one that is well known to be one of the best rescue groups around here.

Henry walked in on Jack and Rosemary to see if he could offer them a beverage, and saw the two of them looking so in love that he almost backed out. Instead, he said, "Hey, you two lovebirds, give an old guy a chance. Jack, you've been monopolizing that lovely and talented wife of yours all day!"

Rosemary blushed, but said, "Why Henry, you know I'd always have time for a fellow photographer!" She motioned for Henry to come and sit with them. The three of them began to talk about rescuing dogs, and looked through the photos on Rosemary's new camera.

I had been walking past the library and saw them sitting there looking at the pictures when Rosemary said, "Oh Jessica, I took some amazing pictures of the flowers and trees out front, and I captured a beautiful doe!" I was very interested in seeing her photos. I had wanted to spruce up my website, and wondered if maybe Rosemary might share some of her glorious photos. The photo of the doe was especially interesting to us both, because the property is entirely fenced in with mostly cattle fencing, except for the brick entrance to the property. It was very rare for a deer to get in. I thought maybe we had a part of the fencing down, and I hoped the young doe hadn't gotten separated from its family. Henry, sharing my passion for animals, told me that he would keep an eye out, in case the doe needed any help. Henry even offered to pick up some feeder corn.

Chase and Melinda were walking back to the house together. They didn't say much to each other, but Chase would put his hand on her shoulder now and then during the walk, as if to say, "It's going to be ok." As they headed towards Melinda's suite to see if Kelly was there, Melinda stopped about ten feet from the suite door and looked at Chase with frightened eyes.

"I'm scared, Chase," she said.

"I know you are Melinda, but it's okay; she is your sister, and I won't leave if you don't want me to," he replied staunchly.

"I know that this is something I have to do, Chase, and it's not that I am afraid of my sister; you know that, right?"

Chase smiled at Melinda and said, "Yes, of course I know you are not afraid of her. It's facing the truth about how you feel toward life right now that you are anxious about."

"Yes, I am anxious, because if I tell her even a little of what I feel, then I'll have to relive the entire pain all over again, and I'll have to tell the doctors, and live it again, and then..."

Chase stepped in to embrace Melinda, as he noticed she had started having what looked like the beginnings of a panic attack. "Melinda, take a breath, and know that you will never have to relive that pain again. You will start to heal when you let this all out," he said, in a sweet, gentle voice. "It's going to be okay; and I won't leave your side," Chase added.

"How do you know all of this will work out, Chase?" she asked before they approached the door to the suite where Kelly was.

"I suffered from depression, Melinda, and I felt like giving up at one time. My Mom suffers bouts of depression, to this day. And, she once felt like giving up." Chase turned and looked away for a moment, and then took a leap of faith. He turned back toward Melinda and said, "I never got to meet my grandmother, because she took her own life when my mom was only ten years old. The sadness that a suicide brings can travel through generations. There are so many people out there, just like us, but we can make it, all of us, if we just help each other out. I made it, Melinda, and you will, too." Chase opened up his heart to her.

Just then, Kelly opened the suite door and said, "I thought I heard voices out here." Realizing quickly that Melinda had been crying, Kelly looked at Chase and asked, "Is everything ok? What's wrong, Melinda?" Kelly reached over and took Melinda's hand. Chase asked if they could all go sit down for a minute, in the suite, and have a talk. "Of course, of course. Come right in," she replied to Chase.

Kelly looked at Melinda for what seemed like an eternity, but was only seconds. Melinda said, "I'm sorry Kelly; I've been dishonest with you." Melinda lowered her head and began to cry.

Kelly looked at her sister and half-smiled out of nervousness and said, "It's ok honey; you know you can tell me anything."

Melinda choked back the tears, lifted her head, and confessed... "I am hurting Kelly, I hurt so badly some days, that I wish God would just take me, too."

With that, Melinda burst out sobbing, and her head fell to her knees. Kelly immediately stood up, and went to sit right next to her little sister, hugging her tightly. Kelly said, "I know, Melinda, and I'm here to help you; the whole family wants to be with you, and to support you. I'm so sorry you have been hurting and we weren't there," Kelly replied, with tears in her eyes. Hugging her little sister, Kelly looked over at Chase, and mouthed the words, '*thank you*' to him. Chase nodded, and felt the need to choke back tears, himself. He had begun to have feelings for Melinda, and was so grateful that she was opening up to her sister like that.

Chase had gotten up to grab the box of tissues on the side table. Melinda lifted her head, and took the box that Chase was offering to her. She wiped her eyes, and looked at Chase with gratitude. "How can I ever thank you, Chase?"

"You don't need to thank me; just promise me that you'll take care of yourself, because the world needs more good people like you, in it," Chase emphasized.

She nodded back at him and said, "Yes, I promise."

Chase knew it was time to leave the sisters alone, and asked them if they might want to have some time with each other to talk. Both sisters nodded their heads, and Chase politely excused himself from the room.

Melinda opened up, and told her sister everything. Kelly listened patiently, and remembered the advice that Jessica had given to her. Kelly insisted that Melinda go home with her on Monday morning, and told her that Ben, her husband, would take care of the details for the move from California to Texas. And, the sale of Melinda's business.

Melinda agreed with her sister, now. She realized that the most important thing was to get the loving support from her family, and the professional help she needed so badly. She needed to be able to really move on with her life. That had Kelly feeling a sense of hope, and relief. Melinda felt fear and anxiety, but also, a sense of release.

Chase returned to the kitchen with a renewed faith in himself. He believed strongly that he could help people with his words, and Melinda was definitely not just a 'stellar audience participant.' No, she was a spark that had ignited his heart. For the first time, Chase felt a flutter in his own chest, but his was the fluttering of a new love. But, now was not the right time. He knew he had to be patient, and just go with life's flow.

Dan was already firing up the grill by the time Chase reached him. Chase looked at Dan and smiled. Dan looked back at Chase, and said, "Well, that's a pretty big smile. What's up, young man?"

Chase shrugged his shoulders and said, "I'm not sure, but I think Melinda is pretty cool."

Dan knew this look, as he had felt the same look in his own eyes, for Aubrey. Dan continued to light the grill and move the charcoal around, as he grinned to himself. "You know, Chase, she is quite the beautiful young lady. Your mom said that her sister, Kelly, asked her to move back to Texas.

Maybe you two can go sailing with us sometime. I have my sailboat docked by Lake Amistad."

Chase smiled and said, "That would be rad; I'll let you know. Thanks, dude."

That was the extent of their man to man talk, but it had Dan feeling like a father figure, something he had never felt before but had always thought about. Dan knew that he could not have children of his own, which was what ultimately ended his marriage, years prior. So it was an unexpected feeling of comfort to him.

The morning quickly turned into afternoon, as the preparations got underway. Everyone was pitching in and offering to help set up for the party. Things were beginning to really 'cook.' I asked Aubrey to take some blankets outdoors for later, while Dan mentioned warming up the grill. Aubrey decided to 'kill two birds with one stone,' or as we now say, courtesy of Henry's late friend Will, 'rescue two strays with one bone,' by taking several of the blankets and covering up the top of the grill with them. She did sort of wonder at the simplicity of the task, but piled on more covers. I just happened to look out the patio door to see Aubrey. I ran out to try to save her any possible embarrassment, but secretly thought, *Thank the Lord it isn't lit yet, bless her heart.*

"Aubrey, no, silly girl. That's not what I meant. I wanted the blankets for sitting on, during the fireworks; and by warming up the grill, Dan meant getting a fire started. Here, I'll show you," I said kindly, as if it was just a joke.

Dan, meanwhile, stared out a window wondering what the hell we were doing! The obvious occurred to him in a vision. He slapped his head and was heard to mutter his trademark expression: "Madre de Dios!" and words that trailed off in his native tongue…

As the guests were outside munching on snacks and drinks, absorbed in their own conversations, Tom nodded to Kathryn saying, "I really wanted to talk to you, Kathryn, but I was hoping maybe we could step back inside the house, for a little privacy."

Tom stood up, and Kathryn followed. Her curiosity overcame any questions. Tom led the way, taking her into the great room where the white baby grand piano seemed to be his destination. Even more curious now,

Kathryn watched silently while Tom sat down at the piano. He played a few bars, and then began to softly sing, as a melody became obvious. The words to Michael Buble's song *"Lost"* became a serenade sung especially for Kathryn.

Kathryn watched and listened, mouth hanging open (not her best pose, she realized later), as Tom sang to her, and only her, in the softest, gentlest voice she ever could have believed could come from this truly complex man. Suddenly, she saw him as the sophisticated, cultured man he really was. As her face turned beet red and hot, she simultaneously felt the chills go up and down her spine. The melody was beautiful; as were the words Tom sang to her. Under this spell, she got up slowly and planted a kiss on Tom's cheek. Tom, caught up in his music, turned a bit and kissed her lips, as gently as he sang. This kiss turned into much more than a friendly kiss. Kathryn sat down next to him, and they continued the kiss until they had to break for air.

"Kathryn, I ..." Tom never finished, as Kathryn put her finger to his lips. "I just want to savor the moment, Tom." Tom fully understood, and the kiss resumed, in all its sweetness, and, yes, there *was* ignition.

After a bit, they broke away again, and Kathryn said, "Tom that was the most beautiful thing anyone has ever done for me. I could feel your words and music down to my toes! Where did you learn to play like that?"

Tom, shy about his accomplishments, simply said: "I had a scholarship to Julliard, after A&M."

Kathryn was a little bit blown away, to put it mildly. "Oh Tom," Kathryn said, "Here I thought of you as ill-tempered and self-absorbed at first; and I'm so sorry. I was so wrong."

She was twisting a tissue between her hands, nervously, but Tom chided her softly: "Relax, honey, you girls from the East can be so uptight."

Kathryn playfully hit Tom with a magazine she had picked up, and suddenly it seemed as if they had been friends forever.

Kathryn said, "Tom, please play more for me!"

Tom was thinking; he was a bit rusty, but he started playing some soft blues.

As if by invitation, some of the others started showing up from outdoors slowly, one or two, here and there.

Unbeknownst to Tom and Kathryn, I had been around the corner, and had heard it all. I felt full of wonder for Tom and Kathryn, and somewhat tearful, myself.

The music and laughter brought some of the others at the barbecue into the house, and some were even dancing. Jack and Rosemary were cheek to cheek to another old *Elvis* love song. Henry soon took over at the piano, and for a time, Tom and Henry took turns, playing some of their favorite tunes for everyone to enjoy. Tom played a few bars, and Kathryn and Rosemary both recognized Tom Petty's "*Stop Dragging My Heart Around,"* and did their best *Stevie Nicks* imitations.

Soon, the party resumed outdoors, as it would be dusk in a few hours. Just as Tom, Henry, and Kathryn were approaching their chairs outside, Tom asked Kathryn if she wanted to take a walk before the fireworks display commenced, and she happily obliged.

"Henry, would you mind if Kathryn and I took little Felix for a walk with us," Tom asked in his even tone of voice.

Henry was glad to see Felix take a shine to so many strangers, and Henry knew the plot that was about to unfold. As Tom, Kathryn, and Felix were walking, Martha brought over the ring that Kathryn had admired at the shop. Since she and Jessica were friends, it was not unusual for her to stop by. In fact, tonight, she was coming to the barbecue, anyways.

Meanwhile, Tom and Kathryn were chatting about their upcoming week-end up in Dallas, and making plans so that Kathryn could learn to ride a chopper.

"Tom, you wouldn't happen to have one of those bikes in blue that I could learn on, do you?"

Tom laughed, saying, "Kathryn, leave it to you to think of the colors. Any color you want, honey! Besides, you are going to start out with your arms wrapped around me, hanging on for dear life!" he joked. "And please, leave any scarves at home, thank you," he added, mysteriously.

Felix was feeling the sense of happiness in the air, it seemed. He became a little frisky as he got closer to the water. The ducks and geese were interesting creatures to him. Tom kept him securely on the leash near this area.

Kathryn and Tom sat on a bench talking for almost an hour, and it was nearing dusk. By this time, Martha, who could not stay for the fireworks display, had gone, having had her share of barbecue and a drink, with a to-go bag for Jenny, her daughter.

As Tom and Kathryn walked Felix back toward where Henry was seated, I approached them and told them how much I enjoyed the music. Henry, in perfect sync with my little plan, walked over and distracted Kathryn by showing her one of Felix's little tricks, while I discreetly handed Tom the small ring box from Martha.

Henry and I then took Felix back to the chairs and awaited the skies to begin lighting up, while Tom and Kathryn made their way inside for some drinks.

Walking into the house, Tom and Kathryn met Jack and Rosemary coming out, holding hands. They seemed so close since spending this much needed holiday at *Luna's Hope.*

"Hi, you two," Tom said with a great big smile. "Out for some romance? It's a glorious night," he beamed.

Jack and Rosemary said, both at the same moment, "what's going on with them!" They just knew, however; it was written all over their faces. Rosemary said, "Jack, I think we missed something *big.* Remember at the antique shop, when Kathryn was sighing over that vintage, garnet ring? Well, I saw Martha here while you were inside, and mark my words, baby; she was not just here for the barbecue." Jack laughed and replied, "Honey, you always had an eye for anything going on!"

"C'mon, snuggle closer-there that's better. Anyway Rose, sweetheart, honestly; I don't remember too much about our little antique shop venture, except a dream or two." Jack pulled her close, laughing, as he kissed her on top of her head. Rosemary punched his shoulder playfully.

The sky was clear, with a waxing crescent moon. The fireworks display began at nine o'clock, and it was incredible. I looked around and saw Kelly and Melinda sitting on a blanket together, next to my sons. Melinda turned and faced Chase, and I got a glimpse of the most beautiful smile I had ever seen. Melinda had not smiled the entire time she was here; not a genuine one, anyway. But here it was, in its entire splendor; and it was beaming right at Chase.

Kelly then reached over and took her sister's hand, and pointed up at the sky where giant green fireworks had just exploded. I can only imagine that she was telling her little sister that she ordered that one special, just for her, as she did when Melinda was a child.

Jack and Rosemary, wrapped up in a blanket and all snuggled up to each other, her head on his shoulders, were in their own little world of love and bliss.

Aubrey and Dan were standing nearby under the tree, down by the lake, sipping wine. With Aubrey most likely sharing a funny story, Dan was cracking up, laughing.

Tom and Kathryn had decided, at the last minute, to take out one of the rowboats on the lake and watch the show from there.

Henry and I were on lawn chairs near the grill, watching our guests, and the beautiful display of lights above our heads. I sat back in my chair and let out a small sigh, which Henry picked up on, and asked: "anything you want to talk about, Jess?"

I looked over at him, smiled, and said, "Pretty amazing what can happen in a weekend, don't you think?"

"Yes it is; but I have a suspicion that you have more on your mind than that. Is everything okay?"

"Did you ever consider going into the business of being a psychic, Mr. David?" I asked.

"No Jess, I just know your looks, so it's pretty hard for you to hide it when something is on your mind. You do wear it on your sleeve, my darling," he said, pointedly.

"Well, as a matter of fact, I do have some thoughts on my mind, and I was going to ask if I could come and talk to you, after the fireworks, when everyone has turned in for the night. You will still be up, right?"

"Yes, the little guy is going to be full of energy tonight, after all the noise and excitement; so, I'm sure we will be up late. You come on over to the RV whenever you are done, and we can talk."

Henry wouldn't press me to say anything more at that time, and we just sat back and watched the grand finale.

Tom and Kathryn had been watching the grand finale from the boat, when near the end, with the entire sky lit up in glorious colors and sounds, Tom mustered up the courage, and said: "Well, shoot, Kathryn, by God, what could you possibly want with a numbskull cowboy, who rides bikes, at my age. But here it is, darlin,' I have fallen for you pretty darn badly, and my life without you would be empty now. I'm not some silver-tongued devil, that's for sure, but look here, Kathryn; I know I'm in love with you, and ..."

Tom produced the little, red, leather box, and opened it to her, revealing the garnet and diamond ring that Kathryn had liked so much at the antique shop, the day before.

"So would you *please* make me the happiest man in the world, and marry me!"

With that, Tom let out a huge sigh of relief, but also felt the tension of needing an answer from Kathryn. In the seconds that Kathryn took to reply, Tom contemplated that if she did say no, he could always jump overboard into the water, and sink to the bottom like a rock. This proposal business was excruciating, and he didn't know if she felt the same connection with him as he did with her.

Kathryn had not been proposed to properly the first time, so this heartfelt speech of Tom's brought genuine tears to her eyes. In fact, she couldn't stop them, and poor Tom misunderstood.

"Kathryn, please don't cry. I don't mean to horn in on your life. I just don't want to lose you, now that I found you, but I understand; I'm moving too fast, and..."

"Stop it, you silly cowboy!" she said with a smile, as she wiped her eyes, continuing with, "this is like a fairy tale to me; for you to care so much about me, and your beautiful speech, and the ring from yesterday...it just overwhelmed me. Of course, I'll marry you, you big jerk. Now give me a proper kiss, and we can seal the deal!"

Tom leaned over, kissed her, and said, "I need to call my daughter, Ellie, and tell her all about you." Then he let out an enormous "Yahoo-o-o!"

"Okay, right now!" Kathryn laughed.

"Yes, right now would be good, or should I wait??" he shakily questioned.

Tom was now lost with excitement. Kathryn then took his face in her hands, kissed him, and said, "Yes, right now, Cowboy. Go call that beautiful daughter of yours, because we are going to want her blessing."

Tom returned to his suite alone, and nervously dialed Ellie's number.

"What is this?" Ellie answered into her phone, "Okay Dad, what tactics were used in order to finagle another phone call out of the prison guards?" She laughed.

"Ellie, honey, you know you will always be first in my heart, right?" Tom started his call with this interesting statement.

Ellie, misinterpreting his statement, fearfully replied with, "Dad, are you okay?" *Could it really be that bad*, she wondered?

"No, no honey, I met someone here. You were right. I never thought it could happen. I mean, babe, it's a miracle! You'll love her!"

"Dad, slow down." Ellie tried to calm him down, yet she was excited, too. She wanted to hear all of the details! *Dad actually sounded happy*, Ellie thought, in amazement.

"Dad, tell me everything," she said. "And don't leave anything out!"

"Well, her name is Kathryn; she is beautiful, and kind, and sweet..."

"Dad," Ellie interrupted, impatiently clicking her nails on the counter. "What does she look like, how old is she, and what does she do? You have to admit that this is happening so fast; although I am crazy with happiness for you, both."

"Well honey," Tom said more calmly, "I just fell plum crazy over her. She loves nature and wants to bike with me. And can you believe it; she is in love with me, too! And Ellie, we can talk; I mean really talk to each other."

"Okay Dad, when's the big day?" Ellie thought she was making a joke, until Tom answered, "Hopefully soon, honey."

"Whoa, Dad, I need more details!" Ellie cried, as someone's phone battery started beeping. Ellie heard, "Don't worry. You'll meet her soon; as we both want your blessing..." as the phone died.

I had finished bringing in the last of the blankets from outside, and I decided that it was a better time than any to take Henry up on his offer to talk with me.

Henry and Felix were settled down for the night. Henry was wearing his pajamas, and little Felix had his stocking cap on with the red pom-pom. It was white, with little red hearts all over. Felix thought he was so cool. He jumped all over the RV right before bedtime, so he could get his cap. It was a ritual for both of them, ever since Will had passed. Henry heard a faint knock at the door. He recognized my signature knock. He grabbed his robe, and headed for the door, with Felix following, excited by the prospect of more nice people and attention.

Henry opened the door of his RV and gave me a gentle look, knowing that I needed to talk. "Come on in, Jess."

I gladly came aboard and said, 'Oh Henry, I have to talk to you, and I was hoping this would be a good time, unless you are too tired; I'll understand."

Henry knew by my look that it was important to me, so he settled into a chair with Felix, and pointed to another comfy chair across from them.

"Sit yourself down, Jess. Let's hear what's on your mind, right- oh?"

He smiled encouragingly, for he and I had been through a lot since meeting on the phone, a few short years ago. Henry became a father figure in my life, and seemed to understand me, sometimes better than I understood myself.

The moment I took a seat, little Felix hopped over to me and kissed me on the cheek. I began petting him gently, as he curled up in my lap, looking lovingly across at Henry. I slipped the postcard out of my pocket, and handed it to him.

Henry did not even question me; he just reached over and took the card from my hand. He took his reading glasses from the table next to him, put them on, and read it. I looked around at the all too familiar home to Henry and Felix. It was spare, yet truly a home. Henry had kept most of the art works that he and Will had collected together. Will had helped Henry furnish the RV, as he and Henry had meant to travel; and Will had excellent taste, too.

Henry finished looking at both sides of the card, took off his glasses, and looked over at me. He said, "Well Jess, think about what your gut instinct is telling you, my dear."

"What if my gut is wrong?" I asked him.

"Jess, is it so impossible that he is reaching out to you? That he has feelings for you, still? Henry asked me these questions with gentle, yet obvious, common sense.

He went on, "*what if you could see your reflection through my eyes?* Think of Will…he had the courage to be himself, and enough left over for me, too. If it weren't for Will, I would be stuck at work, and would never even have taken your call, most likely."

Henry then asked me, "What are you scared of, Jess? Think of replying to the man, at the very least. What have you got to lose, my dear?"

"My sanity," I joked darkly, as I sort of laughed and cried at the same time. I looked at Henry and asked him, in all sincerity, "Henry, what did you mean when you asked, *what if I could see my reflection through your eyes.*"

"My dear girl, you mean the world to me. Look at how relaxed little Felix is, sitting with you. You have a way about you, but you can't seem to see it in yourself. I want you to be happy, that's all. You must give yourself a chance; if you don't, how will you ever know what could have been." Henry smiled, his crinkly eyes full of kindness and wisdom.

"Yes, I know. But you see, there's so much I don't know, about Jay, my heart condition, my future, my past. I just don't know which way to go, sometimes," I repeated myself, wringing my hands in agony over my utter confusion.

"Jessica, none of us know the future, and what if you did…would you change things?" Henry asked.

"How do you mean? Change things; like what?" I questioned.

"I don't think you are confused about your future, Jessica. I think you are still scared because of your past."

"Henry, what if Jay wants to rekindle our love. What if I end up depressed again, someday, and push him and others away, like I did before. What if my heart gives out again, or worse…I end up taking the road my Mom did, and I hurt everyone?"

"Listen to yourself, Jessica. You are projecting things that may never happen. You need to see the Jessica that *we* all see and love. You have come a long way! And, look around at this incredible place! It would not be here if not for you and your grand ideas. Do you not see the happiness that can happen, here? Look at Kathryn and Tom; like a couple of kids, in love for the first time, it seems." Henry laughed aloud. "And, look at me, Jessica. I'm happy, and have been able to live my dreams. That would not have been possible if you hadn't come along, with a purpose."

"Henry, you always know just what to say." I smiled and felt uplifted, as though some invisible force brushed by me, near enough to feel it.

"Well, I don't know if I always know what to say, but I do know that you will make the right decision."

"Thank you, Henry. Your confidence in me gives me hope. And strength." I smiled as I stood up, and handed sleeping Felix over to him.

Henry put little Felix in his bed, and walked me to the door. "Now, go get some sleep, Jess. It's been a busy weekend, and tomorrow's a new day."

I said goodnight to Henry, giving him a hug, and began to turn toward the door. Henry stopped me by saying, "Jess, remember, I love you, my dear, and always; *remember your purpose.* We all navigate our way through this life, and you are headed in the right direction."

I looked into Henry's eyes and smiled again. "What would I do without you? You mean the world to me, and I love you, too." I leaned up and kissed his cheek, and then looked over at little Felix and said, "Oh, I love you, too, little one!"

I lingered, somehow reluctant to leave. "Henry, I feel silly, but; everything is going to be alright, right?"

"Of course, my dear," he replied with that twinkly-eyed, kind smile of his. "Now, get a good night's sleep."

I went to bed feeling a sense of self-worth and contentment with the words Henry had spoken to me. I also decided, after speaking to Henry, that it was time I try to reconnect with Jay.

12

Away, But Never Forgotten

*I*t was Monday, the 5th of July, and I was shutting the front door after saying goodbye to Melinda and Kelly, who were our last weekend guests.

Before Chase and Trey left to head back to the city, Chase had spoken to me about how he and Melinda had become friends, and now that Kelly and her husband were going to help Melinda with her move back to San Antonio, Chase was looking forward to seeing her again. Chase assured me that he was going to take things slowly with Melinda, and that he was going to be there for her, if she needed anything at all. I gave him my full support.

Tom and Kathryn had been the first to leave, early this morning. Kathryn took me aside before she left, and thanked me for the best vacation she had ever had. She showed me her ring, and was beaming with joy. She and Tom had made a love connection. The phrase 'opposites attract,' was never truer. They left in her little, red, Corvette, both filled with the joy that only love can bring.

Jack and Rosemary had to leave Sunday evening after the fireworks, because Jack had a hearing today at court. They left feeling like honeymooners, full of dreams for their future.

Aubrey was packing her things, for she was heading back to the city, too, this afternoon. I decided to have a little chat with her while she packed.

I walked up the stairs, and saw her zipping up her suitcase on the bed.

"Hey Jessica, another successful weekend, don't you think?" she asked, as I walked into the room.

"That's an understatement, Aubrey." I grinned as I took a seat on the bed, next to her suitcase.

"So, Aubrey, I was wondering if I could ask a favor of you?"

"Sure; what's up, girl?"

"Well, yesterday during the fireworks, I saw something pretty special. It may have been the most romantic courting I have ever been witness to."

Aubrey lifted her suitcase off the bed, placed it on the floor, and sat down next to me.

Looking into my eyes, Aubrey pleaded: "Oh? Do tell!"

"When everyone was out by the lake, getting all settled for the fireworks display, I ran to the house to get a few more blankets, and that's when I saw and heard the most beautiful thing!"

"My goodness, girl, tell me already!" she begged, now.

"Before Tom and Henry entertained us with their music on the piano the other night, it was just Tom and Kathryn in the house. Tom played her a song, and he sang it to her! It was incredible," I said, as the sheer memory of it left goose bumps on my arms.

"What! And I missed it! You should have come and gotten me," Aubrey said, as she lightly poked me on the arm.

"I couldn't. I didn't want to move, in case they saw me. I could have ruined the moment," I replied.

"Well, how did it go?" Aubrey whispered.

"They are not here anymore, so you don't have to whisper, silly," I whispered back, as I started to laugh.

"Well, could he sing, or did he just give it a good old country try?" Aubrey asked.

"He was awesome! You know how much I love to sing, Aubrey; and he played the heck out of that piano, too," I exclaimed.

"You do love to sing," she said, as she discretely rolled her eyes.

"And I *knew* he and Kathryn had a spark going!" Aubrey added, confidently.

"Well, I didn't stay after the kiss, but that spark was a full blown flame, from what I saw." I smiled.

"Kiss! I missed the whole thing." Aubrey shook her head in disappointment.

"Yes, you did, but that's not really what I wanted to talk to you about. All of the romance helped me make a decision that has been too long in the waiting," I said.

"Decision?" she asked, curiously.

"Ah, yes…a decision…I never told you this, Aubrey, but a while back, I wrote Jay a letter and mailed it to him in San Francisco. I asked him in the letter if he could ever forgive me for pushing him away. I wanted to reconnect with him, but…"

"A letter…Jay didn't mention that you wrote him a letter, Jessica!" Aubrey stood up and blurted this out, before she could even think about what she had said.

"You've spoken to Jay? When did you talk to him?" I asked suddenly, with both confusion and excitement.

"Jessica, Jay emailed me last week to say that he had moved back to Texas, and he wanted to know how you were doing, and if I thought you might want to see him, or at least speak to him.

He told me that you had never replied to his emails or voicemails, so he was reaching out for my help. He wrote that he had been transferred to Washington, after moving to California; and now he is living back here, in Texas.

I talked to Dan about it, Jessica, and we planned to show you Jay's email the other day, but you were so adamant with Dan that you didn't want to talk about Jay. So, we thought it would upset you too much.

I swear, if I would have known that you tried to reach him, I would have told him, and you, and Dan! Why didn't you tell me about the letter, Jess?" Aubrey was now wringing her hands.

I stood up, and paced across the room. I was trying to figure it all out. "He never got my letter. He must have moved to Washington, and *never got my letter!*"

I looked over at Aubrey with a huge smile, and asked: "Please tell me that you still have his email address, Aubrey!"

"Yes, I do, I do…I'll go to my email right now, and get it!"

He's here, in Texas? I can't believe it. He wanted to know how I was doing…*he never got my letter*…he must still wonder why I never answered his emails. What will I say to him?" I was feeling butterflies flitting all over in my stomach.

184

"It's okay Jessica, *breathe*... he wants to talk to you, and he wouldn't have emailed me asking about you, otherwise," Aubrey replied, as she almost tripped over her suitcase in anticipation.

"Aubrey, he sent me a postcard to tell me that he missed me. It went to Sarah's house by mistake, and she brought it to me on Saturday, while you were all in town."

"Oh Jess, that is so romantic. You are going to contact him back, right?" she asked.

I sat down at the edge of the bed, contemplating the different emotions I had been having this past weekend.

First, my son Trey, and his news of going abroad, then the postcard I had received from Jay...I suddenly felt a little lightheaded.

Aubrey handed me a piece of paper with Jay's email. She smiled at me, knowing what I was about to do, and said, "I'll be downstairs, if you need anything."

I took out my laptop, and I began to pour my feelings onto the screen. I wrote a sentence, and then deleted it, then wrote another, and deleted it. I was able to compose an entire novel, but that one email was by far, the most difficult thing I had ever tried to write. *It has to be perfect*, I thought.

Dear Jay,

I know it's been a long time. I received your postcard, and Aubrey told me that you also emailed her, and asked about me. I was confused at first, because I wrote you a letter awhile back, and it was returned to me, unopened. I thought you were angry with me. You might be angry with me; you should be angry with me. I want to say so many things to you, and explain what happened to me, but an email just doesn't seem to be personal enough. I don't know if you are married, or involved, or what relationship you may be in now, but I want you to know that if you are happy, then that's all I ever wanted. Well, that's only partly true, actually...I wanted more, but I pushed you away, and I'm sorry I did that. I've never stopped loving you, and I miss you, too. If you can find it in your heart to forgive me, I'd love to see you again, and talk...

I must be crazy to even consider sending this kind of email to Jay! That's too much to drop on him, all at once, I thought to myself.

As I was about to delete it all, and start over again, I was distracted when I heard Henry calling for me, from downstairs.

"Jess...Jessica, when you can, please come outside, so we can ask you about this pool filter situation. Dan and I need a mediator, and quickly!"

I took a deep breath, as I obviously needed a short break. I was struggling with the perfect words to write to Jay (if any existed) and went to see if everything was okay with Henry and Dan. I walked down the steps, through the kitchen, and out the veranda doors, where I saw Henry approaching Dan. They were out by the pool, talking about a new pool filtration system that Henry wanted to try. Dan seemed unsure about Henry's explanations.

"There you are, Jessica; Dan and I were wondering if the birds were going to be staying down by the pool?" Henry asked.

I looked over at Henry in confusion, and said, "Birds? Henry, what the heck are you talking about?" I asked, a little bit scared.

Dan looked just as confused as I was, and just shrugged his shoulders.

"Not birds, silly girl, the pool filter. What do you think about the new filter system?" Henry asked, brushing off what he called another 'senior moment.'

I never did like that phrase: 'senior moment,' so I just shook my head, and said, "No thank you, I trust you guys, and anyway, I'm working on something up in my office right now."

"Are you writing some good stuff up there, my dear?" Henry asked, as he looked up from the instruction manual and smiled at me. Suddenly I felt something brush by me again, causing goosebumps on my neck.

"I'm giving it my best," I said, even though he must have thought I was working on my novel. I still felt a bit uneasy.

Felix was behind me in the house, scratching at the door, so I asked, "Henry, have you fed little Felix, yet?"

"No, I was just going to do that, as a matter of fact," Henry replied, as he took down some notes from Dan.

"It's okay, I've got it. You two just concentrate on this pool filter issue, and I'll go in and feed the little guy," I said, as I looked confused, at the filter system, and at the two of them, who were in the middle of investigating it. "I trust you completely, Henry, and yes, you too, Dan!" I added, with some mixed feelings.

"Thanks Jessica; I have a new bag of food for him in my RV. And if you wouldn't mind, could you bring me back my allergy medicine, because my head is hurting, and I'm afraid the mold count is up, again," Henry asked.

"No problem, I'm on it," I said, as I turned and walked back into the house. Little Felix was so much fun to feed and give treats to.

"Does anyone want to go for a walk?!" I asked, in a high pitched, excited tone that I aimed towards Felix.

He jumped up and down, and darted all around, as I grabbed his leash and harness from behind the door in the kitchen, and wrangled it onto him.

Aubrey walked into the kitchen, with a basket of freshly folded towels. "So, how's the email going?"

"It's not an easy one to write, but I think I can do it. I'm going to walk Felix over to get his food in the RV, and get Henry's allergy meds, and then, I'll finish the email. I'll let you read it before I send it out, if you wouldn't mind??" I asked her sincerely.

"I wouldn't mind at all; actually I was hoping you would share it with me. I'll put these towels away, and wait for you to get back."

"Sounds good; be back in a few minutes. And, Aubrey, thank you for always being there for me, really!"

"Yes, yes, now hurry up, and get back here and finish that email girl! Don't you think that you have made that man wait long enough to hear from you?!" She smiled sweetly.

Felix and I walked out the side door and started on our way towards the RV, which was parked in a nice quiet spot in between the house and the lake. I was feeling so excited that my heart was beating quite rapidly, with anticipation and nervousness.

Felix and I were walking along the path, when he suddenly stopped in his tracks and began barking. I looked down at him and said, "What is it, boy?"

He started to let out a low growl, and tensed up his little body. I looked in the direction his focus was concentrated on, and through the trees, I could see some movement across the lake. His keen sense of sound had already picked up on what my sense of sight had not yet seen.

I quickly bent down, to attempt to pick up Felix, so that I could distract him by carrying him to the RV. But he quickly wiggled out of his harness and darted forward.

"Felix, STOP! Come back here!!" *Oh no, not the lake, not again!* I was in full panic. *The little dog can't swim; he'll drown,* I thought, anxiously. It was too late. He was hot on the trail of a young doe drinking from the far end of the lake. All I could do was to yell, at the top of my lungs, "Henry, help!" and "Felix, stop!"

I quickly took off after him; running at my full speed. Then, he stopped suddenly, and pointed his tiny ears straight ahead, focused intently, as if he were a lion hunting a gazelle. I was in reaching distance of him now…I took a leap of faith, and made a flying tackle for the little guy, and caught him in my arms…

But something was wrong. I couldn't catch my breath. I rolled over, with Felix escaping my grasp, as I hit my head sharply on the rock trim of the pebbled path. The pain immobilized me, and my vision began to blur.

Feeling as though I was going 'under,' I fought to stay above, and I heard garbled voices: Jess, Jessica…! I heard panic in their voices…

"Put something under her head!

No! Don't move her; we need to stop the bleeding!" Then I felt what I knew was my last dance in this life. I felt light as a feather, slowly undulating down to earth.

The voices were now muted sounds. Then I felt calm and serene. No more struggling. All was silent. No more voices, no pain, no sound, or light. All memory of my physical existence was now a dream-like fantasy, somewhere.

I tried to move my numb body. I was halfway between being awake, and a dreamlike state.

"Jessica, open your eyes." The man's voice was clear and loving, as it guided me away from the colors and light. As he continued to speak those soothing words of encouragement, I felt a sudden heaviness in my body, again.

As my eyes slowly opened, the room was blurry, with my vision fighting to clear. The colors that had been swirling around me were fading fast, as was the man's voice.

I was lying in a bed, and I began to make out a figure of a person; he was holding my hand and slouched over in a chair, sleeping with his head down next to me on the bed. All of a sudden, I remembered losing grasp of little Felix by the lake, and I asked aloud in a soft, dry voice…"Is Felix okay?"

The man holding my hand woke up suddenly, and said, "Jess, oh, my God!" and then he pushed a button on a remote near him, where a woman's voice replied: "Yes, can I help you?" He replied back, "She's awake, she's awake, please come quickly!"

It was Jay! I couldn't believe it, and I was so confused. He stood up, kissed my forehead, and still holding my hand, he dropped down to the side of the bed, and prayed: "Thank you, God, thank you, God!"

With tear filled eyes, returning to the chair next to my bed, he sat down, and answered, "Yes, Jess, Felix the little dog is fine, but how do you feel? Can I get you anything? Do you hurt anywhere?"

With my vision clear now, I could see that I was in a very familiar place. It was the hospital, and although my memory was slowly coming back as to what happened the day Felix was running after the deer, I was still somewhat confused. "Jay, *the woman in blue…* did you see her, too?" I asked.

Jay quickly looked at one of the nurses in bewilderment. They were now filling the room, rapidly. He then looked back at me, and asked, "Jess, what woman in blue?"

I soon felt panic creeping up inside of me, but then, suddenly, I recalled the voice of the man, who told me to open my eyes, and a beautiful calm settled over me, along with a sense of renewed hope, and love for life. I didn't even take notice at that time, of the date written on the dry erase board, which was on the wall in front of my bed…July 15th 2011.

Grabbing Jay's hand, I looked into his tear-filled eyes and asked, "What happened?"

He leaned over and kissed my hand, held it tightly, and replied,

"Jess, they think you passed out from low blood pressure while chasing the dog, and you hit your head on the rock. You've suffered a severe concussion, and for ten days you have been in a coma."

I heard him say ten days. But this news did not seem to frighten me.

The nurses were all around us now, but Jay never let go of my hand. They were taking my vitals, checking the monitors, and noting information into their computers.

One of the nurses began to ask me: "do you know what year it is, do you know where you are?"

I told her, "It's 2011, and I'm in the hospital."

Then she asked me, "Do you know who you are?"

I looked at her, smiled, and then I looked at Jay, squeezed his hand again, and said, "Yes, I'm Jessica Aries."

The nurse asked me a few more questions, and then she smiled and said, "He is exactly right, Miss Aires. You have endured a serious concussion and brain hematoma. We have been waiting for you to wake up." She looked over at Jay. "This man of yours hasn't let us skip a beat, when it came to making sure you were getting the best of care."

Another nurse announced that Dr. McCain was on his way, and would be up to see me soon. After the last nurse stepped out the room, I looked into Jay's eyes, and said, "Jay, I'm so sorry."

I couldn't explain to him the journey I felt I had just been on, at least not yet. And I was still confused, too.

"You mean the world to me, girl! I don't ever want to lose you again, and I promised God that if he would bring you back to me, that I would always be here to take care of you," he said.

I was speechless. He was so sincere, and I could feel his love, his exhaustion, and his fear, all at once. His sense of hope seemed so endearing and contagious, I couldn't help responding with the three words I had wanted to say to him for so long: "I love you!"

"I love you, too, Jessica. I've never stopped!" Jay leaned over and hugged me tightly, and then kissed my lips.

"Aubrey sent me the email you were writing to me on the day of your accident. I promise you Jess, I never received a letter from you."

Jay ran his hand through his beautiful black hair, and tried to explain what might have happened.

"Maybe, when I moved to Washington, it was lost in the mail, or rerouted. Anyway, I never got it, and I'm sorry. When you never answered my emails or voicemails, I thought you didn't want me in your life anymore, Jess."

"This isn't exactly how I pictured us seeing each other again, when I wrote that email," I said, as I lifted my arms and looked at my hospital gown.

He just smiled and said, "It doesn't matter to me. I'm just so happy you are okay, and that you want me here with you, Jess. I work from home now, here in Texas, and I'm not leaving you again!"

"Jay, I'm happy you are here with me, and I don't want to lose you again, either."

Jay smiled and replied, "I was hoping you would feel that way, sweetheart."

There were tears of joy filling my hospital room, but I had a sense that something was being kept from me. I could see it in Jay's eyes. I thought that maybe it was my heart again, and maybe something else was going on that he was waiting for the doctor to tell me.

Aubrey and Dan arrived together within thirty minutes, and then I knew by the look on Aubrey's face, that she knew something I didn't.

In the midst of the excitement of my awakening, none of them seemed to want to be the one to tell me where Henry was, or if anyone had called him, yet.

I finally asked, "Where's Henry?" Everyone looked at each other. Aubrey nodded to Jay, as if to give him permission to tell me where Henry was. I looked at Aubrey, then at Jay, and he finally said,

"Jessica, sweetheart, Henry passed away from a massive stroke while you were *away*. I'm so sorry, Jess."

I didn't want to believe this news; he couldn't be gone. Henry is so full of life! "He can't be, he was just…I mean, I was going to get him his allergy medicine, then Felix and the deer, oh God, no!" I cried.

That was when it hit me, just how long I was away in the coma.

"Jessica, Henry is sadly missed, and he loved you so very much! You were his dearest friend, Jess. Henry left everything to you in his will, including little Felix, who is fine, and waiting for you to come home. Henry thought of you as the daughter he was never able to have," Dan said, trying to comfort me, as his own eyes began to pour out tears.

Aubrey quickly embraced him in a hug.

"When did it happen?" I asked, as the tears were streaming down my face, and the lump in my throat was making it hard for me to breathe.

"Two days after you were taken to the hospital, Henry passed away in his sleep, in his RV. None of us had any idea that he was even sick, Jess.

The doctors said that Henry couldn't have known either, and it was sudden," Aubrey explained.

"I went to your computer to get information on how to reach Jack and Rosemary Hastings, so I could ask for their help, and that's when I saw your email to Jay, and I sent it to him right away," she added.

"I called Aubrey immediately, and found out where you were taken, and I came right away, Jess," Jay said.

"We asked Jack Hastings to help us with the arrangements for Henry, and he kindly took over Henry's estate, the legal matters of his business, and the reading of the will," Aubrey continued.

I saw strength in Aubrey that I had not seen before. She was the one 'holding down the fort,' and comforting the others over Henry's death.

Dan turned back toward me, and told me that Henry had spent the first two days here at the hospital, praying and talking to me.

"Henry told us that you were going to be okay. He just knew it somehow, and he kept telling you to open your eyes, Jess," Dan said, as he began choking back his tears, again.

Everyone had already spent some time grieving and accepting what happened to Henry; they had held his service, and said their goodbyes, but for me, he had just died. I closed my eyes for a minute, and then I remembered the voice that had guided me back from the lights.

"Jessica, open your eyes. It is not your turn, yet. Live that happy, hopeful life, so full of purpose; that you are now on the road to."

The voice! It was Henry's voice! He was the one who guided me back. Tears squeezed out of my scrunched shut eyelids, as I felt Henry's presence. I nodded my head, "Of course, Henry."

Everyone there knew something was happening, but no one was sure what, except for me.

My cardiologist, Dr. McCain, arrived during this time and told me and everyone in the room that he had a good feeling that everything was going to be okay, with my heart and my head. He apologized for the loss of my good friend, and told me I'd be staying only a few more days for observation. But he had high hopes that I would be able to go home, soon.

Before Dr. McCain left the room, he said, "Miss Jessica, your heart will sustain you in whatever you choose to do, but please keep clear of those rocks!"

I nodded and tried to smile at him through my pain, but couldn't. He had seen me through my heart surgery, and my depression that followed, so he believed I could make it through this.

My sons were on their way back to the hospital, after hearing that I was awake. I was looking forward to hugging them both.

I finally talked Jay into going home to get some very much needed rest, since I had more than enough people to watch over me. He only agreed if someone would stay with me, and call him immediately if there were any changes.

Aubrey gladly accepted, and she took Jay's place where he had kept a vigil for the past eight days.

After a few hours, my family and Dan all went back to the Inn to help get things ready for my return home, while Aubrey stayed with me, as she promised Jay she would.

I looked around the room and saw all the flowers and balloons that had been brought in for me. Aubrey brought some of the cards to my bedside and began reading the inscriptions.

She told me that even the hospital staff had taken turns reading the cards to me in the hopes that I'd hear how much I was loved and I'd come back.

So many people had been praying for me. I never realized how many people cared about me, or how many lives I had touched. How many lives we all touch!

There were bags of cards and well wishes from my readers, family, and friends, past guests, and even complete strangers who just cared.

Aubrey grabbed a little bag from the window sill, brought it over, and handed it to me. It was a small pink bag that had antique calligraphy writing on it. I recognized it right away…*History in the Making.*

I looked at it and said, "This is so Martha; she is always giving me special things from her shop."

Aubrey stopped me before I opened the bag, gently squeezed my hand, and said; "No, no, Jess, this bag is from Martha's shop, yes, but the gift inside is from Henry. I found it in his RV. He had asked me for one of Martha's bags a few weeks ago. It looks as if he made it himself for you. I wanted to give it to you special, after the others had left, and before your sons arrive."

I peeked into the bag, and saw the little blue box. It was all I could do to keep from leaping out of bed. I took the box out of the bag, and in the lock sat the small brass key. I turned the key, and opened the box. It was a little blue jewelry box, with a mirror inlaid on the inside lid. *As I looked at my own reflection*, both tears of joy and sorrow filled my eyes. My purpose, shown to me in such an obvious way, through this tiny mirror. It always was, and always will be, to be true to myself, and to share my love and experiences with others.

Aubrey quickly asked, "Is everything okay, Jess?"

I took a deep breath and said, "Yes, Aubrey, everything is going to be okay, I promise. I am… just really going to miss him." I tried to get the words out, but could barely speak through the pain of losing him.

"I know Jess, we are all going to miss him, but he would be so happy that you are awake, and going to be okay. Like Dan said, Henry told us that you were going to be okay; he was sure of it!" Aubrey said.

"I think I might just need to rest a bit now, Aubrey."

"Sure hon, get some rest," she replied.

I rolled over and smiled, as I thought, *I love you, too, Henry.*

Then I said, hardly audible now, as I held the little blue box in my arms and closed my tear-filled eyes, "I think I had a dream about a box like this…*something about a purpose.*"

Only the Beginning…

Printed in the United States
by Baker & Taylor

Printed in the United States
By Bookmasters